Alison Hennegan, Mary Hemming & Jan Bradshaw   Photo by Jane Munro

Jan Bradshaw has been involved in the Women's Liberation Movement since 1974 and 'became' a lesbian in 1980. Since coming to London in 1975 she has worked for the Marie Stopes Clinic, The Women's Research and Resources Centre (now the Feminist Library) and as assistant editor of Women's Studies International Forum. She worked for The Women's Press from 1983 to 1985. She contributed to *On the Problem of Men* (The Women's Press, 1982) and edited *Women's Studies Courses in the UK* (WRRC, 1980) and *The Women's Liberation Movement* (Pergamon Pres, 1982). SHe is white, working class by birth, middle class by education, lives in Hackney with her seven year old son and is committed to a radical feminist revolution.

Mary Hemming came out as a lesbian in Glasgow in 1974 and became active in the Women's Liberation Movement. She was a member of the founding collectives of Glasgow Women's Centre, Glasgow Lesbian Line, Stramullion Co-operative (Scottish feminist publishers) and Scottish & Northern Book Distribution Co-operative. She lived and worked in Glasgow for twelve years in social work and bookselling and moved south to work for The Women's Press in 1983. She is a student of Washinkai Karate and is white, middle class and 35 years old.

Alison Hennegan read English at Girton College, Cambridge, abandoned her efforts to complete a Ph.D. on turn-of-the-century homosexuality and literature and became instead National Organiser of FRIEND (the national federation of gay self-help groups). From 1977 to 1983 she was Literary Editor of the original *Gay News*. She has contributed articles to a number of books on the relations between gender, sexuality and writing and has written the introductions to modern reprints of Radclyffe Hall's *The Well of Loneliness* and *Adam's Breed* and to Rosemary Manning's *The Chinese Garden*. She writes regularly for The *New Statesman*. A lesbian (just in case you were still wondering), she lives alone in Cambridge.

JAN BRADSHAW & MARY HEMMING, editors

Girls Next Door

lesbian feminist stories

Introduction by Alison Hennegan

The Women's Press

First published by The Women's Press Limited 1985
A member of the Namara Group
34 Great Sutton Street, London EC1V 0DX

Reprinted 1986

British Library Cataloguing in Publication Data

Girls Next Door
   I. Lesbianism in fiction   2. Short stories,
   English
   I. Bradshaw, Jan   II. Hemming, Mary
   832'.01'08353   PR1309.L4

   ISBN 0-7043-2871-2
   ISBN 0-7043-3980-3 Pbk

Phototypeset by AKM Associations (UK) Ltd, Southall, Greater London
Printed and bound in Great Britain
by Nene Litho and Woolnough Bookbinding
both of Irthlingborough, Northants

To Jill
and
To Eleanor

Contents

Introduction	1
Went to a Marvellous Party *by* Marsaili Cameron	9
One Day *by* Rosemary Auchmuty	13
The Two Spinster Ladies *by* Kate Hall	22
Photographs *by* Caeia March	26
If One Green Bottle . . . *by* Sue Sanders	33
In the Camp *by* Ellen Galford	43
Strange Connie from Two Doors Down *by* Pearlie McNeill	48
First Kiss After First Row *by* Berta Freistadt	52
Reunited *by* Rosemary Auchmuty	55
What I Did on My Holidays: a truncated and one-sided story *by* Berta Freistadt	64
Rosemary For Remembrance – or from my diary 1962 *by* Lorna Mitchell	74
The Marina Trench *by* Sigrid Nielsen	86
Kittens *by* Liz McLaren	91
Not What I Mean by It *by* Gillian E.Hanscombe	94
A Bit of Help *by* Anira Rowanchild	101
Distance *by* Sandra McAdam Clark	105
Family *by* Paulina Palmer	111
Julia *by* Caroline Natzler	123
Breakfast in Bed *by* Amanda Russell	128
The Severed Tongue *by* Lucy Whitman	131
The Stranger in the City *by* Caroline Claxton	144
A Country Dance *by* Mary Dorcey	159
Biographical Notes on the Contributors	177

Introduction

Each of the twenty two stories printed here has its beginnings in the life lived, not observed, the life known, not imagined. Which is not to say that they lack either imagination or observation. Their characters inhabit the twenty-first century as well as the twentieth and not all of them are Earthlings. Their authors construct plots, invent men and women and offer insights which draw upon a detailed and intelligent scrutiny of other people's everyday lives. Nevertheless, these stories spring initially from the life experienced by the author, known from the inside. They are not only about lesbians, they are by lesbians. They are 'lesbian' twice over: yet it is the sexuality of their authors rather than of their characters which, I would argue, makes them lesbian stories. Each author has a knowledge and experience of lesbian life which does not come filtered through a heterosexual imagination capable of comprehending lesbianism only as a version of heterosexuality. When these women address lesbian subjects they bring to them a moral authority denied to heterosexual writers.

That first paragraph will be anathema to anyone taught (as most of us were) to believe (as many of us no longer do) in the mysterious and semi-divine power of the Literary Imagination which, somehow (or so we were told), effortlessly transcends the prejudices and limitations of the mind which houses it. Floating free in some purer air, it grasps truths withheld from mere mortals. There is no need to know, only to imagine, for Imagination is its own truth, its own knowledge.

Women in general and lesbians in particular have good reason to be suspicious of the transcendental powers of the Literary Imagination. Through Western European and American literature troops a dreary procession of 'lesbians'. Power-crazed, sexually rapacious, emotionally cold, sadistically cruel, neurotically clinging, spiritually corrupt and physically repellent, they come to us by courtesy of some of the greatest Greats in the literary tradition: Balzac, Baudelaire, du Maupassant, Strindberg, James and Lawrence among

1

them. That each man in his own and sometimes dramatic way experienced personal difficulties with the fact of lesbianism need come as no surprise. And that the difficulties found expression in hostile, distorted or falsely glamorous depictions of 'lesbian' characters is also unastonishing. Nevertheless, the imagination of a man obsessed with fears that lesbians will steal his wife, seduce his mistress, corrupt his daughter, mock his manhood, invade his club and wreck the nation is unlikely to produce a truth which any *bona fide* lesbian can recognise.

Which matters. For fiction offers many delights, fulfils many purposes but one of the oldest and most constant is to teach, inform, show us to ourselves in ways we recognise and acknowledge to be true. The act of recognition can be its own sufficient pleasure or it can be a necessary first step before going on to question, extend or change the self we recognise. But before we can recognise ourselves, we must be drawn true and, for lesbians, truth about us in fiction has proved hard to find. Often we have been caricatured or vilified, sometimes camouflaged, usually ignored. And we still are. The knowledge offered, values endorsed and assumptions made in most fiction remain resolutely heterosexual. It's true that 'literary' novels, appearing in hardback with a print run of two thousand or less, may occasionally contain intelligently conceived, subtly delineated lesbian characters and themes. Some eventually appear in paperback editions. But 'most fiction' means popular fiction, the fiction readily available at railway stations, newsagents and supermarkets:'ordinary' books and magazines for the 'ordinary' reader who is never expected to be anything as 'extraordinary' as a lesbian.

It's no coincidence that many of the stories in this collection deal with remarkably everyday aspects of everyday life. The 'only' difference, it may seem to some (probably not lesbian) readers, is that they are lesbian lives. So, for example, where once the familiar formula ran 'Boy meets girl; boy loses girl; boy gets girl (or loses her once more)', both characters now are women. 'So what?' some may say. Yet, paradoxically, it is that very ordinariness which is remarkable when we remember the tiny, tiny proportion of published fiction which deals – as a matter of course – with 'ordinary' lesbians. That very sense of ordinariness is itself (in literary terms) utterly illusory. There would be absolutely nothing whatsoever 'ordinary' about finding lesbian love stories, let alone a serial, appearing regularly in a mass circulation women's magazine.

As with fiction, so with fact. Where, in the same magazine, do you find systematic attention paid on the family pages to lesbians bringing up children, with or without lovers; or an awareness of lesbian bereavement; or an acknowledgement that lesbians also have mastectomies and hysterectomies, grow old and live alone and that some of the resulting changes reverberating through their lives will be different from those of their heterosexual peers? And where do you see the automatic inclusion of lesbians in the endless articles on finding, adjusting to, keeping, leaving and losing life partners? In both mainstream fact and fiction lesbians, it seems, must still go it alone. (There is, of course, the counter argument which says how lucky lesbians are to be forced to make their own social and emotional maps over terrain uncharted and untrampled, uncluttered by other people's leavings. The contradictions inherent in such enforced freedom are among the many subjects explored in the stories collected here.)

People learn from fiction. They look to it for information, reassurance, affirmation about the ways in which other (fictional) people feel, believe, act and – most important of all, it sometimes seems – love. Some critics may, do, find such a confusion of Life and Books maddeningly, even dangerously wrong-headed. Nevertheless, readers (and different critics) doggedly, rightly continue to seek in imaginary lives and people values and experience which they recognise as 'real' and 'true'. For heterosexuals, fiction often supplements other easily found sources of similar information: it comes via playground lore, popular manuals, television drama, documentaries, films, feature articles. Most important of all, it's part of the daily currency of gossip, conversation and discussion exchanged at work and at home. Its all-pervading presence provides, as it were, the oxygen which heterosexuals never notice but cannot live without. Until recently for many homosexual men and women fiction was their most important, sometimes their only source of the very different knowledge they needed and could find nowhere else. And fiction remains vitally important for many lesbians. It may indeed have become even more so, since our increasing visibility over the past decade and our growing recognition of each other's endless variety means we have more questions to ask, more ideas to exchange, more and different needs which we must understand.

Lesbian lives, like heterosexuals', have their own Rites of Passage, significant moments or events which together make up our Sentimental Education. Most of them appear in these stories. There is the moment of discovery ('I am lesbian') or decision ('I shall be').

Coming out – at any age from eleven to eighty-plus – brings its attendant joys of self-affirmation and risks of rejection. Many make the big move to the Big City, sometimes to avoid coming out at home, often to go in search of The Others who we are sure must be there somewhere. We make love for the first time, break up for the first time, break up again. A job, a home, a partnership or custody of our children may be suddenly endangered or lost solely because we are lesbian. We outgrow or are outgrown by our partners. We raise children who, we realise, are daily taught, by playground insults and curricular bias, to despise the thing we are. We see, and try to stop, our anti-sexist sons growing up into the men we warn our daughters against. We discover feminism and try to decide what it has or doesn't have to do with lesbianism. (Some of us, of course, discover lesbianism and try to decide what it has or doesn't have to do with feminism.) And some of us become extremely irritated by paragraphs like this one which use the all-inclusive 'we' to bind together so many very disparate women in a deceptive and deluding homogeneity. Yet even for us, stubbornly, teasingly, the sense of connectedness remains.

Some of our rites of passage are unique to lesbians, others overlap with heterosexual experience. Or do they only seem to?

There is a comforting belief that Love is Love, and Loss is Loss the whole world over: but it's only half true. When Jack loves Jill who leaves him for Joan the value and significance of the two relationships will not be seen as identical and the main difference is that Joan's feelings for Jill will generally be deemed less important, less 'real' than Jack's. Some loves are less Love than others: an attitude which will be faithfully reflected in the decisions made by the housing officers, custody judges, neighbours, nursing staff and gutter press journalists whom Jill and Joan may encounter in their new, joint future. The two women's love for each other will have a different social significance than heterosexual love, may indeed be denied any significance at all. The women themselves will now be perceived differently and they will know both greater constraints and freedoms.

Those very basic and seemingly self-evident facts, which any lesbian knows, are easily obscured and, in moments of temporary amnesia, can be forgotten even by lesbians ourselves. The unexamined belief that 'Love is Love' is powerful and pervasive. To deny it offends and disturbs traditional humanists who cling passionately to the belief that through Education we learn to cherish and feel affection for Difference. But that's another half truth. We cherish more that which in some way resembles ourselves. It is not difference which delights us, but similarity: we seek the point of identity, not divergence. How else, if at all, can Difference be negotiated? 'Love is Love' is an appealing but deceitful universal statement which, like so many universal statements, is used to obscure and silence inconvenient differences rather than to accord equal recognition, in this case to homo- and heterosexual needs and experience. Heterosexual readers who wish to assert that 'It makes no difference' what the gender is of lovers enduring the lover's common lot of ecstasy, agony, rage and rejection miss at least half the point.

I have lost count of the number of times impassioned heterosexuals have quoted to me W.H.Auden's 'Lullaby' which begins

Lay your sleeping head, my love,
Human on my faithless arm;

Here, they urge, is a magnificent love poem in which the gender of the lovers is quite irrelevant. What they actually mean, of course, is that it's quite unknown since at no point in any of its four verses does a stray pronoun, proper name or anatomical reference give any indication of the lovers' sex. They could be two men, two women or a man and a woman. Imagine what you like: at no point will you be jolted out of your own preferred fantasy coupling. As an example of a universally applicable love poem, it's unfaultable. As evidence that heterosexual readers can empathise fully and give an enthusiastic reception to an overtly gay male love poem, it's a non-starter.

Universality, opacity, obliquity, suggestion are literary qualities often valued above the particular and direct. Their use, it's argued, indicates a greater sensitivity, a subtler craft. It may. But sometimes it mainly indicates fear and concealment. To understate, to hint, imply provides a way of (almost) saying the unsayable. Many a wistfully elegaic piece of gay writing from the earlier part of this century owes its curiously elusive tone to the successfully mastered art of not quite telling.

The writers collected here lay claim to their stories and their right to tell them in a manner barely imaginable by an earlier generation of lesbians. It is, I think, no accident that so many have chosen to use a first person narrator. Two 'I's are at work: the (lesbian) woman who writes the story and the (usually lesbian) woman who tells it. Events

5

recounted, characters depicted and the significance attached to them are contained within an account whose lesbian perspective is guaranteed twice over – by author and narrator. Heterosexual static is kept to a minimum or obliterated altogether. Heterosexuality is there: implicitly, as an omnipresent fact, to be contested, subverted or ignored; explicitly, with its demands, threats and assumptions forming an integral part of the story. But the eye which sees, the voice which tells, is doubly lesbian.

That it should be so seems almost inevitable at this stage of popular lesbian writing. A lesbian author's freedom to address herself publicly to lesbian subjects is a freedom recently and still incompletely won. Small wonder that many of the writers represented here should find a first person narrative the most appropriate in which to claim and convey that new-found authority, to use that newly possible voice.

Only one of these stories has as its narrator a heterosexual woman. She is, unwittingly, intensely anti-lesbian although she prides herself on her open-mindedness and sexual sophistication. Lesbian readers will get her measure very quickly, just as they will immediately understand the story's almost casually tossed away punch-line. Transpose the story to a popular heterosexual medium and much of its meaning would go unrecognised: readers would understand what it was 'about' in the sense that they'd follow the plot. But almost certainly they'd fail to notice the author's subtle yet – to a lesbian reader – unmistakable hints about the relative merits of the lives led by the narrator and her next door neighbour. This, in fact, is a story which can be guaranteed to work only in a lesbian context – as it does, beautifully. Sometimes context is all.

The assumed context of fiction – as of life – is heterosexuality. The writer who wants to change the rules must find a way of notifying the reader. The safest (and, it must be said, the easiest) way is to let a lesbian narrator dictate the terms, establish the lesbian context in which the story is to be read. 'Strange Connie from Two Doors Down', with its anti-lesbian narrator who is nevertheless clearly the creation of a lesbian author, illustrates the freedom and fun a writer can have when, with rules reversed, the subject is heterosexual but the reader's assumed context is lesbian. It will be a long time before every lesbian writer feels it's safe to take that risk.

The stories which make up this anthology were chosen from over a hundred submitted in response to advertisements placed in *Spare Rib*, *Trouble and Strife*, *The Caribbean Times*, *Voice*, *Wires* and various local women's newspapers. Together they provide a fair cross-section of those themes and issues which most exercise lesbians today. Here lesbians seek to uncover their part in the past and to envisage a sometimes triumphant, often frightening and uncomfortably close future. They unravel with patient subtlety the often tangled threads which link lesbians and heterosexual women, explore with sometimes painful precision crucial and dividing differences between those who were 'born' lesbians and those who 'became' so. The violence which is so many men's response to us weaves its way through this collection, from today's rural Ireland, to the twenty-first century and back to ancient Greece, home of the myth of Procne and Philomel, recounted in a version rightly included here because although its heroines are not lesbian the woman who retells it for us brings to it her own lesbian-feminist perspectives and uses them to illuminate marriage, virginity and rape. Whether the subject is serious (learning to live without the drink you've become addicted to) or comic (extracts from a baby dyke's schoolgirl diary), whether the story's realistic, fantastical or science fiction, strongly autobiographical or fully imagined, the overwhelming impulse we can sense at work behind them all remains the same: to try, after so many years of lies told about us and silence imposed upon us, to tell the truths we know as truly as we can.

Alison Hennegan
Cambridge, March 1985

MARSAILI CAMERON

Went to a Marvellous Party

'When did it happen?' The bloodshot eyes were very close; the glass, three-quarters full of some vile end-of-party mixture, was tilted at an angle more dangerous to me than to her. This woman was a menace and she wasn't going to give up.

You want to hear more about her, despite the eyes and the glass? Well, first things first. Let me tell you about me and parties. I hate them. The noise, the people, the dirty glasses, the quiche, the peanuts in the ashtray, the cigarette ends in the peanuts, the elbows in the ribs. All right, yes, some things have changed from the parties of one's youth; but isn't it just a change from the abominable to the ghastly? People don't usually vomit over you now, granted, nor do they have screaming rows over some arcane personal topic. You know the kind of thing. In extreme youth you might hear 'My mam said your mam said you don't even *like* shrimps.' Or, later on, 'You said you'd *burn* that tie she gave you – and, anyway, it's horrible.' Well, yes, that has changed, mostly – but, really, so what?

Suffice to say (must remember to watch my blood pressure – not getting any younger) that the nearer the time of my arrival to the time of my departure, the cheerier I am at parties. (You're quite right, what a frost – cross me off the list for that next get-together of 'just a few friends – and I'll *have* to invite Blah and Blah'.)

Obviously, I never make an appearance near the beginning of a party. Quite apart from that making one look a bit desperate for company, it would involve gearing oneself up to sociability in these precious early and mid-evening hours when even the telephone is quiet. But arriving on the late side has its disadvantages too. For a start, there's only wholemeal quiche left, sitting stolidly beside a pudding basin of undressed limp lettuce riddled with sultanas (quiche and lettuce unthrilling; sultanas poisonous – well, we all have our quirks). And then there is the drink situation. Who *does* bring sweet white wine to parties? Yes, I believe in democracy, but can nothing be done to stop them? And, anyway, if they do truly like it, why do they bloody well never drink it themselves?

Misery-making though they are, quiche and sweet white wine are as nothing compared with the people you meet at the back-end of parties. They haven't 'got off', as our mothers used to say; clearly they haven't or why the hell would they be wanting to pour sweet white wine into your glass? Furthermore, they've often got beyond the stage of the decent restraint now considered the necessary prelude to 'getting off' with anyone. The civilised veneer which they presumably wear to the post office, the bank and the supermarket has been stripped away to reveal what lies closest to the ventricles of every human heart. Their last lover was a psychopath, with a sinister penchant for women in uniform; their mother always preferred their brother/sister/dog; their father had always wanted them to be First Secretary of the Admiralty, despite a clear early aversion on their part even to bathwater.

And so it was that on this particular occasion I heard the words, 'When did it happen?', and immediately experienced one of these sinking sensations. 'I'm sorry,' said I coolly, 'I didn't quite catch what you were saying.' This was unfair in a way: the eyes were un-questionably bloodshot but the speech was comparatively clear. It was true, however, that I hadn't heard what she had been saying. Call it hysterical deafness if you will; why not?

'When did it happen?' she repeated, 'that change – when did it happen?' 'What change?' I asked, a trifle desperately, trying to rid myself of a mental picture of streams of copper and silver coin. 'The change,' she said, a little irritably – well, that was understandable – 'when I became a full-bloodied lesbian.'

Why was this strange woman asking me this strange question about her personal life? I had no idea but, for the sake of saying something, murmured, 'Full-blooded', still in the mood for word correction after an afternoon with a friend's eight-year-old. She gave me an unexpectedly sharp glance. '*You* may be full-blooded, dear, and good luck to you. But when I said full-bloodied, that's what I meant.' 'Oh,' I said, and, yes, it was said feebly. My companion took a swig from her glass: she knew she'd got me on the carpet now.

'It all started,' she said, 'with this girl.' I was silent. I could well imagine that that was true. 'That was *before* the change,' she said. 'You understand that, don't you?' I nodded. I didn't understand at all. She continued. 'For years I'd had these funny feelings about some girls. You know, flutterings in the stomach, cold hands, all that kind of thing. I thought I must be a bit nuts, to tell you the truth.' I nodded again, this time understanding exactly what she meant.

She adjusted her waistcoat, which indeed looked as if it had been at the party for a long time, and went on. 'And then I met this girl. We didn't have a lot in common but I knew there was something important we had in common, I just knew it, even though I didn't know what it was.' I nodded again; even this I understood. 'One afternoon I kissed her,' she said, 'and that was that. The whole world was different: there was just her and me and everything else was there just to give us somewhere to be. I was so grateful – to God or somebody, I don't know who, for letting me feel the things I felt. I can remember the smell of her sheets – isn't it funny? That smell was everything to me.' I nodded again; but rather wished all this was not happening.

'And then,' she said, 'I couldn't put weeks or months to it – they didn't exist then – she said it wasn't right, you couldn't live your life like that, and we had to stop before it was too late. It was already too late for me, I knew, whatever "it" was. But she left one summer morning, the birds were singing, about four o'clock, and I never saw her again, no, never.' I poured some sweet white wine into her glass. 'It was after that,' she said, 'that I think the change happened. I'd loved *her*, her smell, I hadn't really thought about what that made me. But afterwards, when I didn't see her any more, I couldn't forget about it, I couldn't go back to where I was before. I heard about this pub in another town – people made jokes, you know – and I went there; God, I was scared. And there were these girls at the bar, laughing out loud and carrying on. I couldn't see what all that had to do with me and the way I felt; but I couldn't leave either, not without talking to them.'

'No,' I said, 'of course you couldn't.' I gave her more wine and this time filled a glass for myself too.

'And that was it,' she said. 'They were nice to me in their own way, asked me out with them and all that. And I did go out with them from time to time and eventually I went to bed with some of them. And soon enough there I was, one of them, dressed like the rest of them, laughing out loud like the rest of them. It wasn't horrible; it was nice in a way. But it was a bit funny sometimes. Like when a Spanish girl came to town – she was a teacher or something. She was beautiful, really – long black hair and she didn't give a damn about anything. She smoked a pipe sometimes, sitting there in a long dress. Well, we all fell in love with her, though we pretended to each other that we hadn't. One of us would ring her in the morning, another in the afternoon, and another would go around to her flat in the evening before we all met in the pub. What d'you think of that?'

'Amazing,' I said. 'What was in the pipe?'

'Very funny,' said my friend and crunched a peanut – or, possibly, a cigarette end. 'There was something else about us lot then. My name's Pat – but I wasn't the only one called that. We were all called Pat or Jan or Jo or Sylvia or Mo or Barb. It made you think sometimes that our mothers must have known something when they christened us. Of course, it's not like that now. Well, everything's different now, isn't it, this feminism and all that? No one's called Pat or Sylvia any more; you meet someone now and it turns out she's called Pipi Rainwater or something.' She laughed uproariously, drawing considerable attention to herself from se· _ral quarters of the room. I looked round nervously. I had known such jokes to fall flat before. Fortunately, it was that time of the evening when old sixties' records were being played so I think nostalgia had deafened most people to everything except the voices of long-lost lovers.

A comparatively sober note returned to Pat's voice. 'What I want to know,' she said, 'is if it's all really like drink.' Naturally, I asked her what she meant exactly. 'Well,' she said, 'the first drink you have in your life – Scotch, say, – you think, that's bloody marvellous and that's what I'll always drink. And for a while that's all you do drink. But, you know how it is, one night there's no Scotch in the house and you could really do with a drink and next thing you know you're boozing away at the Benedictine. Look at me now – I'd drink anything.'

I looked at her empty glass – what she said was clearly true. 'So what I want to know,' she continued, 'is if it's like that with women too.'

I couldn't think of a thing to say. Fortunately, Pat's attention began to wander at this point. 'There's a nice-looking girl,' she said, peering into a corner of the room where I could see only the merest outline of a human form. 'And she looks as if she's on her own. Bye-bye then. Nice talking to you.' She refilled her glass carefully, seized another full one and stumbled away. The awful thing was that I felt spurned and, yes, bereft. God, I hate parties.

ROSEMARY AUCHMUTY

One Day

Every morning when consciousness broke through Nancy would cast her mind over the tasks that were planned to occupy that day. Her aim was to leave no spaces empty in this mental calendar. She dreaded the day that stretched ahead unassigned, unstructured. That would be a tiresome prospect, long hours of fretful hankering after diversion. Far better to be closely booked and rushing round. With no time for reflection.

Today Nancy is awake at 7.30 which is so unaccustomedly early that she knows immediately some momentous event awaits. Recollection speedily follows realisation. 'I met an Australian woman,' Cheryl Charteris said by way of chit-chat in the common room yesterday. We all know that Australians who live in London love to be informed of the existence of other Australians there, no matter how transient. There is always the chance, one supposes, given a country of only fifteen million souls that they will already be acquainted. 'Who said she knew you, you used to teach her.' When you are a teacher, the probability is increased severalfold.

'Oh yes?' Nancy said, sipping her Nescafé, thinking of that school in Australia.

'She seemed very anxious to see you, so I asked her round tomorrow after work. You can come, I hope?'

Hedging seemed judicious. 'What's her name?'

'Christabel Clark. She said she hadn't seen you for ten years.'

Nancy said, blank-faced: 'I left Australia ten years ago.' She did not tell Cheryl what she had said, on the occasion of her leaving, to Christabel Clark. Which was, 'Come and see me in ten years' time.' She had said this sharply, meaning: you've seen nothing of life yet.

'Evelyn introduced us. She's doing some kind of course at the Royal College with her. She seemed to know you were connected with the Institute.'

'It was a small town,' Nancy explained. 'They kept tabs. They all know what I've been doing although I've never been back. So she did go in for music, did she?'

'Oh, you remember her?' Cheryl Charteris was gratified. 'Then you'll drop by tomorrow?'

'I'll be there,' Nancy promised.

She could see herself still, up on the dais in the assembly hall with the other mistresses at the commencement of the new school year, with a fresh set of prefects directing the children into seats, and a different girl at the piano playing them in. She wondered what Cheryl Charteris would have made of her then, sitting so conformist in her dark skirt and pale blouse – you could not wear trousers to school in those days – with her stockinged legs properly glued together and her feet in low-heeled sandals tucked beneath the chair, so correct you would never have guessed about her, could not have imagined what was to come. Senior mistress she was already in this small girls' high school, although only thirty years of age. A career woman. One had not heard of prospective husbands in her life. Destined for big things: headmistress, perhaps inspector or college lecturer even. And a local girl. Miss Watson has natural authority. She will go far.

Twelve thousand miles in fact, Nancy mused. When people questioned, puzzled, for why would anyone choose to live in declining Britain, she never told them of the need to place twelve thousand miles between herself and her reputation. There were plenty of other explanations to invent, for London is an exciting city after all, it offers a hundred ways to fill your life so that you do not have to think.

She has, for instance, a seminar at 10.30 today at Russell Square, and will cycle. Cycling through central London occupies all one's attention. Lapse and you've had it. But the seminar is as boring as anyone could have anticipated, and on someone's radio next door a concert pianist is playing Brahms, a piece by chance that Nancy knows since Chris played it, maybe not at that first assembly but at one of them: she loved Brahms, and so does Nancy.

Accustomed as they all were to hearing the 'Teddy Bears' Picnic' and 'Colonel Bogey' at school functions the audience could not help but notice, those who had any ear at all, that this new pianist was providing Mozart, Brahms and even Prokofiev. The girls cared less but Nancy was intrigued. She went over to the piano after the assembly and told the musician, sincerely: 'Thank you, I liked that.'

'Good,' said Christabel Clark, not pausing, not even looking up in the act of marshalling her sheet music into a bundle to convey away.

At first Nancy sensed contempt, and was uneasy; then it seemed a natural assumption of equality. Indeed, the girl was an artist, she was in that sense Nancy's superior. Nancy felt humbled, could think of nothing more to say, and wandered off. Meeting the music mistress in the corridor, she ascertained the girl's name.

'Talented child,' Miss Giovelli confided. 'Plans to read music at Sydney. Should study overseas, really. Could make a performer one day. But a difficult personality.'

'What do you mean?' Nancy had asked, curious.

'Full of herself,' Miss G explained. 'Full of her art. Fools are not suffered – you know.'

Nancy did not know, exactly, then.

The second meeting is the clearest memory. Having become aware, Nancy then actually *saw* the girl for the first time: and now whenever her mind dwells on that era which, thanks be, it has not done with its former obsessive persistence for some years, this is the vision it calls back.

An angry girl in a gym tunic, presenting herself sullenly in the senior mistress's office.

'Miss Sherwin sent me to you.'

'Why?'

'I wouldn't do what she said.'

Nancy, perplexed. She remembered her mixed feelings with rueful amusement. No one sent sixth formers to senior staff for discipline. She couldn't imagine what she was supposed to do with her. She didn't care personally for Beth Sherwin and PE was not a subject that caught her sympathy. So whatever the girl had done, the chances were she would be on her side. Finally, there was the matter of the gym tunic. It was very becoming. Nancy was appalled at herself.

(When she went home that night, she recollected, she wanted so desperately to say to Mary, who was older and more experienced: Look, Mary, what's happening to me? But she never did say anything, although of course Mary guessed in the end; and what difference would it have made anyway?)

'What did she ask you to do?'

'It was jumping over the horse. And forward rolls and things. I won't do them. I'm hopeless at gym, and I might hurt my hands.'

'Did you explain to Miss Sherwin why you have to look after your hands?'

'Gail, my friend, did, but she wouldn't listen.'

Nancy was silent. She said at last: 'I suppose you were very rude to Miss Sherwin?'

'I suppose I was.'

Beth Sherwin was known not to handle classes well. Nancy said: 'I don't think you should go back to the lesson if you are going to behave badly.'

Defiant eyes were raised to meet her own. But saw the look on Nancy's face, and grew submissive.

'You'd better stay here,' the senior mistress instructed. 'Tell me a little about yourself.' (I like to get to know the girls personally if I can.)

Doomed, she was, from that day.

The seminar is over. 'So interesting,' murmur Nancy's colleagues on principle. 'Will you join us for lunch?'

Fortunately Nancy has arranged to meet Louise in the Senate House canteen. 'Next time,' she promises, or rather lies.

Louise, she finds, has problems. She wants Nancy's advice, or rather a sympathetic ear.

'And so although I've told him nothing can come of it, I do feel so much better in myself,' Louise explains. 'I mean, *he* finds me attractive, even if Neil doesn't. He must do, or he wouldn't hang around, would he, when there's nothing in it for him?'

'You mean there's no sex.'

'Well, yes, I've told him I couldn't be unfaithful to Neil. Neil may be a shit, well, he is a shit, but he is the kids' father, and I'm not prepared to break up our home, or Jeff's home for that matter —'

'And sex would make all the difference?'

'Well, it would, wouldn't it?'

'You don't think Neil would be upset just by knowing that you see a lot of Jeff and talk to him on the phone?'

'Oh, he'd be upset, but not as much as if I'd slept with him.'

'Does it matter? Do you want to sleep with him?'

The question startles Louise. 'No, not really. It's silly, but I have this awful fear he's only after me for that.'

'And as long as you refuse, you can go on believing that he isn't?'

'I suppose so.'

'Until he gets pissed off, and gives up.'

'Oh Nancy!' and Louise sighs. 'Do you think I'm dreadfully screwed up?'

'No more than most women,' Nancy says, wondering why all her

16

friends turn to her, a celibate spinster, for advice on sex and marriage.

An hour to fill before her afternoon class. She could mark a few essays, do some preparation, read a chapter or two of the current novel. But she delves around at the back of her files and finds her old photographs.

Chris with her hand all bandaged up. Inappropriately smiling: a happy day in spite of the pain. What had been foretold had come to pass. A nasty episode on the hockey field, involving two broken fingers and a special meeting of senior staff. No one seemed to share Miss Watson's excessive apprehension over the incident, but the Clark girl had been removed from Miss Sherwin's PE classes forthwith.

Nancy remembered. Laurel Beckham bringing Beth a cup of tea in the staff room, the latter collapsed into an armchair with interested colleagues grouped about agog to hear the saga. 'Beth's had a terrible morning,' Laurel explained to Nancy. 'Accident on the hockey field. Had to send a girl to the hospital.'

'What happened?'

'Sticks,' said Beth. Then seeing Nancy's blank look: 'Someone hit her with her hockey stick. On the hand.'

'Not on purpose, you understand,' someone else put in. 'It was an accident.'

'I wasn't sure how extensive the damage was,' Beth Sherwin went on in her pompous way. 'There may be a broken bone. I thought it best to send the girl to Casualty.'

'Who took her?' asked Nancy practically. She had a feeling that matters like these were the province of the senior mistress.

'I called a taxi.'

Nancy frowned. 'Did someone go with her, then?'

'The girl's in the sixth form, Nancy. She doesn't need a nurse-maid.'

'We're responsible for her while she's at school,' Nancy returned sharply. She had never liked Beth Sherwin's attitude. 'You could at least have let one of her friends go. Who is the kid, anyway?'

'Chris Clark – wouldn't you guess.'

They could not help but observe the manner in which Nancy received this news. Her face was quite revealing – but of what? (Later they discussed it in grave tones.)

'Chris Clark is a brilliant pianist,' stated Nancy heavily. 'And you say she may have broken her fingers. What on earth were you doing to let her play hockey?'

'All the girls play hockey in the winter months,' Beth replied with dignity. 'I make no exceptions. As long as Chris Clark is in my class she does as the others do.'

'Even if it means her career is ruined,' snapped Nancy, rather over-dramatically the others privately agreed.

She left the room abruptly, and the others closed in on the reclining PE mistress. 'I did not feel I should leave the class,' Beth justified herself, seeking confirmation in their surrounding faces.

It was mercifully a small town, the hospital was but five minutes' drive away. With only one doctor on duty, the waiting room was full. Nancy stood in the entrance and cast her eyes over the miserable crowd. Chris looked up, as they all did, as the shadow filled the doorway, and foolish Nancy never forgot the grateful joy that sprang into the eyes which met hers.

'I knew you'd come,' said Chris.

What sort of girl was this Christabel? Across the years Nancy still cannot explain. Many people have the idea that love is simply a chemical thing. Towards the end several of the mistresses, and more of the girls, knew that Miss Watson had a thing about Chris Clark and believed that this explained why she always stood up for her when no one else did. It did not occur to them that we like and admire people because those people are likeable and admirable, that the qualities come before the emotional response and that Nancy thought Chris was wonderful because she really was wonderful.

She was nice to look at, for a start. And if that was perhaps a personal response ('Perhaps!' Mary had hooted), surely those candid hazel eyes reflected a fine honesty and directness ('Tactlessness and rudeness,' Mary had corrected, but gently as if half in jest). There was certainly a respect-worthy single-mindedness about the girl. Music was her life. But friendship was important too. Chris was a popular kid, she had lots of girlfriends and Nancy would see them giggling and mucking about in the school playground, children in behaviour but women, really.

Then in their last term Chris took to coming round to Nancy's house on weekends. What her parents thought of this arrangement Nancy never knew. Mary would generously absent herself in the garden to dig spring beds and Chris would trail about after Nancy as she hoovered or ironed or prepared food or just sat and talked. When Mary joined them for tea, the conversation became general. When she went outside again, the personal mood returned, the curious exhilaration of plumbing a friendship. There is nothing like it. And they never reached rock bottom.

Time for a quick cup of tea. In the common room Cheryl Charteris waves to or rather at Nancy. 'You haven't forgotten about this evening?'

You might as well join her, though it means being pleasant to that dreadful Beryl Truax by her side.

'No,' says Nancy. 'How's Bob, Beryl?'

'Fine, Nancy, thanks. Business is booming,' and the poor woman thinks, what a nice person Nancy Watson is, always asking after your nearest and dearest as if she really cares. Needless to state Nancy has never publicly articulated her true opinion of Bob Truax or indeed his dreadful wife her colleague. Nancy has learnt to keep her mouth shut.

Beryl cannot follow up with a polite query about Nancy's mate, Nancy not having one poor thing, so she moves to another acceptable script. 'How are things with you?'

What to say? Today is good because I have something to look forward to but tomorrow may be terrible? Now I am nervous but soon I may be deliriously happy? Is anticipation the best phase, in fact? Would we ever really wish to see into the future?

'Not bad,' says Nancy with a smile. What a nice woman she is.

'We must go,' Cheryl announces, rising. 'We're teaching at 3.30.'

'So am I.'

Would things have been different then if she had foreseen?

In October the senior girls had their final fling with a 'study weekend' in the Snowy Mountains. Coaches were hired and mistresses rostered to accompany. Christabel Clark refused to go when she discovered that Miss Sherwin was in charge of her party.

'What does *she* know about study?' she cried scornfully. 'What does she know about life?'

'She volunteered for the job,' Nancy said mildly. 'It isn't easy to get people to take on these extra duties.'

'Why aren't you coming?'

'I've done it in my time.'

Then by a twist of fate Beth Sherwin was selected for some important sporting team and bowed out and the only person who could or would take her place at short notice was Nancy Watson.

That they were happy days by and large Nancy has no doubt, but the memory is a spoilt and partial one, like a beautiful mural defaced by the vandal's graffiti. Thus, whenever over the years she has sought to recapture the joy she can only see – to strain the metaphor a bit – the writing on the wall that she failed to perceive at the time.

They were housed in workmen's huts, long barracks of single bedrooms, a mistress to a block. Chris and her friends attached themselves inevitably to Nancy's block. At midnight when all had seemingly retired Chris presented herself at Nancy's door.

And said, when admitted: 'I want to sleep with you.'

And Nancy said – but who would believe her afterwards? – 'Go back to your own room.'

They argued.

'I shall never have another chance.'

'Do you realise what would happen if anyone found out?'

'No one will find out.'

'And who knows what the future holds?'

'You don't have to do anything,' the girl said miserably. 'Only cuddle me.'

This was hard on Nancy. 'You must go,' she said.

The girl went; and both raged into their pillows till day. The next night Chris did not come. Nancy had not quite realised, until that time, how much she wanted her.

Back at school, the weekend's success was reported. But something had been seen. Miss Sturgeon drew the headmistress aside and had a quiet word with her about Miss Watson and the Clark girl. 'I'm not surprised,' said the headmistress, an unsuccessfully married principal of the old type.

'I've long suspected,' Miss Sturgeon corroborated.

'It's always a danger,' observed the head. 'In a girls' school. Some of the unmarried mistresses . . . I shall speak to the governors.'

Miss Sturgeon withdrew, triumphant. The headmistress spoke to the governors.

Nancy emigrated to London.

'Coming for a drink, Nancy?' Peter Ramsey pauses by her office door; Nancy Watson is generally a good bet for bar company, not having a family to get back to of an evening.

'No thanks, Peter, I said I'd call in at Cheryl's on the way home.'

But she lies; she will go home first, and wash and change for Chris. A drink is nevertheless needed. Cheryl will provide gin and tonic, the best choice of a limited range, so Nancy will pre-empt her by a shot or two.

These trousers and that shirt, clean pressed, a far cry from the dark skirt and pale blouse. What will Chris think? Though she always wore jeans off-duty, even then. And now she is forty, with the grey hairs massing where once they were individual pluckable wires. Though they say you cannot see them, honestly, against that shade of brown, not unless you really look. *What will she think*?

A coat may be required. The summer sky looks stormy. Have I got a handkerchief? Comb? Keys? Come and see me in ten years' time, I said. She will be twenty-eight now.

'I knew you'd come,' Nancy says aloud, for people who live alone often do talk to themselves.

Of course she lies. She never imagined such a thing.

The Two Spinster Ladies

Mrs Jenkins was very surprised when she called in unexpectedly on Miss Jones and Miss Evans, the two spinster ladies who lived in the cottage at the end of Bridge Lane. The door was unlocked as usual and it was not her habit to knock at the doors of her coffee morning ladies. What she usually did do was to telephone shortly before her arrival, giving said ladies a reasonable opportunity to tidy themselves and their homes to a suitably respectful degree. But on this occasion, the unannounced Mrs Jenkins found Miss Jones and Miss Evans standing rather too close to one another, in the front parlour. This in itself, while being a little unusual, could have been explained or even ignored, but the fact of the matter was that the two ladies, in the front parlour, with the curtains closed, were completely naked. Neither of them, and Mrs Jenkins had carefully checked this, had even her earrings on. Mrs Jenkins stood transfixed, staring at them for at least a whole minute, then she turned on her heel and fled.

Hurrying along Bridge Lane, Mrs Jenkins's mind was in a whirl with every possible explanation that would erase her worst suspicions. To her delight and relief nothing but an extraordinary and shocking answer fitted the situation. The two ladies, Miss Jones and Miss Evans, were performing some unspeakable ritual, which would bring ruin on some poor unfortunate soul, maybe even herself! But what could the two ladies have against her? She could harm no one. However, they did say that the innocent always suffered the most in these things, that was why 'they' kidnapped virgins – to hurt the innocent was to hurt Christ Himself. Mrs Jenkins knew that there were modern witches, she had seen a book in the library van, she would take it out the following day when her books were due to be returned anyway. She could still renew the one on Bonsai, providing no one else had asked for it and also borrow two romantic novels, nothing vulgar of course. Until she had read the book, Mrs Jenkins decided, she would do nothing. The idea of telling anyone, until she had all the facts, made her feel slightly uncomfortable.

Meanwhile, Miss Jones and Miss Evans were in a state of total turmoil. Hurriedly they donned their clothes and drew the curtains, patting their hair into place as they went into the kitchen. The kettle was put on. Then Miss Evans and Miss Jones looked at each other and gave into their laughter, hugging each other. They were unable to collect themselves for some minutes, during which time they managed to stutter out, 'Did you see her face?' several times.

Mrs Jenkins, had, at that moment, a face as supremely happy as the proverbial cat: she was imagining all the coffee morning ladies, with the exception, of course, of Miss Jones and Miss Evans, forming a vigilante committee to confront the shameless ladies. She was just trying to formulate quite the most satisfactory ending to her fantasy when she reached her gate and was greeted ecstatically by her poodle, Archy.

The next morning, before the mobile library arrived, as was the coffee morning ladies' habit, they all gathered together in Miss Jones's and Miss Evans's front parlour. The two ladies, as cool as cucumbers, served coffee and homemade biscuits. Mrs Jenkins was truly impressed by their composure. She did, however, notice that they visited the kitchen rather more often than seemed necessary. She hoped that they weren't to be poisoned or worse still charmed in some dreadful way and made to obey the two ladies' every command. She reminded herself that such things were superstitions, old wives' tales. She had often wondered why they were called 'old wives' – surely it was more likely to be old spinsters. Old maids, like Miss Jones and Miss Evans, who were easy prey to the Devil himself, in their childless and disappointed lives, the dark arts must be a way of getting back at . . . she wasn't quite sure whom.

Miss Evans rushed into the kitchen and spluttered into the dishcloth (she could find nothing more suitable in time). Each time that she had looked at Mrs Jenkins, that lady was scrutinising either herself or Miss Jones in such an alarmed way, as if she expected them to grow horns, or disgrace themselves in some totally unbearable way. Mrs Jenkins's expression somehow created in Miss Evans a state of cheerful hysteria which was as unsuited to the front parlour as two naked ladies.

A week later Mrs Jenkins's worst fears had been confirmed by the library book. Secretly, she visited all the coffee morning ladies, except of course Miss Jones and Miss Evans, and it was agreed by each lady that the matter had to be brought out into the open before any harm was done. Provided that the two ladies promised faithfully to give up their shameful nonsense, all the coffee morning ladies were, of course, prepared to forgive and, possibly over a period of time, even to forget what the two ladies had done.

Mrs Jenkins had hoped to bring the subject up herself, she could be quite tactful in delicate situations and they were in any case meeting in her house. However, this was not to be. Almost as soon as they had all sat down, Mrs Thompson, silly creature, launched straight in with 'Miss Jones and Miss Evans,' her face flushed and her eyes glittering at the excitement and daring of the moment, 'Is it true that you are both witches?'

'Witches, Mrs Thompson? What ever can you mean?' Miss Jones sounded almost surprised. Mrs Jenkins decided that she must intervene before she lost all the limelight. 'Come now, Miss Jones and Miss Evans too, how do you explain . . . well, I hardly need mention exactly what . . . I am referring, of course, to the incident the other morning in your front parlour.'

Mrs Thompson wondered, at this point, why Mrs Jenkins was having so much difficulty saying what the incident in question was, since she had found no such difficulty in describing it, in great detail, to almost every lady in the village.

'Oh, that. Why, Mrs Jenkins, we did wonder what you must have thought.' Miss Jones was smiling! Mrs Jenkins thought she must be stalling for time, hoping perhaps that her cloven-footed master would intervene. She trembled at the thought.

Miss Evans seemed even less perturbed than her friend. 'Why, we were doing our exercises, Mrs Jenkins, then we heard you come in and in the rush to grab our dressing gowns we almost knocked each other over. You left so quickly and we could hardly run after you, as we were still undressed.'

'You do your exercises in the . . . unclothed?' The other ladies leaned forward, as this second and equally interesting possibility occurred to them. Had the two ladies discovered some secret way of losing weight? They had, after all, both retained remarkably youthful figures.

'Oh yes, Mrs Jenkins,' Miss Jones assured her. 'Miss Evans and I always take our exercise that way, it encourages good circulation. The body should in any case be thoroughly aired every day. Swiss doctors recommend it all the time, they call it taking an air bath.'

'I'm sure that it is our exercises that keep us so active and well,' Miss Evans added, smiling contentedly at Miss Jones.

All the ladies looked at Mrs Jenkins, who decided it was time to pass around some of her homemade cake which, some of the ladies could not help noticing, was just a little on the dry side.

Photographs

Not to see my child on his birthday. That's a hard one. I went over to his house, the night before, to deliver his present. David, my ex-husband, Tom's father, was pleasant, distant. Tom was already in bed. Unusually early. I went up to kiss him and found that he was asleep. My kiss woke him. (Did I mean it to?) His arm came round my neck: 'Your voice sounds ever so far away, mum.'

'That's because you were sound asleep. Sleep well, lovie. Sweet dreams. Many happy returns for tomorrow.'

I rang him next morning just before he'd be leaving for school.

'Happy birthday, Tom.' (He's ten. Roger's twelve.)

'Happy birthday, mum. Oh. Oops.' He giggled, realising he'd got the message completely wrong. We both laughed. 'I mean,' he said, 'thank you for my money.'

'Did you get lots of lovely pressies?' (Why the hell do I always ask that when I can't stand those attitudes?)

'Yes, thanks, mum. See you tomorrow.'

I'm unemployed except for one night a week. The fact that Tom's birthday had to fall on that Monday was what life's about. Same when you drop the toast and it's sure to fall butter side down.

Each time one of them has a birthday, my body goes through a series of physical memories. Pregnancies, births. I no longer have the memory–labour-cramps, but there's still a faint tightness and a pushing sensation.

Trying to throw off the guilt, the grief. Emotions being washed and dried, ironed till smooth, folded away flat like winter clothes in late spring. In a bottom drawer labelled: Memories, Comfortable. I'm not ready to part with them, like old sweaters in a plastic sack to go to the charity shop. I need to take them out sometimes, try them on, rewash them.

Birthday photos, stored in albums, aren't thrown away either. They are poignant. Symbols of lost years and lost children. Loss through my leaving; loss through the second process of weaning that goes on as children become teenagers, growing up and away.

Yet, I've always felt that my children were only on loan for a while, through their series of stages of gaining independence. Birthdays, theirs and mine, focus the moments of those years, three times a year, as if the sunlight-tinted lens were taken off the camera, and instead there was a glaring light, stark behind the children's heads.

Proudly they sent me their education authority regulation school photos too. I tried for just one day having those on display in my bedroom. But to wake without Roger and Tom rushing in for a cuddle, left me with only the hard-edged frames for comfort. A silence was in my throat where a laugh could have been.

So, now, the photos sit on top of the front room fire, smiling past each other into middle distance. Still. Inert. With pale, ice-blue backgrounds.

When I lived with David he said photos on the walls were old-fashioned. So we didn't have any. I didn't mind, too much. Secretly I decided that once I was a grandmother, long after my golden wedding, *then* I'd have photos on all the walls, as I pleased. There'd be several of Roger and Tom, grown up, and their children, smiling. I like the way people's eyes crinkle in photos when they smile. Besides, you could ski-jump off Tom's eyelashes. He wore a hat everyday till he was five, to discourage the ladies in the street from stroking his head: 'So unfair, dear. Such lovely curls for a boy.'

The school photos are bland. Nothing of the laughter, the love-hating between the brothers. They are their own trade union, but you'd never get them actually to admit that they need each other. The photos also have nothing of the boisterous energy of the access weekends. It used to lead to a squabble after Sunday lunch. Releasing the tension-energy for getting ready to say 'goodbye, mum' again. Switching to home and dad.

David used to say that posed studio photos of Roger and Tom would be a waste of money.

'Just a nice one, dear,' said my mother, 'You know, one that I can show to Ruby' (her best friend).

David said it shouldn't be part of the household budget and I didn't have any separate money.

'Don't worry. I'll take the photos,' he said.

He bought his camera the day we bought my pram. I wheeled it up and down. It was dark blue. Modern. The sort you could dismantle easily. P'raps there's a photo of it, somewhere. But after I left, when

David sorted out the photos to give me half, we found very few of the children. There were several of the car. None of me, except on the end of a family line-up. Many of the photos were country scenes. David was experimenting. Light, texture, colours, focus and filters.

Waking alone, listening to sparrows coughing in the urban eaves, I can also hear a blackbird trying to sing. Pale blue morning filters in, the colour of the school photos.

Choosing when I want to sleep alone is still a liberation for me almost four years on from having left the marriage. I reach my toes to the edges of my double bed, and no one is there to crowd me. Smugly, I meet the furry cover of the water bottle gone cold overnight. I sling it out with my foot. It lands, where I send it, with a satisfying squelchthud.

The blackbird is now singing loudly. The sparrows are chattery, almost laughing. Thinking about the photos, my mind moves to Vie, my lover, and her friendship with my children.

She took them away one summer when I was away with another lover, and there are photos of the laughter. Tom sits there with the horn of a huge stone dinosaur between his legs. Sharp phallus, unmistakable image. He's only old enough to have the vaguest idea of his sexuality. He's far more interested in dinosaurs, gardens and walking out in the country. He loves to watch the sky as I do, and enjoys the changing cloud patterns just like my mother does on her cliffs by the sea.

'We're going there this August . . .'

'I thought we were going there last summer,' said Roger. (Tom nodded.)

'Yes. Well we were, love, but grandma, she's, well she was finding it hard to get used to me being a lesbian, and us all living the way we do now. She wasn't ready last year.'

'But she is now?' asked Tom.

'Yes.'

'Good.'

I knew it to be true. Relief and hope came in like the tide. Re-connecting.

Needing to know that there is not only love, but liking and a real acceptance. When I experience this feeling, I'm almost as young again as Roger and Tom. A small angry girl standing there in front of my mother, wanting so much, so much for her to like me and believe that I'm good.

Before the trip to the island, the family will also re-connect when my sister brings her children south to visit London.

'How about if you give Lizzie and Debbie your electric train set,' I suggested to Roger and Tom.

'What, so as we can have a new one?' said Tom immediately, hardly pausing for breath he was so hopeful: 'An inter-city 125?' (I had to laugh.)

'No. You don't use it. Not now you're busy with dad's computer.' (How does David find the money for all those *things* and wouldn't my nieces just love to get their hands on that train?)

That led to one of our heart-to-hearts about class and the fact that I, as a working-class woman, once married a middle-class man.

My sister married a working-class man.

'I know what you'll do,' complained Lizzie, talking with her mum: 'You'll wait till they' (she means video-machines) 'come down won't you? Then you'll get us one. But I'll be grown up by *then*.'

'That's right, love. When they give them away on the back of the Shreddies packet, you can have one.'

There's a photo of the boys with their girl cousins from Yorkshire next to the school photos. Roger's making faces and Debbie has the sun in her eyes so she's squinting, but you can still see the closeness.

Taking photos, choosing images, messages, priorities. I'd like to learn to make holograms too. Filling my attic flat with holograms of the sea and seabirds and walk through them with lights all round me.

Last week we 'did' the science museum. Again. It's on a sort of rota of museums, parks and open spaces. How many times on access weekends can you 'do' a museum?

We queued for ten minutes behind Mr and Mrs Het and their two point twos. The men had kind faces, like David, and little beards and small runs in the sleeves of their jumpers. The women kept smiling and saying darling, like I would have done. It was like queueing inside a BBC2 play.

Round the corner and about to queue for another five minutes we saw the notice that put the price on holograms. Old people (it said) went in for one pound, children over seven the same, and adults, one seventy five.

'I'm sorry, you two. I haven't got that kind of money, not while I'm still unemployed.'

'Didn't my dad give you some for us this time?'

'Yes, Tom. For your food. But I didn't ask for extra for holograms.'

'She thought they were free,' said Roger putting his arm around me:

'Didn't you, mum? They're s'posed to be free, aren't they?'

People were beginning to turn to see who was talking. I re-read the list but it didn't say concessions for DHSS claimants. We went to the children's gallery instead, pushing buttons like crazy. I could stay there for hours. On the way Roger kept his arm around me: 'Never mind, mum. Seen them on telly anyway.' He half grinned. His eyelashes crinkled too. Tugging me like when he used to spit out his bottle and grin up at me sideways. I hugged him wondering what kind of kind man he might become, in years to come. They don't stay babies, do they?

Roger still snuggles in with me some mornings when he's at my place. I'm in my nightshirt and he's in his almost too small pyjamas. I recall then the times when I'd use the children for extra comfort while I still lived with them. When I first left, my skin used to crawl for want of their huggings. Just to have a child touch my face would have been wonderful.

My children were erotic. Free with their bodies, their affection, beauty and laughter. There was nothing porno about their eroticism. The erotic was for them and me, a gift between child and mother. A delight in the senses, like the one photo I took of Tom naked in a paddling pool in hot sunshine. (He kept his hat on of course. It was a shocking-pink felt cowboy hat.) Water and bubbles were always an erotic experience for both children. But for most adults the erotic has become distorted, to mean just sex, and usually pornography.

I don't know how soon my sons will come under pressure to read 'dirty' books in the school lavs. I don't know how they will respond to that, or how they'll behave, or what theories they'll come up with to justify what they do. I don't know if they will choose to become gay or het. I don't know when they'll come under pressure to show that they can run with the pack, hunting, winning. I do know that the pressures on them to prove that they are 'real' men (what ever that might mean by then), will be very great. I don't even know how I will try to talk with them when those times come. I know that I love them and that they know that I do.

Holograms. Photographs. A price on playing with light. I have a camera now but there's a limit on buying films for 'snaps' of Vie and Roger and Tom. In the past, David's priorities for photographs were different from mine. My films now come out of my household money. But from our household money he chose a different kind of spending. Photographs ready-made: by the porn industry.

It began with *Playboy* and *Mayfair* while Roger was still in the pram. David said pictures of nakedness were part of liberation, and that we all wanted that, didn't we? Usually David was calm, kind, gentle. But censorship made him see blue spots and gave him the willies. He thought the posed photos of naked bodies in magazines would turn me on, liven me up, in bed. The well-intentioned liberal husband of the early seventies would read to inform himself of the latest male theories of women's pleasure. Would go to see *Emanuelle One* and then *Two*. Would see *Ai No Corrida*, the film based on the true story of a Geisha woman. She was acquitted by the courts after cutting off her lover's genitals at *his* request because he wanted to increase the intensity of his orgasm. He did. It was his last.

David was prepared to spend money on *those* photographs.

Then he tried to persuade me to pose for him.

Camera ready? Bedroom scene. Take *one*? Studio portrait? Another scene?

'No.'

Then: 'Have you ever desired to be tied up, dear, for pleasure?'

'No.'

'Just us two? For fun?'

'No.'

If he'd been a callous man I could have seen through it all more quickly, perhaps. How can I know that, looking back from here? Here where the life is full of women friends, with their photos on my walls.

There, despairing, confused and isolated, with no theory of the porn industry, of women's liberation, I tried taking pictures of my life, looking through a self-made lens, myself. There were no photographs of me, independent and strong. Such as there are now on Vie's bedroom wall. Me, laughing into the camera as if it's an eye into the future. Woman-focused. Me, striding in the hills of Dorset, on holiday with Vie. Me at a desk, writing, making my definitions of my liberation.

There, then, there was nothing except a collage of broken shreds, the pieces of me scattered. Around the edges in those days I'd sometimes glimpse bright colours, some of those being beautiful. But all were disconnected, out of focus.

Some mornings, now, if I snap-awake too early, when Vie's still asleep here, I roll out of the bed quietly so as not to wake her. I go through into the front room, to look out over the roof tops at the trees. Sounds of pre-rush-hour London move in layers where the sky meets the roads.

The room round me is almost silent in the dimness. My sloping ceiling, my mirrors and the glass fronts of Roger and Tom's photo frames all reflect back the different parts of me, with clarity: like lenses all angled at different truths. The truth is: contradictions.

'Photographs' is a true story, written in January 1984, and I would like to thank three women for the following works which helped me to create my own words: Sarah Daniels for her play Masterpieces; *Mary Dorcey for her poem 'Photographs' and Alice Walker for her short story 'Porn'.*

SUE SANDERS

If One Green Bottle . . .

She had thought a bit about her drinking when a friend picked her out of the gutter where she was lying by her motorbike, having a sleep before she could ride it home. She was lucky not to have been found by the Aussie police instead.

When she first began to meet other lesbians it was always in the bars and she needed a lot of drink inside her to bring herself to play the games that were statutory when making the first, second or final moves of the pick-up. She hadn't known any other way of meeting dykes and was not introduced to any other. She took a long time learning to like drink but she discovered she could be really funny, a stunning dancer and a wonderful lover all with the help of alcohol, so she became addicted. She finally learnt to drink heavily when she moved to Australia where the wine was divine and cheap. She never gave herself the chance to find out whether she could do all those things without alcohol and there was little chance for her, for where could she go to be with lesbians where the booze wasn't?

As her politics had become more radical, Vicki's drinking became more concentrated into the last half hour of pub closing time, after charged meetings. Her anger and frustration at the manmade world and unchecked violence were swirled round the glass. She would sit with a group of women consciously colonising a space in the male pub. They would find a table sparsely populated by men and gradually take it over. Their laughter challenged the antagonism. Any verbal attacks from the men would be swiftly rebuffed, the women making it clear they knew they were on enemy territory.

The joy of Sydney was that they could so often find their own territory. There were days when Vicki and Lorna would lie lazy in a secluded cove, sure of complete privacy, coddled by the hot sun. Lying on their backs winking up at the blue, blue sky, hour after hour. Listening to the rhythm of the sea, punctuated by the giggling of the kookaburra, the purring of the currawong and the mournful doleful call of a solitary gull as it flapped its way across the finger of sea to the other shore. Then the pulse of the city would recede and as the flagon of red wine emptied so the remembered images of the bush would flash across their eyes. They had driven hundreds of miles camping in the outback, seeing no one for days, soaking in the sun, the sounds of the bush, the rhythm of cicadas filling in the silence when they turned the engine off. For Vicki the adventure of building their own fires, whether it was in their special cove not seven miles from the centre of Sydney, or deep in the bush, never palled. The smell of burning wood and barbecued meat was inextricably linked with the taste of sun-drenched red wine.

Everything was better in Australia – the land, hot sun she could rely on, the wine, the beaches quiet and secluded, or busy with dykes on special picnics when they all rediscovered childhood games with the children of some of the lesbians.

Nights on the verandas or balconies quietly talking to Lorna, music softly playing, stars many and strong in the sky, smoking, drinking, dreaming together before falling into bed to enjoy the urgency of their bodies.

Then, there was the lesbian conference where she had swept out the hall, disposed of all the bottles and cans only to come face-to-face with two drunken women fighting. She had helped to separate them. Then she herself had been stopped from driving her bike home by a group of dykes who woman-handled it into the foyer, and her, pissed and protesting, into a car. The following day the conference talked long about drink and the serious problem it seemed to be for dykes. No solutions were found, but a taboo had been lifted that day in Sydney – where the booze ran freely and to be seen with a fruit juice in your hand meant you were healthy but boring.

Vicki became concerned about her health. She had developed a nasty cough and felt breathless after a swim. She was smoking and drinking a lot. The cigarettes must go! Lorna pissed as a newt one night also vowed 'the end of the fag' and giggling they ritually drowned a pack down the loo. They were born again, discovering the taste of food without nicotine and nagging their friends to stop smoking. They abhorred the smell of smoke in their clothes and forbade smoking in their home, hanging huge 'No Smoking' signs in the hall. They also discovered that the wine tasted better and that they could drink more of it before passing out. They congratulated themselves as they eased into the fourth bottle while their friends were waving their glasses aside.

When a crisis came she found the problem and despair all too much to cope with, so she greedily and guiltily went back to the weed, shamefacedly puffing away with her friends teasing her. She pleaded extenuating circumstances and the need for what comfort she could get.

There wasn't much comfort around when she got back to London. She had been gone a long time. There were only two friends, Ann and Jenny, who really remembered her and helped her find her feet, back in her own city. She had thought that her drinking would drop as she wouldn't be able to afford so much, and European wines tasted like water after the rich Aussie ones. But she adapted. Beer, lager and Special Brew became her companions and more recently, though she couldn't afford it, whisky.

Gradually she began to make new friends and started a relationship with Alison, yet she still relied on the bottle. As Alison didn't use alcohol much she was slow to recognise that Vicki was dependent. Vicki was thorough in the art of disguise.

Sometimes Vicki would go to a meeting with a couple of cans, drinking and smoking while she listened and talked, knowing that she was not fully sober but thinking that the drink enabled her to concentrate and helped her when she made new friends. The can in her hand, like the cigarette in her fingers, was a comforter and a confidence-giver. She was often jealous that other women didn't seem to need such props; that others could control their drinking and just have one or two and stop. Vicki couldn't. One glass of anything and she craved more.

There had been some other moments when Vicki had felt she had existed somewhere else. For instance, the shock and exhilaration of mirrors when drunk. She used them as a game. When she looked into a mirror after however many drinks it took, she knew and did not know who she was. The image that had stared back at her was certainly her face. It would mouth at her when she moved her mouth, but there had been a distance and a difference between what Vicki had felt inside and that face. The face represented someone else and sometimes in toilets, she had talked with it.

Now the game had backfired. Before, Vicki was in control. Just now when she had paced the floor she was not only out of control, but outside everything she knew and understood. She no longer knew the rules of the game. Once the game could control her like that, she had to stop playing.

She had gone to bed earlier that night after a real binge. At 2.30 she had woken from a pornographic dream. The shock of the images still tight in her mind brought her swiftly out of bed. Horrified she made herself drink black coffee then water. As the images faded the panic started. She began to pace the floor staring intently at her feet, concentrating on each footfall. She seemed so far away. She could not feel the pressure on her bare feet, or the texture of the carpet. She was somewhere else watching the top of her head and feet moving. She was trapped outside her body. She could, however, feel a pump surging in her stomach. It was the only link with her body. At first she shied away from the pumping as it only panicked her more, rushing madness to wherever she was, whoever she was. All she was, was that beating signifying panic, nothing, no reality and nothing to hold on to. She could not feel who she was. She could not think what she knew, except that beating of what she presumed was her inner self wildly trying to connect to her body. She had continued to pace the floor willing herself, inch by inch, excruciatingly slowly, back into herself. She had never been so far out of her body, nor so far immersed in fear.

Vicki wondered about Alison who was away with another lover, wondered whether that holiday would make or break the complex arrangements. Alison had offered Vicki monogamy, but she had refused, too full of doubts. Now Vicki had regrets, she had been feeling increasingly left out of the non-monogamous relationships recently and had found herself alone more nights than seemed her share, with only the whisky bottle for company.

Vicki picked up the bottle and used it as a telescope peering at her room, wryly recognising the decision was in the making.

She saw through her telescope the distorted images of her home. She loved that room. When friends came into it for the first time they nearly always laughed, it was such a reflection of Vicki – busy, big and untidy. Vicki saw blurred moments, colours and shapes.

Yes, the decision was made. Out of hope, anger, love and desperation. All things that could just as easily undo her decision, she knew.

This time she would try it slowly, not tell anyone for a few days, struggle alone with it. Test it out privately. Enjoy her daily triumphs secretly. Give herself the praise that she looked for from others. She would try it out quietly for herself for a while, giving herself a gift. There were friends, Ann and Jenny, who would support her. They would hear the news, not just with relief, but would recognise that they had a place in her decision; know when and if to say certain things, or not say others and to listen to her.

It seemed to Vicki vital that to kick the drink this time she needed to care about herself and not be selective about which bits she cared about. If she hated all the drunken bits then she would end up hating a lot of herself. She knew she did that all too easily and this was part of the reason she drank. No. This time let her try from love, or at least a sympathetic interest in herself.

It had taken Vicki a long time to work out that strategy.

She put the bottle in the tall bin by her desk and smiled. There was regret. Sure. She had made friends of bottles. Bottles that had allowed tears to fall which when sober she would have blocked and, hurting inside, hurt others with her bristly bravery. Bottles that had opened up laughter; dancing; words on paper and in lovers' ears. Bottles that had given her a wild excitement. Bottles that eased grief and loneliness. Bottles that had been friends and lovers. That like some friends and lovers had turned sour.

Of course there were things she regretted in her life, wasted opportunities, painful ends to love affairs, her appalling memory her lack of self-discipline.

She wasn't fool enough to blame it all on drink.

Vicki was going to give up drink for herself. She didn't know whether Alison was going to be in her life. She was not giving up for Alison.

At that moment, as the bottle under its own weight gradually sank to the bottom of the bin through bits of paper, Vicki was clear that she should not torment herself with the past. There would be moments of difficulty, when the body and mind would nudge her incessantly for alcohol, but she would not berate herself with the wasted-years routine but would plug into the future, the potential of the unknown.

She waved at her bottle telescope; at the pictures that it had conjured up, bid them goodnight; and went to bed.

In the morning the reality of the decision was clear. She made herself busy, went off to work. As she drove she noticed with fury all the alcohol ads on hoardings. They had never touched before, but now they seemed everywhere.

The first evening was a hell. She had told no one of her decision, and sitting in her room the absence of the bottle was the only thing she could focus on. When she ran out of cigarettes she found herself automatically following the well-worn path to the off licence over the road. She stopped herself, and walked on to the all-night garage and got them there. She could not trust herself to be in the warm, well-lit off licence where she was known, and the bottle would have been handed to her with a smile, without her even having to ask for it.

After a week of such nights Alison came back from her holiday wanting her relationship with Vicki to be monogamous. Vicki felt as if she had received a reward for her lonely nights and absent liquid friend.

But the separation between Vicki and alcohol was not without its hiccups. For Vicki the effects of that decision were uneven, various and not all pleasant.

During the first couple of months of non-drinking Vicki avoided discos, pubs and parties. Alison missed them or went on her own and missed Vicki. Later when Vicki was able to turn up, she found that she got bored with the taste of orange juice; was sick once from seven tomato juices; couldn't stand the taste of pineapple juice and switched to water. The glass in her hand and the cigarettes in her fingers were still props that she needed.

Vicki found that her humour had changed into anger. She was angry so much of the time. As a lesbian she had a lot to be angry about. But why was she spraying it all over Alison and her friends? She analysed where her humour came from and was forced to recognise that so much of it was a diffuser of anger. She remembered with dismay how often she had been crassly rude when drunk and had been forgiven because she had that excuse. In the past she had drunk to dilute the anger, anaesthetise her feelings. Now she had to deal with them clear-headed. Discover how to use it. No dumping on friends or herself.

Dancing now proved a problem. Somehow the music was never right. Vicki complained about the male singers, the awful beat, or the despicable words. They often left parties without having danced at all. Vicki and Alison had loved to dance together, they had had much laughter and sensuality in their relationship but there didn't seem much of it around at the moment. They both hurt at the changes and wondered how long they could last.

Vicki's clothes were loose on her. In the last couple of years she had somehow never been able to buy fashionable clothes and never in the colours she liked. She often found the style she wanted was not made in her size. Without alcohol her body lost a lot of weight and it showed in her face. There were times when women didn't recognise her. With money saved from not buying drink, she took herself off and treated herself. Colourful shirts and tight trousers. The ensuing compliments were encouraging. They gave her the confidence to go to the odd party and disco and dance.

Vicki still had little or no desire, though. Her body, coping with the massive change in chemistry, rebelled and shut down. Then Vicki tried to explain to Alison that she did love her, that the lack of physical need or desire was not a lack of interest or love, merely a resting period while her body adjusted to not having alcohol. Alison tried to believe her, but not knowing other lesbians who were attempting to support lovers through the drying-out process, she had no means of checking.

Alison was hurt with waiting, exhausted with the excuses and had lost hope of a return to laughter, joy or celebration.

She and Alison had found themselves in a sprung cage unable to do anything but bait each other. But the knowledge of how to bait so well came from an insight of each other which they knew was rare and precious. When inevitably the rejection came, it was shattering. The letter Alison left for Vicki was honest. It was not that she did not love Vicki it was simply a statement of survival.

Vicki retreated bruised, this time with no alcohol to comfort her. She sat in her room and stared at the pattern of her walls.

Vicki desperately wanted the bottle that would bring tears, turn her back into the sentimental drunk who cried those easy tears. Now when she really needed them, they were all used up. She had to learn really to grieve. Pick up the rage and grief slowly with her own hands, and soften down the sharp edges. She began to listen to her own voice.

She saw Ann and Jenny often after a couple of weeks of self-imposed solitude.

She then threw herself into a campaign, not heeding her inner voice. She found it difficult and a challenge to work with hetero-sexual women, wincing at times when they expressed sympathy at her broken relationship and compared it to their own coupling problems.

Vicki and Alison attempted to construct ways of meeting and not meeting. The night she arranged to be out of her own home so Alison could collect her things and leave Vicki's, had a rabbit terror for her. When she stepped into her room to confront the left objects on the floor and the gaps in the room, she froze for minutes. The room she so loved was an unfriendly brittle place. When Jenny got the frantic phone call from Vicki she was out of bed and out into the street in seconds, and arrived to find Vicki still shaking. It had taken Vicki a strange courage to make that call and ask for help. She had a perverse pride that rarely let anyone see her that vulnerable. Jenny had recognised that the journey to the phone box to make that call was further than just over the road. They talked a lot about journeys and different paths that night but not about destinations.

Both Alison and Vicki recognised there was unfinished business between them. When they met to talk they were careful, sometimes too careful. So they left each other wondering what it was they thought they knew about each other. Other times they were not careful enough and they would reel from the encounter. Many nights Vicki would sit and stare at the space where the bottle had been.

Four months of anger, bitterness and hope. Then one night of raw need, perception and courage and they accepted each other back into their lives. Neither of their lives were easy. But Vicki had survived the rejection, loneliness and the uncomfortable awareness of the past repeating patterns without alcohol.

The campaign was proving difficult, for Vicki, being the only lesbian, was becoming more and more of a problem for the group. She was working long hours and coming home tired and dispirited. It was Alison who first saw and labelled the difficulty as anti-lesbianism. When the group split, it was vicious, Vicki was out! She ached with the rejection. The work she had done when Alison left her stood her in good stead. This time she had not only Ann and Jenny to help but a new friend as well as Alison. Her anger now fuelled her decision. No one was going to drive her back to drink. She had made her resolution alone. She no longer had to ring women after a party or disco and tentatively apologise for what ever display of silliness she vaguely remembered from the night before. She had been a fool not to listen to her own voice that had warned her about this piece of work. But she had been her own fool, not a sozzled one who could pathetically blame it on drink. She had toughened up. She was not going to wallow in self-pity. She had coped with a much more devastating loss when Alison left her and had worked her way through that private rejection, owning her part in the break-up. She would do the same now with this public rejection.

Vicki relearned how to use her time and energy, for the campaign had gobbled much of both. She planned that she would not fill the vacuum this time left by booze with anything but honesty; that dykes who saw Vicki with a fruit juice in her hand would think her not boring but healthy.

As Vicki recovered, her sensuality grew and with it came a new softness and openness.

She discovered with some surprise that she wasn't the great socialiser that she thought she was. Wild nights of dancing and talking to new women was not always her scene. She found the occasional night with a few friends and their friends, where the atmosphere was light and the conversation could ramble between politics and who was with who, enjoyable and stimulating. When she went to meetings now, she sometimes went to the pub with other women, joining in the discussions and laughing at the jokes, with a glass of water in her hand, or went home to write or read or meet with Alison.

In the new year Ann and Jenny conspired.

They had a plan. Her second dry birthday came. Alison took her out to the country for the day. The two of them alone larking among the trees in an arboretum, kissing in lovers' walks made for heterosexuals; discovering a lake which seemed out of place in the English countryside, mysterious, lacking only, it seemed to them, the prehistoric creature that belonged there. Driving back to Vicki's home where they were to change, she and Alison sang songs, laughing. They stopped off at a pub Vicki had used in her early days and, sipping their fruit juices, laughed again as they eavesdropped on a group of earnest teachers as Vicki had once been, discussing their timetables and the lack of support they were getting in the classroom. As Alison drove Vicki into her street she urged her to hurry and open the doors and get changed. She would park and follow her. Vicki went on, opened her heavy front door and went to her own door, struggling with the padlock as usual, planning in her mind for the thousandth time to rearrange the lock. She opened the door, switched on the light, to reveal twenty women who broke into 'Happy Birthday'. Vicki stood open-mouthed, astounded. The solid reality of all those women welcoming her into her own home was amazing. There they all were on a busy mid-week evening in March at 7.30 to celebrate her birthday with her.

Vicki did not know which emotion was uppermost in her mind: shock, surprise, gratitude, laughter, they all tumbled about in her. There was a range of fruit juices on her kitchen stand and a feast on her desk. They were high all night on the success of the surprise for there were only a couple of bottles among all those women. The presents they brought were all for her room, subtly echoing or reflecting Vicki. The dancing and the laughter shook that old house that night and Vicki was right in the middle of it. It was a memorable night for all of them. For the women who came would never forget the secret organising it took to plan the surprise and the look on Vicki's face as she switched on the light. For Vicki it was a unique statement of friendship.

Vicki sat at her desk, reading. It was now two years after the night of her decision. It was late. To her right was a green bottle. The page was in a pool of light. To her left was a test tube stand which gripped an electric light bulb shaded by a fake Victorian leaded light lampshade. She leaned over and smelt the pink flowers that Alison had left for her. Then she picked up the bottle and walked over to the cupboard and rummaging found a stub of a candle and a box of matches. She pushed the candle into the bottle and carefully lit the wick and carried it back to the desk and switched off the light.

She lit a cigarette from the flame, leaned back on her chair, enjoying inhaling the smoke, sharing with herself her own private anniversary.

This story is dedicated with thanks to the friends who supported me during my 'drying out'.

ELLEN GALFORD

In the Camp

We didn't take them all in.

It was the ones who make such a fuss about it that we were after. The ones who shout it at the tops of their voices, wear little symbols dangling from their necks and earlobes. You know, the conspicuous ones. Who spray-paint it on to walls, incise it on the doors of public toilets, and feel the uncontrollable urge to bring it up in conversation, when they are not actually occupied in flaunting it up and down the streets. They're the ones who will insist on marching all over town waving flags and banners. The type who have a quaint and rather unhealthy attachment to labels. I can tell you, they wear a lot more than just their hearts on their sleeves.

Now, we're not fools. Or illiterate. We know this sort of thing has been with us since the ancient Greeks. But then, so has cancer, come to think of it. We know all about Sappho and Radclyffe Hall, and those two appalling American women in Paris (funny how many seem to be writers; must get the Research Department on to that). We know perfectly well that we couldn't possibly hope to stamp it out altogether. But then we're not concerned with the ones who are discreet and sensible. They don't bother us; we don't bother them.

The collection process was quite a challenge. We started with Operation Pied Piper. This entailed slight diversions in the routes of marches and demonstrations, hiving off groups into small, well-sealed side-streets, and then into vans and buses. But these large-scale outdoor events didn't take place very often, and our schedule didn't allow for an open-ended intake period, so we extended operations to certain publicised conferences and political meetings (some of these we set up ourselves, others we just took over 'spontaneously'), as well as a few carefully selected bookshops, discothèques and cafés. Thanks to considerable cooperation from the telephone people, we were able to achieve our objectives without undue waste or interference.

As anticipated, there were eventually some questions asked about the disappearances. In spite of the fact that these were marginal people, they seemed to have considerable networks of friends and family, who soon noticed that they were missing. (To be quite honest, if I'd been the relatives of some of these specimens, I'd have been profoundly relieved if they'd dropped out of sight. But we all know that this fundamental loyalty is one of the sterling qualities of traditional family life, and a good thing, too.)

However, we made the publicity work for us, and used the opportunity to carry out a significant number of raids upon known gathering places, in the course of the usual police missing-persons enquiries. Eventually, with the assistance of our colleagues in other departments, and some quiet words in the ears of a few highly-placed individuals within the media, we successfully managed to 'lose' several hundred people with minimal fuss. This, I suppose, is an interesting reflection on the times we live in – dangerous drugs, dangerous drivers, lots of plausible explanations for unexpected vanishing.

In the camp itself, the induction process ran less smoothly. We encountered more than the predicted degree of resistance, running the gamut from physical violence (even some of the puniest can pack a surprisingly powerful punch) to Gandhi-style passivity, hunger-strikes, physical immobility and stubborn silences. Part of the problem, of course, was the tendency for some of them to plot their rebellious acts in concert. Until the requisitioned drugs and other restraints arrived (they were some days late, unfortunately) we had our hands full just keeping order. The Chief did wonders with what was, to be frank, a pathetically inadequate allocation of staff.

Our initial plan was to sort them all into categories. By age first, which was simple enough, once the technicians had installed the VDUs, got rid of the bugs and had the necessary data-sources onstream. Then we tried to classify them by race and ethnicity, which was far more difficult than expected, because there are some extraordinary mixtures. I sometimes wonder if all that mongrelisation isn't part of the problem. Next we attempted to place them according to class. This proved to be equally impracticable, and most embarrassing, to boot: it's amazing how first impressions can deceive. I was quite horrified to discover that Judy O'Grady and the Colonel's Lady are indeed sisters (if not worse) under the skin.

It required three six-hour staff meetings (and that entails a considerable sum in overtime, not to mention an extremely unhealthy amount of instant coffee) to come to any sort of agreement on definitions.

Then, and this was the tricky one, it was suggested that we divide them into Redeemable and Hopeless cases. It was proposed that those within our sampling possessed of previous heterosexual experience could, as it were, be turned back again, and properly reorientated. Indeed, once the dossiers had been examined, some of my colleagues expressed surprise at how large a group this proved to be. There ensued a rather heated discussion on the whole issue of nature versus nurture, and whether the sexual deviant was a genetic freak, or born normal and later corrupted, by parents, peers or some adverse circumstance.

We had already been taken aback, not to say alarmed, by the considerable number of mothers we found in our sample, many of whom – in spite of the so-called alternative birth technologies now available – apparently had experienced normal heterosexual relations in the course of conception. In fact, some of them had obviously decamped from the marital home, taking their offspring with them. (Incidentally, a number of infants and toddlers had been caught up in our original drag-net – it's incredible the places some mothers see fit to bring their children. However, these have all now been placed in satisfactory foster homes.)

Anyway, to return to the point, it was within the heterosexually-experienced group that we encountered some of the most fanatical resistance to reorientation. We tried a very varied repertoire of approaches, ranging from post-hypnotic suggestion to sleep-deprivation accompanied by the repeated screening of classic Hollywood romances, to electrically-assisted aversion therapies. But none yielded any measurable success, so this tack was soon abandoned.

The Chief was extremely depressed during this period – she sometimes confided her doubts to me over our after-dinner brandy. All her life she'd been motivated by the highest ideals of social service, wishing to perform noble experiments for the benefit of mankind, and she was deeply disillusioned by the negative attitude displayed by what she liked to call our clients. In an effort to summon up enthusiasm (and improve our staff morale, as well as theirs) she initiated a series of recreational events, with music, biscuits and inspirational chats from a variety of dis-tinguished – and completely trustworthy – visitors, who kindly gave their services free of charge (which was quite lucky, because there was absolutely no money in the kitty for this sort of thing).

I wouldn't like to say that our little cultural programme was a disaster, but it didn't have anything like the desired effect. Chief was on the verge of tears when she talked about the total lack of social responsibility on the part of our client group: they simply did not appreciate the fact that we were all embarked together on a great exploratory adventure.

Of course, it would be naïve to expect these creatures to show anything like gratitude. I'm not sure if they even realised, when the budget was cut, that the Chief actually diverted funds from staff catering so she could continue providing basic rations twice a day for the inmates. Unfortunately, this move was not particularly popular with the staff, and Chief almost had a strike on her hands until the ring-leaders realised it would be more advantageous to their career prospects if they took out their resentments on their charges instead.

It was around this time that we began to have some problems with the perimeter fence. Electrification had been ruled out after a few unfortunate incidents with straying sheep, because it was judged imperative to maintain good relations with the local farmers. Escape attempts were infrequent, and always unsuccessful, thanks to the well-spaced trip-wires and the dog patrols. But we soon noticed an unusual number of hikers frequenting the area. Our suspicions were rapidly aroused – this district, in the northernmost part of the country, is of no scenic, geological or touristic interest, being occupied primarily by military and civil nuclear installations, pipeline terminals, and a few farms supporting a very large population of extremely stupid sheep and cattle.

Surveillance revealed that the large majority of the outsiders were female, and that they were not simply sightseers looking for a picnic spot. In answer to our enquiries, an interdepartmental memo confirmed that rumours about the camp were circulating in the subculture.

We considered several options for dealing with this situation, until Chief, in a stroke of genius, ordered a few amateurish-looking holes cut at strategic points in the barrier. Those foolhardy trespassers who entered were immediately apprehended. Assessment revealed that, just as we'd expected, they were suitable candidates for treatment.

The subsequent increase in numbers put more pressure on the staff, but there were compensations. Predictably, overcrowding in the huts sparked off angry and sometimes violent outbursts among the occupants. The resulting feuds provided us with a convenient means of control. We played them all off against each other, over such bones of contention as extra rations, shower privileges, and the positioning of heaters – if any – within the huts (winter was coming on). However, we soon discovered that every time we identified a faction or spotted a schism and tried to develop it, things broke up and regrouped again. So the well-tested principle of divide and rule met with only limited success.

Privately, Chief confessed to me that she was becoming irritated. Direction from on high, about what we were supposed to do with them now that we had them, was conspicuously inadequate. But we just soldiered on without complaining, trying this, then trying that.

At this point, Research wanted to initiate some experiments in food deprivation, which was just as well, since the dock and haulage strikes were preventing supplies from coming through. Chief tried, once more, to instil the subjects with a sense of pride and self-respect. She explained that all the knowledge thus gained would one day make the difference between life and death for the victims of famine and disaster everywhere in the world, irrespective of their race, creed, colour, gender or, indeed, sexual orientation. We should all be proud that our little community was thus contributing its own fair share to the alleviation of human misery.

Soon thereafter it was decided that the condition of the surviving inmates no longer warranted the presence of such highly-trained personnel as the Chief and myself; in short, we were no longer cost-effective. However, our superiors were so impressed with her running of the scheme that she has been seconded to the Americans, to train their personnel in the same techniques. I am absolutely delighted, because she has asked them to send me along with her, as her second-in-command. She says that we make an ideal team, and she couldn't possibly carry on without me. Of course, I'm deeply flattered, and also very relieved to be going with her. We would have missed each other terribly, so terribly that it would have undoubtedly affected our work. The Chief thinks so too. Even professionals have private lives, she says. But that, of course, is our little secret.

Strange Connie from Two Doors Down

When Rod and I moved into the new Harrison and Harrison housing estate, we only had the two older children. Cheryl was four years old and Sammy, well, let me think, he must've been just over a year. I met Connie shortly after we'd moved in. Mind you, ours was a more expensive house than theirs and that didn't go down too well with Connie at all. I used to tell her that she should accept what she had within her own four walls and not worry about what other people had. But Connie wasn't the type to listen to anyone's good advice.

She was always a bit strange. Trouble was, it took me too bloody long to work out just how strange! She'd had a good job in an office and kept on working after they moved in 'cos they were struggling to pay off a second mortgage. I can't remember if she had one miscarriage or two before their first son was born but I know she insisted on working right up to just a few weeks before the birth.

It was after their second son came along that she and Matt started to have problems. The baby had been born with some kinda tumour in his stomach. He used to vomit all the time. Connie raised quite a ruckus in the local doctor's surgery, insisting that she be sent to see some specialist with the child. Seems the doctor thought it was just gastric trouble. Anyway, Connie got what she wanted in the end and when she saw this specialist fellow, he told her that the baby needed to be operated on right away.

Poor Matt couln't get away from his work to drive her to the hospital, so I sat in the front with the baby while Connie drove the car. I remember we had to leave the hospital almost straightaway 'cos I had to get back to pick young Cheryl up from school. It was Matt who had to sit in the waiting-room and chew his nails.

Connie used to go on and on about this incident. I never could figure out why she was so upset about it. I put it down to worry about the baby and her not fully recovered from the birth sort of thing. Still, it did seem unfair her not trying to at least look at things from Matt's point of view. Funny thing was, though, that when the baby began to get well, Connie started to go downhill. It was impossible to know how to help her really. One minute she'd be crying and carrying on and the next she'd be dashing around wild-eyed and crazy-looking.

But I did stick by her, by God I did. When the doctors said she'd have to have a spell in that hospital I made it my business to get there at least once a week, sometimes I was visiting three and even four times! I used to tell Connie that I'd rather we talked outside on the grass instead of indoors. Some of them people looked pretty peculiar and I didn't want little Sammy getting any nightmares with things he might've seen in those wards. I used to sort of joke about it with Connie and tell her she had some funny friends.

She'd been in and out of hospital several times before they suggested shock treatment. Neither Matt nor I were very happy with the doctors about that whole business. Matt'd been told that Connie needed one or two treatments but she must've had a dozen or more before Matt was able to get hold of one of the doctors in charge and find out what was going on. Connie looked dreadful for quite some time afterwards. Her memory was none too good either. Poor Matt. It was very hard on him too. You could tell how worried he was.

It was several months before Connie managed to pull herself together. Personally, I have no wish to go through that sort of thing ever again. The things that Connie said to me are over and done with but, believe you me, it's not a pretty story and I guess these things are probably best forgotten. I'd begun to think she was settling down at last, when one night, she ups and tells Matt she wants a separation. Boy! Did that man take it hard. Connie had a part-time job by this time and her younger boy had just started school. It didn't seem too clear to me at the time but I can see now that it was probably things happening for the best.

They were separated for a year. Then, just about the time of one of the kid's birthdays, Matt came up for a bit of a family tea. That started them talking again and they decided to give their marriage another try. I remember I told Connie straight that I didn't for one moment believe she loved Matt. I told her she was kidding herself. She didn't listen to me of course, didn't answer me at all, just gave me one of those eyeball-to-eyeball looks of hers and humphed her way out the door.

We didn't see too much of each other for quite a while. I'd finally got a job working the late shift at the chicken freezing plant which left Rod looking after our four. With my job, the house and four kids, two of them under five, I had more to do with my time than think about Connie and her problems. I kept that lousy job on for almost two years. Meanwhile, Connie and Matt sold their house and bought a bigger house a few miles away, over near the football ground.

I still saw them occasionally; birthdays, Xmas, that sort of thing. Then, lo and behold, not eighteen months after buying the new house, they split up again, only this time it was Connie who moved out, taking both kids with her.

Matt put the house on the market almost immediately but it was quite a long time before he found a buyer. Not that Connie bothered to help him in any way. I heard she'd started to go to one of those women's libber groups and then she told me herself, some time later, that she'd moved into a communal household. And I can tell you, I wasn't at all surprised when Matt phoned me in tears one night to tell me she'd become a homosexual. Connie reckons the correct word for what she is is lesbian but it's all the same to me; they're all weird!

But it's funny how things work out you know. I was so busy, I guess, looking at what was going on with Connie and Matt and their marriage, I hadn't noticed what was happening in mine. I had a suspicion one day that Rod wasn't telling me something and I began to get this queer feeling. Like, when we were out with his workmates and their wives I had this strange sort of feeling, as if they knew things about Rod that I didn't.

It took weeks to drag the truth out of Rod. His affair with that stuck-up receptionist where he worked, had apparently been going on for three years. Finally, after much prodding, Rod confessed the whole sordid mess to me one Monday night after I'd got in from work. I can still see him sitting across from me in the lounge room, his head in his hands, and me thinking that he'd somehow changed from the man I'd married into a stranger you read about in sensational articles in the Sunday papers.

He left the house the same night. I had to give up my job right away as there was no one to look after the kids. It was a long time before I felt I could leave the house with my chin in the air. I couldn't tell the kids about it. The very idea made me sick. I told them he'd gone on a trip to do with his job.

In time, Cheryl picked up the drift of things. When I look back I just don't know what I would have done without that girl. When Connie came over at Xmas I told her and made her promise to keep it a secret or I'd never talk to her again. But when she started to ask me questions about the future I just clammed up. After all, it wasn't her husband who'd gone off with another woman, was it? We had quite a to-do about it there and then. We did manage to patch things up before she left but I never felt quite the same about our friendship. I did tell her I'd never speak to her again if she ever spoke to Rod and she seemed to understand. But that was a long time ago now, and, as I say, these things are best forgotten.

I did get my life back into some order. I put the two little ones into a nursery, made Rod pay the bill, and got myself an office job. Cheryl helped with the house quite a bit and even Sammy was persuaded to mow the lawn and generally make himself useful occasionally. Rod married his shady lady and I got on with the task of picking up the pieces of my life.

Mind you, I still can't understand why Connie was so upset when Matt and I got married. After all, she didn't want him, so why was she so worked up is what I'd like to know. But Connie wasn't really wanting to talk about it, she kept screaming something about how I'd betrayed her and something about double standards, whatever that is, and the way she threw herself around my lounge room, like a child in a tantrum, I could tell there was no use whatever in trying to reason with her.

I've not seen Connie since. Which is just as well really. Matt and I certainly don't want any more trouble in our lives and that's all Connie seems to be about when you really think about it. I guess some people are just like that, aren't they?

First Kiss After First Row

'Give us a hug then,' she says, smiling like a crab with one leg missing. I twitched fractionally, my arms flexing and my body reaching, responding automatically, dancing to its own tune. It's a moment before I remember the hurt and the row. I want to, but the other me, the one who is often wise, often stupid, won't.

'You nearly did,' she is still smiling, happier now having seen my struggle.

She is seated on the bed close to me, touching, has been stroking my back as I wept. I had fled the garden to cry here, on my beautiful new pine bed (and orthopedic mattress). She has never seen it. It had arrived on the day we parted. It was partly her bed, her idea at least that I could own such a piece of furniture. Mattresses on the floor had been a legacy from some hippy, that I'd just accepted; to sleep on a new mattress and a new bed, off the ground – goodness! She had nagged, almost. She had a bad back, well so did I. But wasn't the floor the best, the firmest place? After only two nights in the air it was as if second-hand mattresses had never been. It was at once a cradle, a sofa, a place to be. I could see my garden over the headboard. With my own bed I was grown up at last.

But she had never lain on it. My fleeing and flopping dramatically was a way of saying: 'See how I suffer, see what you have missed, how much I have done for you, a new bed, ours. You weren't there!' Also I sensed that a touch of drama is probably useful at this point, since talking has got us, and in particular me, nowhere. My words have failed to move her, touch her; perhaps my instincts are more reliable. At least she had followed me. I could have sobbed myself dry, I realise, if she'd chosen to let me get on with it. Surely it's a good sign that she has plodded dutifully after me and is sitting closer than you'd expect after that earlier chill anger.

Then I see a gap in the clouds, in the veils of sadness that have clothed us both so separately and so completely for the past two weeks. Something to do with her smile. I feel rather than think; so what my pain, so what it was her fault, so what I don't understand why. I know what I want. Like testing a hot iron with one finger I touch her arm, and clumsily we reach for each other. How else can I describe 'falling into each other's arms'? Is there any way original and new to tell of such an occurrence? Later, she said when she'd walked into the bedroom that she'd deserted for two weeks and had seen the new bed, she'd wanted to laugh and to cry.

We were seated, me lying, her sitting sideways. And at that moment when she reached down for me with her arms and I reached up for her, there was an abandonment of our differences, of unresolved difficulties, of old pain and resentments, as the complicated need we had of each other pushed us to a cleaner, empty place.

Her arms still felt the same, we still fitted and she still takes my breath away. I have to remind myself that this is just a hug. Not to pressure her with my needs. Not to expect. This is a hug for forgiveness, for friendship, to say I still like you. Isn't it? The rest is mine, my selfish hopes. How can I feel aroused at such a time? How crass. Her face is warm. And that soft mouth near. We are somehow stumbling, sitting here. And then our mouths meet, brush each other. Breath gets critical and my stomach caves in, crumbling with relief, memory and desire. So fast comes my breath, so fast and loud seems an inner trampling in my body, my blood, my heart, my mind, that I have to stop. Am I fainting, dizzy with sensation, or stalling, waiting for her to make an acknowledgement of what is happening? Is it a mistake? An accident of mouth on mouth? These arms, are they my lover's or those of a comforting friend?

Then the air in the room seems to grow soft and sharp as it becomes clear. Sensation becomes strong. I feel hers. Unmistakably those old, dear familiar sensations. My shoulders and chest a hive of bees, my mouth electric on hers. The moisture slipping between our gasps making our lips shining, as though gorged on honey. And from the belly and below, a salt, hot painful clutching of pleasure nearly too great to bear. Again I stop.

'What is it?' She is worried, will I punish her, will I make her suffer in revenge? She is big, tall, can obliterate the sky as she kisses me, but her fears make her as small as a child.

'It's too much,' I say. She is still smiling. I lean away and the charge runs from my belly to between my breasts. We are scarcely touching, but I am alight, incandescent. Do I do this? Does she? We joke about

53

our bodies getting on so well, about pheromones, those mysterious chemical magnets, that work overtime with us. I pull her to me again.

ROSEMARY AUCHMUTY

Reunited

The Librarian
Women's College
University of —

Dear Madam,
   I have been asked to introduce and edit a collection of Eleanor
Kingdom's stories and poems. As you probably know, they've been
out of print for fifty years and Kingdom herself is virtually forgotten.
As she was Principal of Women's College from 1918 to 1928, I
wonder if there might be records of a personal or official nature in the
College Archives that might be relevant to my research. If so, would
it be possible for me to visit the Library to see them? Yours sincerely,
Eleanor Conwy

Dear Ms Conwy,
   The Library holds all College records for the period when Eleanor
Kingdom was Principal, and you are welcome to consult them. We
have no personal papers or memorabilia in a separate collection, as
Miss Kingdom did not leave these to the College, but there are letters
and photographs among the papers of some of her contemporaries. If
you wish to see them, perhaps a weekday over the Easter break might
be the best time, as most of the students will be away and you will
have the Library more or less to yourself. Let me know which day
suits you and I will have the material ready for you.
Sincerely,
Margaret Oxenham
(College Librarian)

The librarian was unexpected. Thick-set, incisive, clad in an
Observer-offer suit. Eleanor, sensing her own surprise, wondered
momentarily what she must have been anticipating. Something

altogether more languid, she supposed: faded and dusty, perhaps, like the books.

Margaret Oxenham was not faded or dusty. She was vividly dark-complexioned, vividly dark-voiced, a young middle age. She shook hands with Eleanor and offered her coffee. 'We can have it here, or would you prefer the Senior Common Room? There's a portrait . . .'

'Won't we be disturbing other people?'

'Not at this time of year. Hardly anyone is around.'

'I hope I haven't obliged you to come in specially today.'

'Well, you have,' Margaret admitted, conveying a kettle to the tap in an adjoining cloakroom, Eleanor trailing after in polite earshot. 'But I don't mind, there's always work to do, accessioning and cataloguing, and to tell you the truth, I'm terribly interested in this project of yours.'

'I'm glad,' said Eleanor warmly, not taken aback, as they returned to a power point.

'Quite a few people come here to use the college archives for their research,' her hostess went on, 'and of course an official history has been commissioned for the centenary next year; but no one so far has shown much interest in the principals for their own sake, and they were all fascinating and outstanding women – women we must reclaim.'

'If every feminist undertook to research the life of one forgotten woman . . .'

'. . . then I should have a library to be proud of.' Face unseen, it was impossible to guess Margaret's real thoughts. The kettle boiled. Eleanor waited, but no further reflections were forthcoming.

Coffee made, Margaret took up a tray and led the way down the corridor. A door gilt-labelled 'Senior Common Room' gave into a long, high-ceilinged chamber of leather chairs and low tables. Tall windows the length of one side overlooked the heavily pruned stumps of a summer rose garden, jealously hedge-sequestered. The other walls, inevitably wood-panelled, were hung with portraits.

Eleanor gazed. 'All those strong women,' she murmured; and Margaret, watching, seemed satisfied.

'That's Miss Lightfoot, the first principal. Miss Paine. Miss Preston. Dr Battye.'

And paused before the fifth, ill-lit, in a corner – yet it still caught the eye. 'Miss Kingdom.'

Eleanor approached, confessed: 'I thought at first it was a man.' The sitter had cropped hair and collar and tie. She stood out from the silver coiffures and flowing robes of her predecessors. The face was potent yet serene, eyes directed with artless honesty at the viewer. The hands, too, though loosely folded, suggested power as well as gentleness.

'I've always liked her best,' remarked Margaret Oxenham.

'I've seen photographs,' said Eleanor, not exactly ignoring but storing the statement away for later contemplation, 'but there is no comparison, is there?' She turned to the librarian, to tell her, awkwardly. 'She was my aunt.'

'Really?'

'My mother's aunt. I'm named after her.' The explanation must be given. 'She died just before I was born. My mother thought the world of her.'

As if embarrassed, Eleanor looked away, her eyes ranging over the other portraits in the room. Miss Leslie, Miss de Lisle, Mrs Simpson-Clarke. None so striking as Miss Kingdom.

'I don't suppose,' intruded the librarian, hesitant, 'you have any of Eleanor Kingdom's personal papers in your family?'

'We have all of them,' was the blunt reply. 'But she didn't leave much. A handful only. She destroyed her diaries and most of her correspondence before she died.'

'I wondered what had happened to it.'

Dame Isabel Neville, Mrs Shanks, Professor French, in ever-decreasing verisimilitude. The latest addition, Dr Jenny Lowe, was an uncompromising blotch of pink in a sea of red. Only by the spectacles might one have known her, if one had known her.

'She retired last year,' explained Margaret, following Eleanor's visual circuit. 'Miss Neville' – nodding at the Dame, small, jolly, approachable-looking – 'was principal in my time.'

'You were a student here?'

'Yes. A long time ago. Miss Neville died last November and we've just received her papers. I'm sorting through them now; they make interesting reading.'

'I was going to give Eleanor Kingdom's papers to the college,' said Eleanor, frankly anticipating. 'I rather hoped, when you said you had some letters from her in other collections, that they might prove to be the other side of the few bits of correspondence she didn't destroy.'

Stopped then, because a queer look – alert? surprised? – had crossed the librarian's face as she listened, silent. It was as if Margaret were not accustomed to collaboration – but she must be! – suspicious then, or did not know how to receive the offer. Eleanor was startled, thinking it straightforward and the situation understood.

(But the misunderstanding was hers, in fact.)

'Who are they from, your letters?' Margaret asked.

'I haven't seen them yet,' Eleanor confessed. 'My mother has them, she found them after my grandmother died, years ago, but of course I wasn't interested then, so never asked to see them. I'm going to get them on Friday.'

'I look forward to seeing them,' said the other woman conventionally. Giving nothing away.

Back in the library Margaret brought college reports and governors' minutes and odd letters penned in Eleanor Kingdom's wilful hand and first editions of her poems and stories. Eleanor read and jotted. Meanwhile Margaret in her office worked on the Neville collection. After lunch she took Eleanor to the college chapel where a polished plaque on the chancel wall commemorated Miss Kingdom in company with her sister principals, Dame Isabel Neville most recently added alongside.

'But she isn't buried here?'

'No, in the old churchyard. They're both there, in fact. I went to Miss Neville's funeral as it happened and saw Miss Kingdom's grave at that time.'

'I should like to see it,' said Miss Kingdom's grand-niece.

Again that funny look, bemused, abashed. Eleanor, puzzled, did not dare to press the point.

Margaret drove her to the station.

'I'll let you know what's in the family letters as soon as I've looked at them,' Eleanor promised.

'Thank you.'

'And you'll let me know if you come across anything new?' she pursued.

'Of course.'

'Good. I'd like to keep in touch.'

And Margaret evidently surprised herself by saying, 'So would I.' And turned away, perplexed.

Every day when Margaret gets home from work the cats come flying and oh the pleasure of kicking off work clothes and into jeans, pottering, tending the plants, a quiet drink and the news. It is a ritual, set in her ways she knows and unashamed. They had asked her if she wished to live in college, but no. When you are young, communal bathrooms, cold spartan bedrooms, surroundings in which expense has had to be spared (for this is a *Women*'s College after all), these are all part of an adventure; but Margaret at forty is past dreams of adventure, cannot bear the memory of tousled dressing gowns in corridors, wants her own space, her own silence.

Except. The Neville papers in her briefcase, the tinkle of the telephone just set down, and the vision – could she call it up? – of an adventure, perhaps, not expected. The voice reminded her. Lank elegance, brown hair was it? shaggy on thin shoulders, not like Margaret, casual in trousers – *she* could wear what she chose. Younger, prettier, stylish. So relaxed. So in command. Had her aunt been like that too?

But how presumptuous. The clever scholar and the dull librarian.

Margaret fed the cats and then herself, taking no pleasure.

But found joy in dear Miss Neville's letters later, re-reading, recollecting, anticipating.

Meanwhile, Eleanor, a packet of letters retrieved and to hand.

At the top of the pile, a postcard:

> Hotel Post
> Pertisau-am-Achensee
> 2nd April 1920

Dear Miss Kingdom,

Arrived in Pertisau yesterday in the middle of a snowstorm, but overnight the snow cleared off magically and after a hearty 'English' breakfast we ventured out into the sunshine. Elspeth has already done her ankle in on the ice, wouldn't she just. Most of us tried ski-ing, and Madge is showing impressive proficiency. I am not I'm sorry to say! *Don't* you wish you'd come with us? But I hope you are enjoying your break. Did you go to Sussex as you planned? Seems strange to think of primroses and daffodils here. All the girls send their love.

Isabel Neville

Isabel Neville. Isabel Neville. Where has she heard that name before?

Margaret's brisk tones come back to her, prompting remembrance: 'Miss Neville was principal in my time.' And the plaque in the chapel. 'Dame Isabel.'

And the Neville papers, bequeathed to the college.

Evidently a student of Miss Kingdom: but why keep this guileless missive, of which a thousand must come a teacher's way?

Unless it was the first, and sentimental.

The next, a letter from Weybridge, dated Christmas 1932, and quite different.

Dearest Eleanor,

I am sitting at Mother's desk in the drawing room, well wrapped up in rugs and woollies for it is as cold indoors as out, and wishing desperately, *hopelessly* that you were here . Mother seems a little better today, but no one, even at her best, could call her *festive*. She's having her nap at the moment ... Did the cats like their presents? ... I miss you so much.

Signed: Ever yours, Isabel.

Three more letters in this vein, each apparently written during a separation which must, by deduction, have been temporary, and all the more painful for that, prompting unusual outspokenness. But the last is otherwise. It is still in its envelope, still sealed, addressed to Eleanor Kingdom at the Sussex cottage where she spent her last years. The postmark, smudged, is it April 1950? The year she died? (Eleanor knew, having been born in that year.) Did she never open this letter? Has it never been opened at all? There is no return address, but the writing is Isabel's – precise, almost fussy – and someone (Eleanor's grandmother, perhaps; her mother?) has placed it in the Isabel-bundle.

Eleanor feels voyeuristic, but does not really hesitate.

Women's College
31st March 1950

My darling,

Just a quick note in answer to your invitation which came this morning. Yes I would love to come. I always feel so washed out at the end of term, a weekend in the country is exactly what I need I'm sure. Had the governors bickering about new appointments for *four* hours last night. Oh my dear I am not cut out for this job. Haven't got your strength or your tact. You always got what you wanted didn't you and yet everyone was happy. Must stop this maundering, Iris tells me the builders have arrived. Look after yourself my dear and I look forward to seeing you tomorrow evening, expect me in time for supper.

But never did, never again.

Phoned Margaret. 'There was no warning, she hadn't been ill,' Eleanor recalled. 'My grandmother went the same way later. It must be in the family.'

'It's a good way to go, and she'd a full life,' was Margaret's comment, unintentionally banal; but what to say? 'She was about seventy, I think?'

'Rough on Isabel, though,' said Eleanor. 'Being so much younger. Margaret,' (accusingly) 'you knew, didn't you? Why didn't you tell me?'

A silence, seeking the right words. Then: 'I suppose I didn't want to share the story with just anybody – with someone who might not understand.'

'But when I said I had the letters . . .'

'Yes. Well, there was nothing I could do about that. I knew if she kept any they'd be Isabel's. But by then, it didn't matter.'

'What do you mean, it didn't matter?'

'I'd decided you were all right.'

Eleanor's smile was wasted on the sightless telephone receiver. But all she said was, 'You must have Eleanor's letters to Isabel.'

'Yes.'

'May I see them?'

'You show me yours,' Margaret proposed; 'and I'll show you mine.'

'Bring your wellies and a mac,' Margaret had instructed. 'It's very overgrown and likely to be muddy. They cleared a trail last autumn but . . . I don't suppose anyone else goes up there now.'

She was waiting at the station. The train was late and Eleanor had meant to be apologetic. But in her pleasure, forgot. The librarian was transformed. In the college, in her work clothes she had seemed distant, intangible. Not quite right. Today's trousers, boots, parka with hands thrust deep in pockets – a happier uniform. One sensed she was at ease. Windswept. Woolly. Tangible. Eleanor kept *her* hands at her sides, with an effort.

'You look nice,' she told her, inadequately.

Margaret's manner made it clear she could not take compliments gracefully. 'The car's outside,' was her brusque response. And marched off.

They drove to the old church on the hill above the town. Once there, they must walk. Margaret had got the key to the cemetery from the rector. She unlocked the gate and led the way along the path, uncomfortably overhung as predicted, and dripping and slippery in the drizzle.

'What an odd place to choose to be buried,' Eleanor remarked by way of making contact.

'It would have been neat and kempt in Miss Kingdom's day,' Margaret reminded her. 'But it must be thirty years since they closed it, it was full, and now they only open it for people to be buried in family plots.'

'How come Isabel Neville is here, then?' demanded Eleanor, guessing anyway.

'Wait and see,' teased Margaret, she knew she knew.

The graves they sought were insignificant, easily overlooked without foreknowledge, twin oblongs of earth low-fenced with a single headstone, like a double bed with one pillow. And on that pillow, in worn lettering first:

Here lies
ELEANOR MARY KINGDOM
1879–1950
Principal of Women's College 1918–28
Poet, Teacher & Friend

while below, more freshly incised:

And her Friend & Pupil
DAME ISABEL ALICE NEVILLE
1902–1982
Principal of Women's College 1948–63

And then the one word:

REUNITED

'Reunited,' read Eleanor, as if . . .

'Miss Kingdom bought the double plot before she died,' explained Margaret. 'But I don't suppose either of them dreamt they'd have to wait so long.'

'Reunited now, though. A happy ending.'

'If you believe in such things,' but Margaret was looking at Eleanor, no longer at the tombstone.

And Eleanor?

'Shall we go and read the letters?'
It is agreed. And off they go together.

BERTA FREISTADT

What I Did on My Holidays: a truncated and one-sided story

1. At the seaside

I sat at the edge watching her and let the waves, clean, cool and faintly green wash over me, like love. They came from an inexhaustible source, far from the still, hard commanding horizon. I half lay on the stones, tired from a swim. I was waiting for her to come and join me, so we could play together. Swim together. But I'd swum away from her feeling only the water, forgetting the shore, and she'd stayed where she was. Had she noticed how well I'd swum? I wanted praise. She knew I was afraid of the water, that I was a poor swimmer. I am unused to swimming, to any hard physical activity except riding my bicycle or making love.

At first the waves washed my feet, and I could admire the gloss on my body performed by the water. I could catch my breath, pleased that I'd been out of my depth without fear, without drowning. I'd not minded the taste of salt and had felt the great swell of water support and surround me. Then we'd been in partnership and I'd used the power for my pleasure and achievement. Now passive, tired of my part in the dangerous watery game, I was aware that the sea, like love was not to be trifled with.

As if teasing, indeed the sound of the surf had that same quality as soft laughter, the waves began gently to take me. I felt embraced, desired; the waves' urgent pull felt like a claim. The sea became animal with needs and qualities like my own. This constant return should be my lover, ever urgent, ever eager. Always there. But as I day-dreamed, lulled by the rocking of the water and the pride of my swim, I didn't notice how the sea was changing. Or rather was being the same; itself, alterable, nothing to do with my fantasies. Do I ever see things as they really are? Things, the world, lovers?

Soon, in a minute or two, the water that had splashed over my feet in play, had risen to my chest and was lifting me powerfully, demanding something from me, threatening me with its depths. I had been deceived by my triumph. And all the time the shining sun let the sea glisten and sparkle innocently, turning dull stone to polished marble. And she was a tiny faraway figure, a swimming doll with no recognisable face, intent on her own exercise. Lover, I called to her silently against the roaring waves. Are you constant? Are you honest? Why are we here together? Then soon I was being dragged a few inches back and forth over the stones. I got up and dried myself, and lay down on the sand. She emerged like a sleek seal flicking water from her head, dripping, gleaming. She smiled at me and lay on her towel without speaking.

2. The beauties of nature

'Come and look at the sky' – she said. It was an unremarkable orange with only the silhouettes of trees making it dramatic. Earlier when we hadn't been speaking it had been more unusual, pale streaked with both silhouette and shadow. One night before when she had turned away from me and not sleeping I had crept from the tent before dying or crying or something, the sky had, as it often does in crises of love and hate, astounded, humbled and comforted me. A great dark blue panorama with stars dancing in their lovely formations and the luminous Milky Way a tearful streak that seemed to laugh at my distress.

In London, that dirty, tricky collection of towns, the sky was punctuated with the loud exclamation uprights of buildings. Never a long flat horizon to rest the eye. Never the soft breeze or the eternal motion of the sea. Buildings. Grimy and neglected. But inside, in some of them, were my friends. Soft arms, kisses warm as toast; my support, my life-line. Here I was alone except for her. Here was the sea, the sun, the wind, the open sky and a heavy band of cold constraint between us. We spoke, or rather she spoke, all smiles and charm, faultless. I responded. Almost in grunts. I was unable to burst from my cocoon, my strait-jacket of fear, of premeditated pain. I should laugh at her demands, thrust myself boldly at her, claim from her what I wanted. I should dance lightly before her like the stars did for me. Exist, enjoy, live for myself, ignoring her moods. But I was concentrating too hard on keeping my balance as I tumbled at full screaming pace towards the end, the edge of this love. 'Yes' I said, 'it's lovely, a lovely colour.' Even that a lie. Anything to please her, to win her. Look, I'm trying.

'I love you,' she'd said. 'You don't trust, you'll see. We'll grow old together.' Now she no longer wanted me. We had no future as lovers. 'It isn't enough,' she said, 'just to be turned on by your body.' There was nothing to say then. No more striving. I lost my words. My reason abandoned me. I was passive. If that's how she felt then of course we should part. I scarcely asked why, not wanting to hear those words from a mouth that had given me so much pleasure. And now I was being invited to come, to view, to admire, to communicate. Be loved again? But it was nothing. Neither her distant smiling nor the sunset warmed me. I could raise no enthusiasm. Which was a mistake in the game we were playing whose ground rules had been lost somewhere. If there had ever been any. She was visibly irritated by my blankness.

Adrift in an alien place, I remembered it had happened before. Another mercurial love had boiled and evaporated. Then fifteen feet of snow had prevented me running away, but had aptly echoed the ice in my heart. Now sun and sea persuaded me to stay. She did too – 'We can still be friends, still be nice to each other.' It was her holiday as well. I sat in the dying light, the air still warm, in my bikini. So my body is all right is it? Or is she just saying that? Or is what she isn't saying even worse? Which part of me was unacceptable? All of it, some of it? It, do I mean me? 'I'm crazy about you' – she'd often said. How quickly it had gone. And even now we weren't doing it right, being honest, working it out, talking, telling each other what was wrong. We were, I was, just letting it sail away. A paper boat on a strong tide.

Sex was important to us, to me. With other lovers it had been just sex; with her we flowed right off an electric current. The same one. The same river of joy. But last night, trying to make love, she'd said it was the exposed nature of the tent that had inhibited her. 'Sounds carry for miles in the open,' she said. And I'd felt a dying fire.

So I stared at the sky obediently, awkwardly, and knew suddenly that the beauties of nature were for me only made lovely when illuminated by another kind of beauty. I could be happy down a coal mine, if only she loved me.

3. Going home

Slowly she drives us over the bumpy track. Slowly, carefully because of the fragile suspension, past the tent with the barbeque stand, past the lines of washing, the communal loos, the swings, past the girl putting curlers in her friend's hair. They are not lovers, but see how tender they are to each other. We stop briefly at a jam at the entrance and I sink down in the seat not wanting to be seen. I'm sure it's written all over my face, all over hers, all over the hastily packed car. All over. Another lesbian fight. They all do it. No security in those relationships. I feel the criticism, the world's blame. I'm no different to the rest. My loving is not special.

I want especially to avoid The Man. He either owns or manages the site. Short, very tanned with sleeked back hair and a knowing smile. A strange smile that embraces the places you'd rather it didn't. But even more unnerving are his eyes. One has a wild and crazy squint. It goes with his smile, together they attack a world where most eyes face the front. He is a good-looking man and his wild eyes give him a delinquent air that is almost frightening. I knew one like him before, years ago. A man who played judo. He was very successful. He would grimace at his opponent at close quarters, scaring and horrifying with his bad eye, as well as fighting. But once also I knew a teacher, a sweet woman who had a squint. I knew she would look straight at me when she spoke to me, so I simply looked into the eye that was on me and disregarded the slothful wanderings of the other. But with The Man it didn't quite work. As if he didn't want to be caught in normal communication, neither eye ever seemed the right one to address, and his smile mocked as he sold milk or took your booking fee.

He's right there, wandering around outside the shop. I feel that if his eyes and then his smile should alight on us in our carload of misery, he would know all, be filled with amusement, and I would expire with grief and shame. But he turns away, the jam clears and we are off on our journey home. Maybe the smile was what we needed. Someone to laugh at us, at our seriousness. Someone to bang the importance of our feelings out of us.

Remember that first night? You put your arm out as I went by and I was folded to you. Into the fold. Home to roost. So big you were, and that was so good. Was it my mother who was so big, was comfort, all love? Was that why it felt so familiar and easy? She's tiny now, an old lady; but when I was little, she must have been big as a tree. A tree certainly, no rock. For if I remember the lovely sanctuary she was, then I must also remember that it was as wavy and dangerous as a tree in a gale when the tempest raged. And if it was her I was re-creating with you, I should have been perfectly happy, for that's what you are like. Sanctuary and tempest.

It is now four hours since I woke. Of course I was not hungry then, waking up and finding the day worse than the night. Usually you can wake from bad dreams, from the hauntings of rejection that play in the night cinema of your mind. You can greedily grab the daylight's sanity, throwing off those remnants with a shower, some cold sharp juice, a phone call. Ironically I had slept dreamlessly, exhausted and hunched away from her, but well. As I woke aware of a painful heaviness in my body, I remembered it all and was instantly in tears. I needed to face the day, get through it without disgracing myself; she offered me breakfast but food was out of the question. My whole body was turned inwards consuming the pain, the loss, the humiliation and was without a doubt eating itself. My gorge was in my throat, my glands were swollen, my head was sick and my eyes were blurred. There was a barrier between me and the world, between me and her, invisible, intangible, but tough, and to me very familiar.

I was desperate for safety, could not possibly live out weeks here in civilised friendship. I wanted to go home. 'Just drop me at a station.' But nothing I could say would persuade her to stay, she was affronted by the idea that I could leave her alone among the heterosexual families. So I packed, she packed, we folded the tent into the car and divided the food. Even that was contentious. I threw away a bulky white loaf that she'd bought. This she saw as provocation and revenge. Now four hours later, my body is of course hungry, though I couldn't contemplate food. Or maybe it's the other way round. Maybe I need the food and my body is the rebel. I'm not sure how to make that split comprehensible to myself. I, me, my body. We are all one in my head, but today different things were happening in different departments. If I'd been less involved with my pain I could have had some fun with the image of myself as a castle under siege, with the drawbridge raised, the moat full of alligators and boiling oil being prepared on the battlements. But that was to come later, weeks later. Now I was in tatters, hungry but not hungry. Beginning to shake.

She asked me if I'd got any food. Presumably, since I'd wanted to come home and she was driving me, it was my job to provide sustenance. Of course I had. A packet of biscuits was somehow there and I ate at last, knowing I needed the sugar to give me strength, wanting a ʃhe had last night to be alone, on a train, on a coach, anywhere but close to her in her car. She had some nectarines; so we ate together, honey biscuits and nectarines. A lovers' supper you might think, except we weren't any more, and weren't going to be ever again. The dry crumbs and the sweet fruit made me choke and salivate in turn, while she smoked fag after fag and watched the road.

Remember when I used to slip my hand under your thigh as you were driving? Anything to get nearer, closer to you, my beloved. Beloved; I mean that word in its true sense. Not joking this time, not being ironic. You were beloved, though I knew you didn't really believe it. Any more than I did when you said you loved me. We both thought ourselves unworthy. And that time you took my hand and steered the car with it. Laid it on your thigh after.

Remember when you asked me to hold your head? It made you feel safe. Remember telling me to lie on top of you? Often you said that. And we'd get lost sharing passion. Exchanging warmth and moisture. You'd feel me next to you and be getting into that. I'd be feeling you next to me and feel how you were feeling. Would be getting off on you getting off on me. Such a happy roundabout. So many horses to try.

Coming back in the car, in four hours we'd scarcely spoken. I'd been ironic again, she obtuse, turning everything I said into more reasons for our separation. We stopped at a motorway café. Where was it? Somewhere. There were more families, youths, little girls in frocks, the angry travelling faces of the other world. Again the feeling of exposure, of being naked: that I was playing in an old familiar movie, that everyone knew the plot, was whispering my lines beneath their breath. She seemed oblivious, she whose surrender two nights before had been half-hearted, almost disinterested because of other people hearing, could sit unselfconsciously with a trembling, tearful, white-faced companion. Of course, that's my subjective view; after all, she has lived as an outsider far longer than I.

She bought an orange squash, I had tea with cream, no milk. Too strong, and white sugar making a bad taste. Beginning to feel dizzy, with the car, the loss, the silence. That car, yellow as a canary. Or a crocus. What did she call the colour? I never asked her. I remember once we had a fight over the colour of my new shorts. I only bought them to impress her. I've never worn them since we parted. I called them golden, she contradicted me saying no, I was wrong, they were primrose. She was right of course, they were primrose, but I fought though somewhat defensively and certainly without humour, for my

69

right to call them what the hell I liked, amazed that she should correct me. Such arrogance. Later we learned to laugh at the incident. It became history for us.

She offered me her squash when I said how awful the tea was. But that was just as bad. I was often amazed at the dreadful food she ate. I loved her body as it was, big, fleshy, erotic. But she hated it, and fed it a diet of coke, pizza, cake. Not that my diet is any better, but I only hate my face, not my body. I didn't want her squash anyway. I wanted her to love me.

Side by side we sit, sat. Shoulder to shoulder on a bed, suffragettes of love. I can remember that this happened, I know it did, though now I'm so cut off from that time that I've lost the ability to re-create the smallest, the slightest shiver of feeling. We were just sitting. I turned my head and our eyes met, immediately we desire each other. Immediately I am drawn into a whirlpool where she is a centre and the rest of the room, the world, is spinning unrecognisable and forgotten. I feel the breath in my body lift me towards her, though I'm sure I don't move. I'm loosened, near to fainting, need to lean on her. She sees it all in my eyes as I see it in hers, the same thing. 'How did you know,' she says, 'the very moment when I was turned on?' 'It's written all over your face,' I say.

We'd had such a nice day. Finally being able to be nice to each other. I can hardly remember it now, except that it was hot, I was hopeful and there were at least ten more days of this. I remember too writing postcards. I saw one later at a friend's house, it was cheerful, jokey and so hopeful. I had come doubtful, feeling a sense of impending disaster. When we first arrived we were so formal and silent I'd been reminded of two women at the open-air swimming pool in Hampstead. Eve, my best friend, and I had watched them sit on the same blanket, each occupied with her own book without speaking for three hours. 'Guess who's a couple,' I'd said and we'd laughed. Now I felt there were three of us on that blanket. But I wanted so dreadfully for this to work. A holiday in the sun with my lover. I was going to take reels of photos of her looking happy, beautiful and loving. Looking at me in the eye of the camera and sending a message of love that I could photograph and keep for ever. This is her, she loves me, look, you can see it in her face. So I'd ignored the warning bells. So far I'd only taken one picture of her. She none of me, I think. Maybe; I remember so little of the externals of those few days. Only the tumult of my inner self.

The night before we'd talked, made peace and made love. Today we'd been on the beach, now it was tea time and we were sitting eating cream teas. There were families seated around, busy with each other. It was fascinating if sobering. You could see who was boss, who was underdog. Who was assertive, who always gave in. Before me was the whole of our civilisation in miniature; the hierarchies, the systems, the laws. All reflected in how these men and women, who would say they loved each other, ate tea together. The interplay between members of one family in particular reminded me painfully of my former life. Cold waves of memory hit me and as we'd sometimes talked before of how different our lives had been, she a lesbian since young, full of self-loathing till recently, me with long years of failed heterosexuality, I joked that nothing, even her suffering, could compare with trying to love one of those strange creatures who are so other. It was as if I had cast a spell. I could almost feel a wind as she withdrew from me. An apology was no good, that's not what she wanted.

At the camp site I still hadn't fully comprehended what was happening, what was to happen. I could scarcely believe what I was hearing. What she was doing. Taking offence over that remark. It was nothing, half a joke anyway. Inviting her to laugh a little at herself, in sympathy with me. Not enough to end a relationship. Was she looking for a way out? Had she been? It felt like it . . . 'Is there any hope for us' – I was being ironic again. Making a little joke. Still not understanding that she'd gone. That I was already talking to a stranger who had made up her mind. I was like a saleswoman trying to hard sell a beggar. I never noticed her going, only suddenly that I was here and that she was there and was untouchable, wanting cruelly to be alone and away from me. Why did I give her that opening? I made it easy. Why didn't I see quickly where her land lay and creep quietly like a harvest mouse into the lining of her pocket? Maybe later she would have been calmer, sweeter, would have wanted me again. Was I so tired of the long haul, that I could no longer fight? No longer hang on to this rollercoaster love? Just once more. Had she forgotten the promises and the ecstasy? Apparently she had. 'Is there any hope for us?' 'Not as lovers there isn't.' The prompt answer, as if on a cue she'd been waiting for, immediately stealing what was most precious to me. Killing at a stroke the animal that was our love.

We sat in the tent looking at each other. My skin was hot from the sun. Still felt hot in the cooling evening air. She crouching over the gaz stove was a creature at bay, ready to spring and kill me if necessary. I mustn't waken her anger. Was it too late to pacify her, she was pre-menstrual, wasn't she? I must try to be light. She'd laugh at this tonight in my arms, when I kissed her. Kissing her I would sometimes open my eyes to watch her. To catch the fire on her face; to check she was really there, a woman. That it really was true I was in a woman's arms, kissing a woman's mouth; aflame for a woman. For how long did I try often in vain to catch alight in a man's arms? So many years. And now I watch her, and see her eyes avoiding mine. I even feel nostalgic for the few men who did cherish me. Right now I need any shelter, any balm. I want to rush to Eve, to Caroline, Jill, Kate. They see me as I see myself sometimes when I am depressed hating the sight of myself, just before I cover my mirror. And still are fond. They don't reject me because I'm imperfect. Cannot bear that cold clarity. I feel naked and ugly without the soft-focus lens of your love for me. Not that I want to hide the truth, only to have some kind of advantage, a little colouring on that truth of myself. So you will know me kindly, with good thoughts. Don't we all love our friends in that way, doesn't our care and love for them give them a little glow so we don't see their faults, their pettinesses quite so hardly. Just a touch of mascara.

'See you then.' 'Right,' I say, 'see you.' Not looking into her eyes, not touching her fingers as she hands me the last pile of my things. Between us is a well where once there was a bridge. A well full of bitterness, disappointment and misunderstanding.

I haven't seen her since, though she keeps coming to my house to see my flatmate. I'm always out. I hope this irritates her. I'm getting over it quite well. All my friends are proud of me, and though pain lingers in my emotional stratosphere, like a nuclear death cloud drifting over my abrasions when I least expect it, I've almost forgotten her. Forgotten her snake-like whisperings in those moist clutching nights, forgotten her great and desirable beauty, her passion, her promises and her languishing erotic power.

4. What I liked best in my holiday

A few weeks later, away in Wales with friends to recuperate, I met two women. Old, white-haired. 'Good,' I thought, oppressively. 'They'll know how to make pudding.' They were mother figures. It was my turn to cook the dinner and pudding always seems too much trouble to cook, though not of course to eat. They made a lovely pudding and after we'd eaten mountains of soup, casserole, pudding and seconds of everything, we fell into deep, raggy chairs to talk to each other. The subject of love, with its allied interests sex and loyalty arose. One of my mother figures smiled and looked at her companion. 'Well,' she said, 'she and I have been together for twenty-two years. And we're still in love with each other.' It wasn't corny. The room fell silent. Thunderstruck, we could only grin at each other and gape. Though I couldn't resist one of my half jokes. It got a laugh, but I think I meant it. I said, 'Can I have your autograph?'

Thanks to Jacky Taylor for her skilful and beautiful typing.

LORNA MITCHELL

Rosemary for Remembrance – or from my diary, 1962

Thursday 17 February 1962

The big problem is, do I look straight at her when she's on lines duty on the stair or not? As it is, I get thrown into a depression if I just glimpse her gazing at the floor in one of her really sour moods. If a look like that landed on me, that would be it for the day. The last time I got a smile from her was that for-ever memorable day last month. I was late in for school and she was outside Room 36 working at the guillotine and she threw her head back in that wonderful way she has and gave me a really friendly grin. I do love the shape of her mouth. I worry about her face being a bit manly. I worry, because now that I come to think of it, that's what I like about her. I really must buy a book on homosexuality. I know what a state of ecstasy I get into when I see her walking into the science lab. for her coffee at the interval. Oh that walk, that slow elegant almost swaggering way she moves and I really like her legs. But are my feelings sexual? I mean it's not as if I want to stand up the close with her and put up with boring slobbery kisses like I had to do with John Ferguson last year. Maybe its just more heroine worship like I had for Grace Kelly and Audrey Hepburn and Ingrid Bergman and Mary Ure. But I worshipped them for their beauty and what I feel for her is more physical. I remember reading in the *Spectator* that there are a lot of queers in boys' public schools and they explained it was just sexuality rather than homosexuality. But boys in public schools don't get a chance to see girls, but I could go out with boys if I wanted. But I don't. I mean look at what happened with John Ferguson. I sometimes think we spent all that time necking at the pictures because we couldn't think of anything to say to each other. And then he threw me over for his cricket anyway. Cricket, I ask you? I mean how could I have talked to him about D.H. Lawrence or Piero della Francesca? With her it would be so different, I'm sure I could make her understand all my ideas. Oh I don't know, I can't really believe I'm queer, but I do love her with all my heart.

But anyway how do I get her to notice me? If I keep smiling at her will she eventually notice and say 'Why are you staring at me with that imbecile grin on your face? Haven't you got better things to do with your time?' – and that would be just awful. Maybe I should practise perfect posture, knowing how keen she is on that. Trouble is that when I do think I'm being conspicuous, I just get self-conscious. It all seems so hopeless trying to plan anything. Every night I'm carried away with my dreams 'tomorrow something will happen to bring us together, tomorrow she'll look and understand', and every morning my hopes crash on the rocks. Nothing, absolutely nothing.

Monday 15 March 1962
Yet another lousy day and no sign of her anywhere. And I had Miss Gorman yelling at me at maths for doing a sum while she was working at the board. God how I hate her bawling, and her clichés, 'I've got my certificates, I don't have to sit exams,' etc., etc.Today she said to me, 'You're the laziest girl I've ever come across – you make me sick,' and I wished I'd been able to stand up and say, 'You make me sick, Miss Gorman, I'll tell you why, I'm not interested in maths, because I hate you. I hate you, you rude crude bullying loud-mouth *Philistine*.' I didn't, of course, I just sank into my seat and she went on about 'Give me boys every time, none of this whingeing and moping,' etc., etc. The woman is a prime example of what maths does to people. Everyday I sit there, gazing out at the trees and the sky, then I look down at the lines marked A,B,C, and my soul dies and my mind goes blank. What do lines A,B,C, tell me about people? About love and hate and the purpose of living? It's so utterly abstract, the epitome of D.H. Lawrence's deadening intellectuality, the enemy of sensual knowledge and blood consciousness.

Dinner time was the usual going over the weekend's debauchery. This Saturday it was a party at Jane McKay's house. They were playing 'chicken' apparently. I didn't lower myself to enquire exactly what 'chicken' was but I can guess the sort of thing. Two boys stood outside the door and told Mrs. McKay they were playing 'Hunt the thimble'. Some parents must be pretty gullible. I try to restrict my comments on these parties, but I don't want to look as if I'm too shy and innocent, so I try and throw in a few sarcastic comments here and there. I have tried to deliver the odd lecture about dragging sex in

75

the mud but mostly they just ignore it or look at me as if I was cracked. 'Petting' is a good word for it. It's got a sordid sound. And that's what it is, petty and sordid. Not sex at all in my opinion. I certainly am never going to demean myself by getting involved in it, ever. No, I shall only have a complete sexual union or not at all. When I meet a man with whom I have spiritual rapport, sex will be fulfilment, an ecstatic union of both the spiritual and sensual. I don't agree with Lawrence when he opposes the spiritual and sensual; the intellectual and the sensual are opposed, definitely. To be lost to intellectuality, to sink deep in blood consciousness, that's what sex is all about. It's what Rupert Birkin in *Women in Love* calls 'the mystic conjunction beyond love, in the realm of pure being like two stars together in constellation'. Really, what has all this fumbling about and rolling around in piles of coats and slobbering and showing off red marks on your neck got to do with 'mystic conjunction'? I have so much feeling about this that I know I won't be able to concentrate on these Latin verbs I've got to learn for tomorrow.

And I have to do the map for geography because I forgot to take in my atlas today. As a matter of fact, I also forgot my arithmetic book, algebra jotter, French Dictionary, and my *Approach to Latin*. Oh my sins! I'm so utterly lazy and undisciplined. What I need is a guide, a guardian angel. She could be that, I'm sure. Oh, when will it happen? When will our destined paths merge?

Wednesday 21 March 1962
Today I had a wonderful revelation at prayers. I had managed to get to the end of the line, and had her in full view. This week she's been wearing that black band of hers round her neck, like women do in Impressionist paintings. This morning it came to me: Renoir's 'The Umbrellas' that's hanging in the top corridor opposite the Latin room. The way the woman in that painting stands: with her head tilted, that slant of her hips. Oh yes, it's just exactly how she stands at prayers. What a remarkable coincidence! I wonder if it's because she and that woman have attained the same depth of blood consciousness? What puzzles me is how she has evolved that far. I mean, she must be a virgin, she's not exactly a raving beatnik or anything, quite strict really. I can't imagine she believes in pre-marital sex like Careen Levison's mum who gives her pills and all that. What's more she's not exactly the youngest person on the staff, must be at least 30, so she's obviously on the shelf already. Yet she's no dried-up old maid.

She has this amazing physical magnetism that makes me want to hug her everytime I see her.

Wednesday 21 April 1962
Talk about the 'agony and the ecstasy', that's what this afternoon was. Usually they're just plain agony, Wednesday afternoons. God, how I hate art. I get worse and worse every week. I've completely lost my confidence. I always have hated them prowling around looking at everything, but now I just die of shame and embarrassment. Thank God I don't have her for art, I'd have had a nervous breakdown months ago if I had. So now to the ecstasy. Well, she came into our class and asked for people to come and help her clear up. Naturally I sprang up first, but Andrine was a close second, so I don't suppose it meant anything to her, but it was certainly worthwhile. First of all I got a big smile when I asked her where a brush went. Then, when I was at the cupboard, she came up to me with a drawing pin. I lifted up the box for her to drop it in and then absent-mindedly put out my other hand and took it from her. I didn't even think about being embarrassed, it was such a joy. I replayed the whole episode over and over, wondering how I could have communicated my feelings more clearly. Oh, imagine if the electric current that shot through me had gone through her at the same moment, a mystic fusion wrought by a drawing pin.

Now the rest of the news: the scandal of the week. One of the parties of course. It's Marlyn this time. Apparently she went to number 8 (downstairs inside). Carol came into one of the bedrooms and Marlyn said 'Go away, I'm busy.' Everybody was disgusted. But Marlyn said, 'Oh, we wouldn't have gone any further. He's Roman Catholic, his religion won't let him.' What a thing to say! At least three of us protested, 'What do you mean, his religion won't let him, does her religion let her?' Then Margaret Stewart said, 'It doesn't say anything about it in the Bible, and that's what we follow.' Have you ever heard anything so ludicrous? What I don't understand is what difference it makes what number you go to. In fact, I sort of said this and was told that number 5 was the furthest anyone went. Well maybe, but I think putting numbers on sex is equally disgusting whether it's 1 or 8. I mean, can you imagine Rupert Birkin, saying to Ursula, 'What I really want is a mystic conjunction in pure separateness beyond love, but in the meantime, we could just go to number 5.'

Oh it makes me want to scream with rage and frustration. How different my feelings are for her. Thank God for *Women in Love*, for rescuing me from all that muck, making me know what love really is.

This week I can say almost certainly was the nadir, the slough of despond, the pit of blackness. Of course, it was all the fault of my stupid crazy egotistical optimism. It was *Women in Love* that catapulted me into a state of bliss. I discovered at last what it is I want. It's what Birkin wanted with Gerald. As he says to Ursula, 'What we have is enough, between a man and a woman, but I think it's necessary to love a man purely and fully too.' That's it, that's it exactly. One day I'll find a husband, but I also want intimacy with a woman, to make a vow with her of *Blutbrüderschaft*, like Birkin wanted with Gerald. Of course, this got me dreaming like mad, that it had to be with her. I was sure it must be significant, finding this book and being in love with her at the same time. Surely that's fate. I worked myself up to such a pitch, that I did absolutely no homework at all, in spite of the fact that I had a Latin prose, and an English essay and yet another geography test to swot for. Of course it was terrible, twelve and a half out of twenty. I was downright lucky even to pass. I know it was what I deserve, for my sinful laziness, but I still feel terrible about Eleanor, and Fiona, and Winnie, and Andrine getting seventeen.

But the anguish of the test was nothing compared with dinner time. I had brought *Women in Love* with me and I was plonked on the back row with it open. I'd just got to 'Gladiatorial', where Birkin and Gerald wrestle by the fire in the nude and achieve physical closeness. I didn't deliberately pretend I was at that chapter, I was completely innocent. 'Surely this is fate,' I thought. So I sat half concentrating, on tenter-hooks – will she come in or won't she? Ten minutes later, in she comes, goes straight to the cupboard behind me, my heart was in my throat, I could hardly contain myself. Then she moved. She had a pile of folders with her. She dumped them down, only the third desk away from me, my heart leapt a beat. Then as she opens one of the folders she flicks something away from it in disgust. She turns in my direction, but is looking above my head at no one in particular and says, 'Who was eating here? Surely you 3L2 girls are old enough to clear up after yourselves? What a pity there has to be a form-class in the art room anyway.' Olive, typically, rushed over saying she would clear the desk up. This seemed to stop her continuing the lecture, but she picked up the folders, put most of them back in the cupboard and walked out. 'Bad-tempered old rat-bag,' said someone and they went back to their gossiping. I wanted to go out and bury myself in the hockey-pitch there and then. Oh, what utter folly, imagining this was to be the day. What a total egotistical fool, not only was there no coming together, but she doesn't even want us to be in the art room! How will I ever recover from this utter humiliation?

Monday 15 May
For once in my life, I managed the after-school timing perfectly. A few feet behind her all the way along the road. Right behind her in the queue at the bus stop. Along comes the trolley-bus, on she gets. And then what happens? I get on and it turns out there's only two of us on the bus and it's heading off to the land of happy ever after? Flaming fat chance. Oh no, the world's biggest coward doesn't even have the nerve to get on the bus. After all this time, hoping and praying for just this opportunity. I left the bus stop and meandered off home through the park, with a heavy heart, wondering what I would have done if I had got on the bus. I was going over and over the possibilities until I heard laughter behind me. I turned round and there were these blokes mending the road, all looking at me. I had been talking and gesturing to myself as usual. What a fool I make of myself with my day-dreaming. By the time I was inside the park, I'd forgotten them and I floated away again, wiping out the disappointment at the bus stop.

I'm on the bus sitting behind her and I ask her where she's going. 'Into the station,' she says, 'to get a train to Helensburgh. That's where I live.' 'Gosh,' I say, pretending to be surprised, having already invented an aunt in Helensburgh, and got an address from the telephone book. 'Fancy that! That's where I'm going.'

So we travel together and I tell her about *Women in Love*, and when I talk about Birkin and Gerald her eyes seem to light up strangely. When we arrive in Helensburgh station she says, 'Are you in a hurry? Come and have a cup of tea at my house first.'

An hour or two later, as the sun is setting over the Argyll Hills and sending a path of sparkling light over the Holy Loch, we gaze deeply into one another's eyes and our hands reach out to touch across the table. It grows darker, she lights a candle and sets it between us. Then she takes out an old, jewelled, very sharp, Arab knife from the bureau, cleanses it in the candle flame and cuts a tiny wound in my palm. I do the same to her. Hand clasping hand, we mingle our blood and make our vow of life-long *Blutbrüderschaft*. And thus we sit, hand in hand, into the night in pure, final, mystic, conjunction.

Monday 30 May 1962

Dinner time got me to a high pitch of excitement today. It all started when Andrine declared that she was sure Miss Sherriff was in love.

'Why?' we asked.

'Haven't you seen her? New tight skirt, high heels, and wearing eyeshadow. It's *got* to be love.'

'Well, that's nice for her,' said someone.

'Let's hope it makes her less horrible to us,' said someone else.

'Oh, it's bound to. When you're in love, you love everybody,' said Margaret Stewart. A few faces were pulled. 'Oh, yeh, you know,' we said.

'Do you think she'll get married?' I said, making sure the conversation didn't shift to Margaret Stewart's sordid sex life.

'Well you can never tell,' said Andrine, 'Things can go wrong.'

'Yeh, right,' came in Jane. 'How do we know he isn't married already? I mean, she's not exactly a spring chicken, is she? And women of that age often have to have affairs with married men, because there aren't enough single ones to go round. That's what my sister says.'

'Hey, doesn't she get a lift into school with a man?' said Winnie.

'Maybe it's him and he's got a little boy, so he must be married.'

'Oh, what a scandal,' cried Andrine, 'If Miss McVicar got to hear about it, she'd be out on the streets in no time.'

'Well, I can't imagine anyone fancying her, she's really ugly.'

This was a golden opportunity. 'Who do you think is attractive?'

Everyone put in their candidates, including myself, naturally. No one seemed to agree but it did lead to a heated discussion about her. Half were very 'pro' and half were very 'anti'. I wasn't bothered by the 'antis' since it proves she has a strong personality and the 'pros' were mainly Joan and Dilys who I like best anyway. But what a thrill to hear her discussed for at least ten minutes. It filled me with pride, as if it was my own sister. And that wasn't all, Andrine went back to Miss Sheriff, wondering if her fancy-man said, 'Oh, Jessica, darling!'

'That isn't her name,' said Jane scornfully, 'It's Isobel.'

'How do you know?' said I. It appears her big sister Sheila knows practically all the teachers' first names. Naturally I wanted to know if she knew *her* first name and Jane said she would ask. I tried not to sound too desperate, but I hope and pray she'll remember. I won't be able to badger her or anything. I couldn't bear them getting wind of a crush. They'd get up to all sorts of tricks like making faces when she comes in. Maybe exposing me in some way she'd be disgusted by and leave me devastated. No, I won't have them dragging my devotion in the mud.

Tuesday 31 May
Amazing! Wonderful! Sheila came in and Jane remembered to ask. It's Rosemary!!! I was with Dilys at the time and she said: 'That's a romantic name.'

'Yes,' said Sheila, '"Here's Rosemary, that's for remembrance", that's Ophelia in *Hamlet*, we've just been doing it.

'Why does she say that?' I asked, instantly wishing I could be in fifth year studying *Hamlet*.

'Well, you see, Ophelia's gone crackers and she wanders about giving flowers and herbs to everyone, and the plants stand for different things, "Rosemary for remembrance, pansies for thoughts".'

'Sounds lovely,' said Dilys.

'Actually I think it's pretty boring, except that bit; because Moira McPhie has an unexpurgated edition and Ophelia sings this really dirty song. But those fuddy-duddies in the English Department don't let you read it and tell you off for not having the school version. I'd rather have Mr Brown for biology anyday,' and off she waltzed.

Well, I just couldn't contain my excitement and Dilys gave me a penetrating look and said, 'You've got a thing about Miss Caldwell haven't you?' She'd guessed after yesterday's conversation. I told her not to blab about it to anyone else, and she promised. It turns out Dilys knows quite a lot about her. She's heard it from Moira McPhie who's in the dramatic society.

Oh, it's so unfair not being allowed into the dramatic society till fourth year. Apparently she's very friendly out of class. I'm sure we'd come together through that. Mind you, there is one problem. It turns out her and Miss Walker are great friends. She makes all the costumes for Miss Walker's plays. And they go on holiday to Italy together. They have a marvellous time and spend all their money too quickly, and they go to Italian lessons together. Do they have mystic conjunction? Surely not, I mean even if Miss Walker is a producer she's still a maths teacher. Oh but Italy! I just can't settle down to these Latin sentences at all, it's been whirling around my head all evening. An amazing memory jumped into my head while I was thinking about it. I read in the papers a month or two ago that a boy had been kidnapped by his teacher and they had run off to France, but they got caught. Imagine! If she could kidnap me, take me off to Italy, and *not* get caught.

For hours I've had us wandering through all those places, Florence, Ravenna, the Pieros in Arezzo, the Giottos in the Arena Chapel in Padua – that's where we are now: we're alone and we stand opposite Judas and Jesus, with Judas about to give Jesus the Kiss of betrayal in Gethsemene, our heads are parallel with Jesus and Judas and we turn and gaze rapturously into one another's eyes. I say 'Rosemary,' (God, it does embarrass me thinking of calling her by her first name) 'I know I will never ever betray you.' And she replies, 'Shall we then give ourselves to each other, finally?'

'Yes, now,' I say. 'Now, with a kiss, not of betrayal, but of eternal fidelity.' So our lips meet (fortunately neither of us is wearing glasses at this point, which might be awkward) and we kiss. Long and lingering, incredibly passionate, but with exquisite lightness of touch. There we stand, united in the depths of sensual knowledge and aesthetic ecstasy. Oh take me away! From the prison of school and family and middle-class convention and let us live the free artistic life, like D.H. Lawrence and Frieda. Painting and writing and drinking red wine in our villa hidden in a grove of cypress trees, 'mid the rolling hills of Tuscany. Oh, Italy, I can't wait!

Friday 3 June

Oh, I get so mad with frustration sometimes. First it's Mum getting me to put out a new tablecloth and napkins for tea just because Hilda's boyfriend turned up. I shouted 'Where do I put the napkins?' in front of him and, oh my God, did I regret it, dragged in to the kitchen: 'You're just getting above yourself, Lorna Mitchell. You think courtesy is just for ordinary folk,' etc., etc. Honestly, telling me I'm getting above myself when she kowtows to Peter flaming Bennet, just because his dad's stinking rich.

And now it's Caesar. Really, what do I care about the minute details of building a Roman battering-ram or how many Gauls the Roman soldiers can slaughter in a day. Oh hell! I think I'll give up and go and watch *Rebecca* on the telly.

Saturday Morning

I was so elated by *Rebecca* I stayed up till four o'clock in the morning. There was a beautiful full moon and because I wasn't wearing my glasses I didn't see the mountains and it looked like a round window letting in the light of heaven. I imagined drinking the light in and it became a reservoir of divine love within me. How will I ever be able to burst the dam and let it pour out of me! Only by someone needing it, wanting it. I tossed and turned with so many inspired thoughts until the birds were singing. It was then I came up with an idea. Why don't I take control of my own destiny? Bring about the fated meeting by my own action? I could write her a letter telling her my problems (well not *the* problem) and ask her to talk to me. Yes, surely this revelation I had from the moon is a sign for me to go forward, to open the dam myself.

Saturday 11 June
Hilda and Elma heard me on the phone to the janitor trying to get her address, and they both jumped on me at breakfast.

'Miss Caldwell is still your dream girl is she?' asked Hilda.

'Are you lovesick for her?' said Elma. 'What are you going to write to her? Ah hem, My darling . . . do you know her first name?'

'It's Rosemary, but I'm not going to . . .'

'Rosemary, how terribly poetic, I can just see her, a sort of tall wispy Pre-Raphaelite beauty . . .'

'Hardly,' butts in Hilda, making a face, 'Actually she's kind of horsey and her face goes red in the sun and when she's running up the stairs.'

'Oh well, then,' quipped Elma, 'Lorna can serenade her with "My love is like a red, red Rose(mary)", So what are you going to say to her? My Darling Rosemary, come up and see my etchings as soon as possible. I can't wait any longer. Yours ever, Lorna.'

'No, I'm just going to tell her my problems . . .'

'Tell her your problems?' said Elma, 'You think she'll understand your problems? I doubt it. It would take a psychiatrist to understand you. What is it you find attractive about her? If it's not her Greta Garbo face?'

'Well, I . . .' (I'm blushing), 'I like her walk.'

'Good heavens, so its her body you're after. I hope you're not going to shame us with this woman. It would bring scandal and disgrace on us ten times worse than Marie Thompson running off with that thirty-year-old man!'

'Oh, don't tease her,' said Hilda, being kind for once. 'I expect she just feels lonely and wants somebody to talk to about God and religion and all that.'

'Well I wouldn't pin my hopes on a teacher then,' said Elma, 'She's probably a frumpish old maid, who'll tell you to pull your socks up and get on with your school work.'

Saturday 25 June
Oh God, Oh God, Oh God. How will I ever get over this terrible humiliation! How on earth could I have imagined this silly letter of mine could lead to even a friendship, let alone mystic conjunction. Her reply was friendly enough but full of all the clichéd advice. What else did I expect given the corny old stuff I trotted out, that was all beside the point anyway. Then this week we met. I managed to mumble a bit about 'a schoolgirl crush'. First she said she was leaving at the end of term so I'd have plenty of time to get over it. Then she said it was unhealthy! I didn't ask her exactly what she meant by that. Then, oh my God, I'm embarrassed to write about it, she said she thought we ought to get more set homework and didn't even approve of me listening to classical music, if it kept me off my work! I nearly died when she said that. Damn Elma for being so prophetic. But it wasn't really her fault. It's me, me, me. How could we possibly have got to know one another? I was ridiculous. I stood there like a complete moron, at my worst, totally shy and awkward, managing a few incoherent mumbles. I'm even too embarrassed to write down the things, I said. Why, why, why couldn't I have predicted how paralysed with self-consciousness I'd be? Oh no, of course not, carried away by my folly, my egotistical dreams. My preposterous arrogant ideas about my reservoir of divine love. What a fool! All this wallowing in emotions! It's just sheer bloody selfishness. Instead of just going about humbly doing my duty, I indulge myself. Mum's right about me getting above myself. And now this humiliation. God has punished me for my arrogance. Oh why does my life have to be so difficult?

Sunday
I can hardly believe the twists and turns of my life. I spent all last night, wide awake, thinking over my sins. Eventually the solution came to me: suicide. Not out of self-pity or loneliness but because I ought to. Why should an arrogant egotist like me be allowed to continue on this earth? I thought. I should put a stop to myself before I got dangerous.

I got up at nine o'clock and went outside. It was a beautiful morning. I felt like crying at the beauty of it. I went along the track by the river to one of my favourite spots, by the big bushy clump of elder trees. I stood and looked at the water, watching the frothy bits round the stones. I started to shake, how far would I have to wade out? What if I slipped and banged my head on a stone, and didn't know I was dying? I stood there shaking and shaking. Then suddenly heard footsteps. Oh no, what if instead of a dignified suicide, I ended up being assaulted by a bunch of nasty yobbos. No, it was one person with a dog. I'd have to wait till they went by or they'd rescue me. Then I saw who it was. Mrs Johnston the Bible Class teacher's wife. She saw me and came right over. 'Hello Lorna, what's the matter? You look ill. Come out for some fresh air?'

I couldn't think of anything to say and she gave me a long look. Then she put her hand on my arm and that was it. For the first time for a long time I dissolved in floods of tears. She took me home and not only gave me a cup of coffee but a sherry as well. After a few sips everything came out. I couldn't believe how easy it was to talk to her. And she understood *everything*. Turns out she studied English at college in America and knows all about D.H.L. Can't stand him. But it didn't put me off. In fact I was completely convinced by her argument. She asked me if I'd read *Mornings in Mexico*. Would you believe it, she's been to see the Hopi Indians' Snake Dance. She thinks all that 'blood consciousness' talk is absolute tripe. The Hopi are highly articulate and intelligent people, not in the least 'dead to the intellect'. Then she said she was going over to Colorado to see her family in the summer and would bring me back something, a piece of hand-woven cloth to hang on the wall, maybe. And then, oh then, she even suggested one day, I could go out with her and visit her family.

Oh isn't life extraordinary! To be rescued from the pit of despair and fly to the heights of ecstasy in one morning. Surely God must be planning something for me after all. Imagine: Ellen and I together, in our hacienda in New Mexico. The sun is setting a deep burnished red over the stark rocks of the Rio Grande. A vulture perches menacingly on a cactus, and the coyote sends out its weird unearthly call. We have just finished our first chapter on the folklore of the Hopi and we sip our – what was that drink again? oh yes, tequila, and we open our hearts to the ancient spirits of the Great Southwestern Desert. Ah, New Mexico! I can't wait!

SIGRID NIELSEN

The Marina Trench

On maps, world maps, it appears in purple. The coastal shallows are marked in bands of warm, light blue; the open sea is a pure primary blue. But towards the edge of the map there is a crescent-shaped place, where blue shades to indigo and indigo to purple: the lowest valley under the sea.

The bays and gulfs and straits in the open sea have long, flowing names. I used to say them to myself, like the names of a dynasty of mythical heroines, when I looked at the map. But the purple place has only its own name; no one goes there to explore it. Light disappears in the depths, and the pressure of the water grows so great that nothing can live. A few small, grey fish, strangely shaped, sometimes go down that far. I used to wonder if sound itself could travel in the deepest places.

The colours on the map stood in my mind for the characters of the sea, and not just the depths of the water. I thought often of the warmth of the continental shelves, and the wilderness of the ocean centre. But somehow I always caught sight of the purple crescent at the edge of the map. I misread its name and called it the Marina Trench, as if it were the real place: the one that gave its name to the sea.

The air flows in the trees overhead; on the street it only shifts and settles. Never quite making up my mind to catch a bus, I drift along the city floor. My armpits are moist; my arms are enclosed in the city's breath. I look at my map, orient myself vaguely, and forget the street names until they drift me to the women's house.

The women's house is the last in a row of red-brick terraces; it has no gate. The front door is open, and I knock and knock again; there is no sound but the leaves turning over in the trees.

I walk through the hall past the stairs and into the room at the back; there are papers on the table; their corners lift now and again in the breeze. Light comes through the leaves and stems of the tomato plants which grow from the bottom to the top of the window. I look out and up into the tree-tops at the sun, which jumps and shifts as the leaves move.

It's a good house, this. I'm sorry they are all out. I leave the pamphlets I've brought on the table, write a note with my phone number and the date I'm leaving, and start out through the shadowy front hall. It's then I see Valerie coming in.

She doesn't notice me at first and nearly runs into me. Then she is embarrassed. She looks as if she were just awakening, as if she is not sure how I've arrived here.

'It's nice to see you.'

I think she means it.

'I was going to call you.'

'Yes, you said you would.'

Silence. She looks around quickly. 'I came to see Karen.'

'They're all out.'

'Oh. Bother. Then I've made a journey for nothing.'

She looks around again: she is hunting for something to do next. 'Would you like some tea? I'm sure Karen won't mind. I was practically living here for a while.'

I am touched; I feel this gesture is slightly more than I can expect. 'Yes, that sounds fine.' We go back into the big room and she boils the kettle. I breathe very slowly and try to think of nothing. I have wanted to see her and been afraid to ring her or write. Not afraid, precisely. Hesitant. Stopped by doubt, like a hand laid gently on my arm. Because my feelings are very strong, and I do not know hers. I know nothing about them at all.

She pours out the tea and tells me what she is doing in London. She smiles. She has an innocent simple grin: her eyes crinkle up behind her glasses. I know now, having felt her body very close, that she is a strongly-made woman, and I can see it a little in the way she leans forward on to the table. She leans as if she were about to catch some moving object: something she cannot see well, whose size she does not quite know.

'Maybe we could see a film,' she says.

'Yes, that sounds good.'

'Do you know what's on?'

I name a few, but she shakes her head impatiently. The fact that I have not come up with the right one at the very first try seems to disturb her, like a bad omen.

'We could have dinner.'

She takes her glasses off and rubs her eyes.

'I'm very tired.'

'There might be plays.'

'I really am . . . awfully . . .' She wipes at the lenses. 'I think I should go home, really. This woman I'm staying with needs my key, you see.'

I feel cold.

'You could eat something there.'

'If she won't mind.'

'It's a long way. You'd have a long journey home, I expect.'

I'm spinning. I don't know what she is trying to say. I can't ask. 'Do you want me to stay, or go?' This is supposed to be an ordinary conversation.

But I recognise this place. I have been here before. I feel the pressure around me, holding my jaws all but shut. I am one of the fishes of that world. I am all eyes and no mouth.

'I'll go back with you for a little while.'

'All right,' she says.

I would like to tell you that I sat straight and looked unruffled when I felt the cold current around me. That I said, 'Oh, this again,' and went home and got into bed, and thought about the next day's business before going to sleep. That is what you are supposed to do. Courage is an old-fashioned word, and stoicism sounds positively neurotic; but everyone knows what to do.

That is part of the Marina Trench: silence. You cannot speak; if you open your mouth the water will rush into your jaws. No one has ever been able to explain to me why that silence falls between women. It is simply something that happens. It is a place on the map of the women's world, that silence. It is not a passive silence, but a tangible presence, like a wall of water which resists everywhere at once.

I was nearly ready for it. If I protested, you never heard me. This story is not a protest, no more than the purple spot on the map, the sounding in feet and meters, the name in boldface type, the warning to proceed cautiously.

We come out of the underground in a part of the city I have never seen, near the docks. The buildings are old and small; we elbow our way through the crowds, buy vegetables from a street vendor, and turn into a narrow lane without cars. We stride, we nearly fly. 'I don't want Margo to have to wait without the key,' she explains, but we move faster and faster, half racing, half showing off for each other.

For a moment I think this makes it all enough: striding down a strange street in a strange part of the city, with my arms bare and my heart pounding and my mouth open, not knowing even an hour ago that this place existed. I had wanted to see her and she was there. Surely that's enough to set against the silence.

It's not so different from the last time I saw her, which I cannot mention now. It was late at night, in another city. She turned to me in bed, and smiled suddenly. We lay against each other and rocked until the motion seemed larger than our bodies, and in the end she touched me with one finger which she drew round and round with an even, practised pressure. I felt all the women in that practice. At my centre were absolute stillness and absolute astonishment. They grew and grew and I burst out of myself and fell back into my body, which was wet with sweat.

These last words are not printed on this page. If you saw them, you saw them like shadows cast from above, from the surface into the depths of the water, wavering and glowing, catching beads of light. If you try to touch them, your hand encounters nothing; their substance lies in some other layer of the sea.

'This,' says Valerie, 'is a friend of mine. She's come to stay for a few hours.'

She emphasises the last sentence, and since Margo, Valerie's friend, would not understand if I followed impulse and said nothing for a moment or two, I take a deep breath and ask how she likes living here.

'It's quite far from things. At least the tube station is just around the corner.' Valerie had mentioned it, but preferred to walk; the trains ran only twice an hour. 'Sit down, have some tea,' says Margo. She smiles at me; I sense that she doesn't have many visitors, so far from the city centre. The people in her flat are quarrelling, the landlord is about to sell the place: 'Let's go to the pub,' she says. Valerie asks if she can make a phone call first. I hear the cornered tone in her voice drift through from the hall while I ask Margo where she comes from.

'She hung up on me,' says Valerie, appearing at the doorway.

'Why?'

'I don't know. I just wanted to talk to her,' she adds quickly, 'I hadn't talked to her for a while. You know.' She picks up her jacket. 'Are we going?'

Outside the evening is light, the air is still warm. We take our glasses out the pub door and sit on a fragment of concrete wall in a field by the river. A cat advances out of the grass, lies down, folds up, and looks at us. We talk about books, our lives, other people's lives. I talk quietly; I keep the note which says this is a special conversation out of my voice.

Little by little Valerie begins to meet my glance; briefly, and not every time. And little by little the conversation becomes interesting in itself. We are three women friends, three lesbians, talking about ourselves in turn, in that way women have. It grows dark around us, and I hear Valerie's voice growing lower and softer as I disengage. I look at my watch. I hesitate.

'I suppose I'd better be going.'

Valerie turns toward me. 'Are you leaving already?'

'I'll never make it back otherwise.'

The anxious note returns to her voice. 'I'll show you where the tube station is.'

'I saw it,' I answer flatly.

Valerie says nothing. Margo glances at me quickly.

'You're very observant,' she says.

'I'll get you up the road, then,' says Valerie, more firmly this time.

I hesitate. 'All right,' I say.

Down there, under miles of water, the pressure reaches tons per square inch. The fish have only the tiniest fins: they cannot move far at once, only little by little. If anyone were to live there, she too would have to learn to live with little movements, but I have no doubt it could be done: after long enough, she might love the resistance of the water, and find she was very strong, if she ever came out of the depths.

90

LIZ McLAREN

Kittens

Jo switched off the TV set and the kittens woke up. One of the little ginger toms (called Fred, for identification purposes only), dashed over and began to lick her bare toes. She was thinking vaguely how nice it was to have the kittens running around, when Fred sank his tiny sharp teeth into her foot. She drew back her foot quickly, but not to hurt him and he jumped away, startled, stiff-legged.

She wanted to cry, the lump in her throat rising. As usual, she forced it down. Maybe she should cry, but a nip from a five-week-old kitten was hardly a good reason. Again, as usual, she wondered why she wanted to cry.

She sat back in the armchair. It was her chair – whichever child was sitting in it got up when Jo came into the room. She thought of all the hours spent in this chair, doing nothing, being lazy. Not doing the housework, not going to the office, not listening to the kids.

Waiting for the bad feelings to go away, waiting for some energy to do something constructive – like washing the kitchen floor, cleaning the windows, mending the boys' trousers and other worthy things like that.

She slid further down into the chair and pulled her legs up. 'Foetal position,' she thought, 'nice and safe. Stay here and don't go out into the big, bad, patriarchal world.' She made a face at herself.

'Poor, lonely little lesbian,' she whined and conjured up a mental image of pathos dripping off her in thick gouts, like curdled milk.

'You wouldn't be so trusting, young Fred,' she thought to the oblivious kitten curled up in the crook of her arm, 'if you knew what a seething mass of piteous, pathetic anxiety you were sleeping on.'

It was late, she should really go to bed; but she sat on, her thoughts trundling on the same old treadmill. Bloody kids, not her fault, she'd had them before her consciousness was raised. Great thing, this consciousness-raising. Became a feminist, got a good job, chucked that useless, soul-destroying husband out, got her life organised and cracked up. Quietly, of course. No screaming, no mental hospitals, just fear and panic which no one else could see until she started staying off work for weeks at a time with 'nervous debility'. Antidepressants, another man who had to be better, but – no. Tranquillisers, psychiatrist diagnosing 'difficulty with relationships' – silent rage at that. 'It wasn't me, it was them!' Good friends and parents trying to help and understand, then off work for a year and a half. Thoughts of lesbianism – was she? Or did she just want to be 'right on'? No, thank goodness, she really was. It was like a dear, familiar dream, being held and loved by a woman. These relationships short-lived, or never started, but they stayed as friends, and the friends stayed. Back to work, still with the fear and the tranquillisers. Almost a year, now.

The kitten slid slowly off her arm, still sleeping, on to the arm of the chair. Carefully, she lifted him up; but he woke, jumped down and began to fight with the strap of her bag. The other two came scampering up to join the fight, the little grey female shoving her two ginger brothers out of the way.

'We'll have to call you Amazon,' Jo told her. The kitten stopped trying to kill the bag for a moment and looked up at her solemnly. Then she went back to the all-important business of learning to survive.

'Hard business, this surviving,' Jo thought, as she had thousands of times before. Anyway, she was now getting off the pills and had finally realised why she was afraid. Getting rid of patriarchal values and attitudes was OK; but it left nothing, recognisable as yet, to hang on to. There was not a complete void, but it's hard to reject most of society and flounder around with only a few women to reach out for, to trust. She knew she felt defective only because of patriarchal stereotypes and opinions – she also knew she was afraid to commit herself to a relationship with a woman in case it should go the same way as those with men.

'Chance would be a fine thing!' she thought wryly. Her spine ached with tension, but she moved slowly and carefully – Fred was asleep on her foot.

She watched him for a few moments, envying his total relaxation. Then she eased her foot gently from under him and smiled as he stretched, yawned and went determinedly back to sleep.

Jo unfolded her legs, wincing as rheumatism twinged her right knee, and pushed herself to her feet. She walked slowly through to the kitchen and heated milk for her cocoa. The house was quiet; kids and kittens all asleep, but her mind had now shut off so that she didn't think to savour her solitude. She made the cocoa, filled her hot-water bottle and took them upstairs to her bedroom.

She put the mug on the table, set the alarm clock and wrapped her pyjamas round the hot-water bottle.

Downstairs again, to collect the science fantasy novel she was reading and her cigarettes. She looked down at the sleeping Fred, then picked him up and took him up to bed.

GILLIAN E. HANSCOMBE

Not What I Mean by It

When something's as hard to digest as that was, it takes – well – it takes time, longer than you think. However clever you are and however many books you've read and however well you can explain away in complicated language the nuances your senses told you spelled love, so that there you are, lofty and unyielding, it's still bitter on the palate when you remember. Not exactly sweet with humour or salt with irony. However much you may be used to winning some and losing some, it's a defeat when you lose, none the less. Even if it is only one.

Take April, for example. Her mother named her for the spring and willed her to be chic and fresh and so she was. Not sickeningly sweet, mind you; she had what the teachers called 'character' and was brighter than was comfortable for people, including herself. But she had winning ways; she was the feminine of debonair. On her way through growing, she did their bidding, more or less; but as soon as she was an adult, she let them have it. Not only up and left her husband, but her three children as well.

'Got to follow my star, like it says in the song,' she joked to anyone who asked what or why. 'Got to be who I am.' Not so unusual, that, considering education at the time – the way it mixed up individualism with democracy – but certainly worrying, when you stood revealed as the sort of person April turned out to be.

'Don't you worry about her,' said one of April's friends to another, who was worried. 'She's rock-solid and never cries inside. She's a survivor.'

'I'm a lesbian now,' she told her mother, who put down her teacup and stared. She'd agreed to take the children in for a bit, April's husband having responded with what they called a breakdown. 'I've got to earn my own living and set up with my lover and it's going to be no life for kids. Not for a while, anyway.'

She wasn't at all cruel, April. She kissed them all warmly and phoned twice a week and took them to the zoo on Sundays. Sent her mother money from her salary. If she'd been their father, no one would have thought twice about it. But being their mum – well – people talked. 'It's not natural,' they said, over and over, not knowing what else to say. Whether they meant the lover or leaving the children or both wasn't all that clear, even to them, but April bothered them, that's for sure.

Anyway, it didn't last too long with that lover; it's hard to change mid-stream, perhaps, and take on subtlety when you're used to habits. But she acquired a taste for it. Really. She was potty about women; besotted, entranced. They were soft, tender, sentimental; but also determined; they had 'character', just like her. The lesbians did, anyway.

It was Karen who started the trouble. At least, that was April's version. Karen said April started it. It was never really clear to anyone else who had started it, but that something had got started was obvious to all the world. There they were, staring into each other's eyes all over the place, just like Hollywood originals. And talking half the night.

April said afterwards that she couldn't understand any of it. Nothing happened, she insisted. They never *did* anything. Well, you know. She'd stare and frown and look weary. And then give up. Karen wouldn't say anything. Not for a long time; then she phoned up Susan and said she was drunk. 'Very fifties, isn't it?' she slopped into the mouthpiece while the pips went frantically on. 'Put some money in the box,' said Susan severely. 'Where the fuck are you?'

Karen said 'That pub. Where I used to sit with April. With the red woodwork. Don't know its name. Want to die.'

'Don't be ridiculous,' said Susan. She was very aggravated. No way for lesbians to be carrying on. 'Get a cab and come here now. I'll put the coffee on.'

Karen did. She looked awful. She had a skirt on with the hem half down and her face was all blotched. 'Tried to change my self-image,' she said stupidly and tottered into the bathroom. She was sick for ages.

'Well,' said Susan finally, when they were settled.

'It's April,' wailed Karen. 'I can't get her out of my mind. I don't understand it. Why she doesn't want to see me any more. Blowing hot and cold like that. I feel humiliated.'

'Happens to all of us,' said Susan, thinking about someone else. Well, it does. No denying that.

'But it's so unfair,' Karen went on. 'I love her. I don't know what I did wrong.'

'Nothing to do with it,' said Susan. 'Can't rationalise it. April's in a state, anyway. Needs a break. She's getting the children back next week. Probably got her mind on that.'

'But what about me? I thought she cared about me.'

'Maybe she did. Who says it has to go on for ever?'

Karen slurped some coffee and rubbed cream into her face. It made her look red and shiny. Susan patted Karen's knee. 'You'll get over it,' she said. 'We all do.'

There wasn't much more to say, so they said that over, in different ways, half a dozen times until Karen was exhausted. Susan put her to bed and felt lonely. It was so often like this.

It was true about April. She was thinking about the children coming back and wondering. She didn't think she was the best mother in the world, but she didn't know how to be any different. Anyway, she hadn't thought her mother was the best, either. May as well have them with her. What was love anyway? Nature and nurture and a smile sometimes. When it worked. Otherwise, just a black hole that never got filled. 'No one can love me,' she thought, flapping a duster round her flat, 'not even them. Not what I mean by it.'

Karen phoned. 'Can I see you?' she whined.

'Of course you can see me,' said April. 'Why ever not? What's the matter? You sound so peculiar.'

'Nothing,' said Karen lying. If April didn't know by herself, there wasn't any good trying to tell her. 'When?'

'This week's awful. What about lunch next Monday?'

'But that's ages away,' said Karen without thinking.

'I know, but that's all I can do.'

There wasn't much point meeting. Karen couldn't think of anything to say and April couldn't understand why not. She got up as soon as she decently could and said she had to get back. She was framing pictures for a show and couldn't waste the whole day. 'I'm not a waste,' said Karen feebly. But she knew she was in the wrong.

It was Susan who eventually went to the hospital. No one could find Karen's relatives. None of them answered the phone. Strange, that. They got Susan's number out of Karen's address book.

'Barbiturates,' said the sister accusingly. 'D'you know where she got them? She'll be all right but she'll have to see the psychiatrist. It's hospital policy.' That, and the way she tore off her rubber gloves, forestalled any protests.

'Why?' repeated Karen dully at the man in white. He was young and pink and had short hair and glasses. 'You wouldn't understand. I'm a lesbian.'

'Oh, I see,' said the man in white knowingly.

'No, you don't see. You couldn't possibly,' she insisted.

'Why don't you tell me about it?' he soothed.

'No' said Karen. And she didn't.

They locked her up for that. Uncooperative, they said. Deeply depressed. Immature. Paranoid fantasies.

Susan told April about it. April was shocked. And really sorry. But she couldn't see what she could do about it. It didn't occur to her that it might have anything to do with her. Until Susan said so.

'But we never did anything,' said April. 'She didn't even want that. She said so.'

'Maybe,' said Susan. 'But love is more than going to bed.'

'But it can't be that,' April contested. 'She can't have done – that – to herself because of . . . Nothing happened, I tell you.'

April went to see Karen. They talked across the table with a nurse listening. 'It wasn't because of me, was it?' April wondered.

'No,' said Karen. 'It was because of me. Not you. I wanted you to love me and you didn't.'

'You didn't give me time,' said April. 'It takes time for me to feel like that, if I'm going to.'

'No,' said Karen. 'I'm not talking about that.'

'What then? asked April, defeated.

'It doesn't matter,' said Karen. 'I made a mistake. That's all.'

'But you can't do that to yourself just because you made a mistake,' said April passionately. It shouldn't be this important. It couldn't be, or she'd have noticed.

'No,' said Karen. But she had.

Karen got over it and they let her out, but it took a while. April was kind to her and put her up for the weekend.

'Children are a bit irksome,' she said, 'but they're not so bad when you get used to them.'

Karen sighed. Her heart was so dead she didn't even notice when the children turned up the television and spilled their Coke on the carpet.

'It's nice having you here,' said April, at the end of the weekend. 'Why don't you stay for a bit?'

'No,' said Karen. 'I have to get back to my life.'

They didn't meet for a long time. April forgot to phone, she was busy with a new course and there were the children and the cooking and the cleaning. And teaching at night for money. Karen got on with things and started to feel again. Not too much and not too often, but a bit. She got her pride back. Had Susan round for supper and put on records.

They bumped into each other in the pub with the red woodwork. April was delighted. 'Karen. You look so good. Christ, it's been ages.'

'Yes,' said Karen. She was having a drink on her own before a party. She did look good. Dressed up.

'I'm going to a party.'

'God, it's so long since I went to a party.' said April, realising. 'Can I come?'

'You wouldn't like it,' said Karen confidently. 'They're nearly all teachers.'

'Lesbians?' asked April.

Karen smiled. 'Mostly. All women, anyway.'

'Well then,' said April.

'No,' said Karen. 'Better not.' And she left.

April sat there for a long time, remembering. Karen had sat there with her often. They'd touched each other, somehow, in some way of women when they touch though their hands stay separate. 'I could love her,' thought April, 'if she'd let me.'

Karen went to see Susan. 'I don't know what to do about April,' she said. 'Does she just want to torture me?'

'Don't be ridiculous,' said Susan. 'She likes you. She always liked you.'

'I can't get into all that,' said Karen.

'Just be nice to her,' said Susan. 'She doesn't mean any harm.'

'She's heterosexual,' said Karen. 'They don't change. Not really. The body, maybe, but not the habits.'

'I know what you mean,' said Susan.

April wondered if she was going mad. She was desperate about Karen. She could hardly think about anything else. 'It's like drugs,' she thought, feeling out of control.

She went to see Karen, without phoning. 'Come in,' said Karen, surprised.

April was half crying. She put her arms around Karen, kissed her face, her mouth. Karen let her.

'I love you,' said April.

'I can't,' said Karen.

They met again at Susan's, who was having a supper party. She had long spells between lovers, getting over it, and filled up some of the time with cooking. It was light enough; no one drank too much and the arguing was good-tempered.

'I'll drive you home,' said April to Karen.

'Thanks. I've given up cycling at night since Mary was attacked. Sure it's not too much out of your way?'

'Come on,' said April.

Outside Karen's flat April turned off the engine. 'I want to come in with you,' she said.

'No,' said Karen. 'I'm tired. And there's no point.'

'But I really want to talk to you. Have contact, like we used to.'

'That's gone now.'

'But why?'

'I've suffered about that and it's over for me now.'

'But I don't know what I did wrong,' April insisted.

'You didn't do anything wrong. I just made a mistake, that's all. It happens.'

'In the hospital, when I came to see you. Do you remember? You said you'd wanted me to love you.'

'Yes, I remember.'

'And I didn't understand that. I didn't think you wanted to go to bed with me. I thought that was clear.'

'I'm a lesbian,' said Karen. '*Au naturel*. A real one. I mean, I've always been a lesbian. It makes a difference. You can't understand that. Your history is too different. I worked that out in the end. You can't have the same reactions.'

April felt insulted. 'I regret my history,' she said. 'But ever since I've been a lesbian, I've never once wanted a man. It's never occurred to me. I'm just as much a lesbian as you are.'

'You can't be,' Karen said. 'When you grow up lesbian, there are hundreds of things not the same. Fine shades of feeling. This girl's face, that one's; teachers, other people's mothers; gestures, looks, going places, being excited the entire time. It's the emotional air we live in. Interchange between women is highly charged, all the time. Nearly all the time, anyway. It isn't a direct pathway from intensity to orgasm, like it is for heterosexuals. Like it must have been for you.

I've had learning you can't have. You can only have it on the way up, not once you've got there.'

April was angry. 'Look . . .' she began.

'No, I won't,' Karen interrupted. 'I'm going inside now. I don't wish you any harm, but I'm not tangling with heterosexual habits of feeling. I'd get hurt again. You didn't even notice what happened between us, but a real lesbian would have. Sex is just part of it, that's what you can't see.'

'You didn't give me time,' said April. 'That's arrogant.'

'Maybe,' said Karen, 'but I know what's true for myself. You do too. But we're different.'

April couldn't forget. She went on looking after the children and earning money and seeing friends. She took a lover called Agnes who was enthusiastic and took her mind off things. She was fond of Agnes and it was fine in bed, but she wasn't in love; or, she didn't feel loved, that was it. One day she was washing up and staring out of the window and not concentrating and it hit her. 'Karen could love me,' she thought. 'I want Karen to love me.' Karen, who was soft and strong and could do things.

April phoned. 'I really want to see you. It's important.'

'Why?' asked Karen.

'Please,' said April.

They sat in the pub with the red woodwork. It was called the 'Red Dragon', Karen noticed and didn't forget. April was chatting and laughing, over-excited and selfconscious. For more than an hour it was catching up and gossiping. Karen felt confident and interesting.

April said, 'I'm so involved with you. I keep thinking about you. Wanting to know where you are, what you're doing, who you're with. Everything. I want to be with you.'

Karen was embarrassed. 'Don't,' she said.

'But it's true. I mean it.'

'I can't,' said Karen. 'It's not the same now. It doesn't work when it's not the same. When you have to explain things.'

'I'm charmed that you're so romantic. But you shouldn't be unrealistic. We could just go on from here.'

'We are,' said Karen.

ANIRA ROWANCHILD

A Bit of Help

Linda Evans looked up from the bath of washing she was pummelling
to stare at her youngest boy.

'Mam,' he was shouting, 'I seed a funny woman. She be coming
here.'

'Have you filled them buckets yet?' she replied severely. 'I asked
you ten times if once this morning. How am I to get this washing
done, may I ask, if I don't have no water?'

'There she be,' said the boy, more quietly, retreating behind his
mother to watch from safety – but Linda cuffed at him and he had to
back right into the kitchen.

Sighing, she looked across the orchard to where the boy was
pointing. Indeed there was a person coming down the path and
straight for the house.

'Here! She be coming to see we! Why didn't you say so you little
goat!' She hastily wiped her hands on her apron, tidied a few stray
hairs off her forehead and yelled into the house.

'Be that kettle a-boiling yet, Mary-Ann? Put a stick on the fire.'
Then she stepped forward to greet the visitor.

She frowned a little and wrinkled up her eyes when she saw it was
the tinker woman they'd seen at Brampton Fair last week. Recognisable at once by her voluminous trailing skirt, ragged woolly
and shapeless felt hat. And the brown bony face and hands. And the
big wicker basket on her back. Come to stay, has she, wondered
Linda, we'll see about that.

The woman came up to the yard where Linda's tubs and basins and
baths of washing stood about, set down her basket, and looked
around her in a pleased kind of way, smiling at the opposite hillsides,
and the hole in the roof where the tile fell off on Jimmy's arm one
wild Sunday last winter.

'How be ye?' she said at last. She had a nice voice, friendly.

'Not so bad,' replied Linda cautiously. 'How be yeself?'

'Middling,' said the tinker woman, with a broad smile, showing how much more than middling she really was.

'Ye'll have some tea?' said Linda formally.

She led the way into the house, watching as the woman removed her boots at the door and lifted up her draggling skirt. Nice manners, though.

The kitchen was a cramped little place with a stove and gas bottle, a stone sink, and a big cream-painted cupboard in the way of the door opening – oh, and little Jimmy standing behind it, too. Linda spotted him and dragged him out with a slap at his bottom. 'Water, me lad!' she growled. Jimmy ran off sideways, staring back at the tinker woman disappearing into the inner sanctum.

Mary-Ann had built up the fire in the range and the kettle was boiling. She was a lovely, round-faced, brown-haired girl with wonderful strong hands and a way with all animals. She sat herself down on the bench behind the table and waited for whatever was to begin. Linda made the tea and from the sideboard cupboard took a tin of fruitcake and a tin of biscuits. Put before the visitor a big slice of the first on a plate and a mug of tea.

'Set yourself there,' she ordered, pointing at the big chair at the head. The tinker woman sat down. For a while they all supped their tea and munched their cake with the silence broken only by the attendant noises. Gave the visitor chance to look round the room at the photos on the walls and the clothes-rack of knickers and teatowels over the range and the shelves of tiny ornaments and ever-lasting flowers in cups, and out of the window at the sunny veg garden with its borders of pink roses. Gave Linda and Mary-Ann time to admire her slow jaw movements, her bony hands, her fine dark eyes, the greasemarks on her hat, the darns on her jumper.

'Another cup?' said Linda.

'Ah, but you take your time,' smiled the tinker woman leaning back in her chair and staring full at Linda.

'So you be Linda Evans as was Linda Meredith,' she said.

'I be. And what be that to you?' Linda retorted sharply.

'Well, only as I remember ye as a little lass what played in the lane with the tinker children and ran away in the bushes with one of them one night and stayed there learning summat else and got a thrashing for it when ye got home. That's what it be.'

Linda's face had grown flushed, perhaps because she was bending over the hearth intent on building up a fire that roared.

'Mary-Ann, us'll need more kindling afore long. Go and get it, there's a good girl.'

Mary-Ann left her seat reluctantly. Only when she was sure she was well away did Linda turn round.

'Zinnia Wild!' said Linda then. 'So here you be again. And you got no reason to talk like that afore the child. Dirty talk.'

'T'aint dirty,' returned Zinnia with composure.

Linda tossed back her hair and put her hands on her hips.

'What you want with we? You got baskets for sale, you say so, and us'll get on to business.'

'Oh, business,' with a contemptuous wave of the brown hands. 'Now there be jobs need doing round this place. I seed that old door be hanging on for dear life by a thread, and them beasts'll be out on the road afore long. And you need help around you.'

'I got help, Zinnia Wild. What you think these three great kids be for if not to help their mother? Our Mary-Ann she's as able as her dad with the beasts and young Jimmy's willing. And I can still pleach a straight hedge without I need help from anyone. When Jackie's through college he'll be back here with a bit of cash in his pocket.'

'Maybe,' smiled Zinnia.

'Maybe it is. Maybe it is. I won't say us have had an easy time since the old man went, but us've managed. Hasn't us, girl?' said Linda to Mary-Ann coming in with a box of kindling.

'Ah, so I see. You got a fine family, Linda Evans. But t'aint quite what I got in mind, you see. I say, as you needs a bit of help.'

'I inna following your drift, missis. And if you finished your tea I got work to do.'

'I got me things outside and I got a present for you, Linda Evans.'

'Get on with you,' snapped Linda.

Zinnia got up slowly and walked to the door.

'Us always was kindred spirits, Linda Evans, you know that, and us'll always be.'

She went out into the yard closing the door carefully behind her.

'Kindred spirits,' muttered Linda. She turned to glare into the fire. 'I'll give her kindred spirits.'

After a few minutes she took off her apron and smoothed the creases in her trousers. Took her comb and pulled it through her hair, tucked in the grips to give it shape again. Looked in the small brown mirror on the sideboard.

The door opened and little Jimmy stood there, the picture of the old man with his pale face and round blue eyes.

'Mam, be she staying? She say as she be staying.'

Linda took the kettle off the hob.

'Fill it up, lad. Ah she be staying – two three weeks maybe – till Jackie get back, anyhow. I need a bit of help, you see.'

SANDRA MCADAM CLARK

Distance

I imagined you on the train – no, before that, on the platform, even at
the ticket office. I saw you buy a ticket, holding your shoulder-bag
with one hand and your suitcase firmly lodged between your feet.
You always took the red, samsonite suitcase with you, even though it
was too small and crushed everything you put into it. Then on the
platform, waiting and looking at the clock every so often. I felt sure
you would be thinking of me unless those other thoughts crashed
through your head in persistent, white waves; thoughts which were
also mine, of grey windows and closed doors, envelopes quickly put
through the letter box, the houses and rooms you'd change almost
daily, the wet streets with no street lamps apart from a solitary
yellow light which had escaped from the savagery of poverty.

You were going to Britain to carry on our fight, and I was staying in
France since it wasn't my turn yet. At the Gare du Nord, still
functioning and full of dirty plastic seats and used paper cups, I
would meet you on your return and every time I did, I would think, 'Is
this where my mother came back?', although I knew it most probably
wasn't. But each time I forgot I'd asked the question when I saw you
half-running down the platform, in green in winter and blue for the
summer, holding your suitcase high as if you were waving. I never
moved, too stunned and unbelieving.

That evening it had been a particularly long wait; most of the
trains had been cancelled and there was virtually no news from
Britain, just snippets we managed to get on the radio. We knew it was
almost the end and I dreamt that the whole island was sinking into
the sea, weighed down by the full prisons, police cells and new
rehabilitation camps by the coast; only the few pictures of isolated
rebellions, some in the cities and some in the country, were in colour,
dark red turning into starlight. The rest of my dreams were in grey.

Finally the train arrived after my fifth cigarette, still cheap in
France, as I stood crushed right at the front of the barrier. I recognised

some of the exiles and had moved up quickly to the front of the queue to avoid them. Seeing you immediately seemed more important than giving or receiving their comfort. You took a long time to reach the exit and there was a delay as the ticket collector and police checked your ticket and passport yet again. I didn't think you saw me although this time I waved and called your name, loud and unmistakable.

'Susan, Susan!' I shouted and still you didn't look up.

When you were through it was the same as other times. We held hands and I touched your hair which was springy and slightly damp as if spray had caught there. You kissed me once on the lips, very firmly and suggested we go and have a drink.

'Wouldn't you rather go home – I cooked a meal and got in some wine . . .'

'No, no I'd rather have a drink round here – that place we went to once, you know, down the side-street.' You sounded tired so I agreed. I still didn't understand.

We walked down the main boulevard where the shops were full of goods and had bright, white lights in the windows and you found the street. I remembered it then, we had first gone to it after we had both arrived in Paris the year before. We had laughed and sat close, trying to suppress our loneliness that we had felt even on the boat. You had ordered drinks, saying, 'I might as well get used to speaking it.' 'You speak very well anyway,' I had replied.

We sat down at a table near the back with candlelight that hid the dampness on the walls and the cracked glasses. The café was almost empty and the radio was on – American music, merry and cold. Then you told me about the trip, how it was going to be difficult to go back, how our friends were, those that had disappeared but were probably underground, the street we had lived in, the rumours of revolution, riots, uprisings, the tanks on the streets.

'What's changed?' I said shortly. Knowing I had never been back filled me with hatred.

'I met someone, we had a kind of relationship – she might be coming here if she can get out . . .'

'Kind of relationship? what do you mean, who?' You looked into your drink and I wanted to hit you.

'Someone called Sophie, she's half-French and has been over there for two years.'

'Like me then, except I'm here.' I wouldn't cry in front of you.

'Her father's French, not her mother and she was fairly safe there at first,' you said quietly, though I could see your hand twirling the beer glass round and round.

When we got home, which was a room at the top of an old block of flats, one of the 'maids' ' rooms the rich rented out, I sat down on the bed while you unpacked. Then we ate, a vegetable casserole smothered in thyme. We drank the wine. I got up at one point and drew the curtains to shut out the rain that had just started and to shut out the lights opposite. We were cold, the gas fire wasn't working very well, so we went to bed.

We were still together for the next few months although both of us knew that things had changed. At night, you would usually get to bed earlier and I would sit at the table by the window, working on a leaflet or an article until you were asleep. Then I would turn round and watch you. One night you woke up, shaking and pulled up the sheet over your shoulders. Before I could go to you, you said, 'You're like a cat, always watching me in the dark – I can even see your eyes.' I turned away and poured out another glass of wine. When I looked at you again, you were asleep. So I talked to you as you slept, your body stretched out under the green blanket.

'What is she like; how could you, now of all times when we're fighting for our lives, for others,' and finally, 'don't you love me anymore?' It always ended with me saying that, as you lay in bed or were out of our room, and often I wondered how I could still think the way I had before we went into exile, before Britain was taken over. Then I thought about my mother coming back to France from the concentration camp during the last war and I wished I could speak to her, but despite her uneasiness at the new regime, and her own bewildered retreat to the south of France, she wouldn't accept that I was living with you, that we were like those others, lesbians, who were imprisoned in England.

One morning in February, when the light was getting longer in the evenings and daffodils were being sold in the market, you sipped the coffee that I had made and told me you were going back one more time, to find Sophie.

'This is my last chance, the boats and trains are definitely being cut off next month. Jean-Marie has information; he must have told you?'

'No, he didn't,' I said, thinking, 'he doesn't trust me'. You touched my face briefly, always alert to my doubts. 'He probably didn't want you to know that he knows about her.'

'Yes – are you going?'

'It'll be at short notice, but yes. I'll find a way of telling you when I'll be back.'

I almost offered to go with you, but you were going for her. I reached over the table and kissed you, giving you strength, I hoped, and with a desire so overwhelming it jolted both of us.

You packed to be ready to go suddenly and we carried on as usual, although we went out more as it felt like spring. We avoided the red suitcase in the corner of the room and we went to bed at the same time, sleeping close to each other as we had done in the beginning.

Perhaps it was the way you looked at me, the way you spoke, always directly as you were incapable of games, perhaps it became clear to me that our lives had changed so radically that the old rituals were now meaningless, but I was no longer jealous of Sophie, only so afraid for you that I could hide my fear with ease and laughter during our walks along the Seine, in the cafés and in our room. This was a new ritual, one that fitted.

You were gone for two weeks and I hadn't seen you leave – I was in the Centre collating material for a television 'debate' and when I returned, the suitcase had disappeared and you had left a note on the table. I read it and tore it up.

Françoise came round a few times and talked; Jean-Marie was difficult to find. I wondered if he'd gone too, but then at the end of the first week he came to see me. He looked round the room approvingly, presumably it was neat, no papers lying around, no evidence that you had ever lived there, and also no evidence that I was not 'coping' as he put it. What did he expect? That my love would spill out like blood and taint the furniture or that the fear I couldn't even feel, it was so deep, would transform itself into half-drunk glasses of wine, fag-ends and an unmade bed? I hated Jean-Marie, hated his self-importance, his understanding and most of all his voyeurism. Yet he was a good comrade, not a brother, but nevertheless a passionate speaker and he worked. He was looking at me, his head deep in his shoulders.

'You're very quiet – I hear you've been looking for me. Sorry. I was in the south, then I had to meet some people.'

'Oh? What's the news from Britain?'

'Well, my wife heard that there's a couple of trains coming through, some deal with the French I expect – I've got the possible dates down,' he passed me a piece of paper, 'You'll have to go to the station and hope for the best.'

'Thank you,' I said formally.

He left soon after and I was ashamed of feeling so ungrateful.

The week passed and I went to the station; the first date on Jean-Marie's list came. You weren't on the train, you weren't one of the hundreds of people who were carrying suitcases, carrier bags, string bags, rolled up sheets, fold-up prams, wearing dark, thin clothes and looking only at the exit and the police and at the other side. There were a few black people, but very few. Most of them had been interned, some had escaped earlier and others didn't have the money to leave. There were more white men than white women and hardly any children. They stared at us as we waited at the barrier, all of them unblinking even when they knew someone at the barrier.

I went home, having given some of the exiles addresses and cigarettes – no one had taken up my offer of a room.

The Tuesday after, I was at the barrier again and the train arrived after a four-hour wait. There were more people at the barrier and more police at the exit point, and we could see the blue rotating lights on the stationary police cars at the entrance of the station.

You were talking with a group of people and moving slowly, looking white and hunched. Nearly at the barrier, you moved forward, apart from the group and I saw you look up. I lifted my arm, waving a scarf you had given me, a red and golden wool scarf, you waved back, half lifting your suitcase. They let you in and you pushed through the crowd to find me.

'My love, my love, my love,' I said as you caught me and cried into the scarf, your whole body moving sideways, back and forth like an animal gone mad.

We walked all the way home and I tied the scarf round my neck to dry it. I felt it blow like a banner in the gusts of wind that shook up the rinds of oranges and apples lining the market street. You told me that Sophie had managed to get away to Mexico with someone else, others had found similar, illegal ways out and London was dying, dying. I held you then, as the old newspapers flew round our feet and a dustbin lorry drove past, squirting the street with bright streams of water, as an old lady tied her remaining daffodils and irises together, and you said, calmer, 'But the other towns are changing, they can't control every single one and the movements are coming together – the guerillas have got closer to Edinburgh, to Cardiff, even to Belfast . . .'

We walked on.

'Perth has had an uprising – whole areas of Glasgow are ours . . .'

You told me over the next few days of the new lights glinting in separate parts of the country, flashes growing into flames, growing into black and red torrents of lava, and I told you of the struggle here and how some of the groups were preparing to go over there with the French comrades.

We arrived home and sat at our table, closed the curtains and you had been away and were back.

Family

Hazel raised her hand, flicking back her fringe of greying hair. Sensing her lover's irritation, she picked up the letter and replaced it in the envelope. 'What's up?'

'It's a bit of a cheek, if you ask me—' Jo spoke sharply, expressing her views in her usual forthright manner, 'your sister asking such a thing. Foisting her daughter on to you like this and expecting you to give her a free holiday here. All these years she's never contacted you and now, when she wants to make use of the fact you live in the country, she suddenly writes.'

Hazel looked upset. 'You're being very unfair . . .'

'You don't even know the kid, you say, you've only met her once at some christening party or other, years ago. You'll regret it if you do invite her here. You'll never have a moment's privacy, you'll never be able to call your home your own.'

Hazel glanced round the sitting room – at the white plaster walls and chintz-covered settee. Her gaze fell on the breakfast table, with the remains of toast and coffee the two of them had just shared – and the vase of pink and mauve sweet-peas Jo had picked for her from the allotment the previous night. Sweet-peas were her favourite flowers and Jo, who used to work at the local garden centre and had a way with plants, had grown them specially as a gift for her birthday. Her fifty-third one it was . . . Contemplating the familiar interior of the cottage, Hazel nodded pensively. She was trying to picture a teenage girl living in the place, sharing her home. 'Mandy isn't a kid and she wouldn't thank you for calling her one. She's all of nineteen and has just completed a secretarial course in London. She's feeling a bit depressed about the job situation. A week or two's break in the country will do her a world of good. It's just what she needs.'

'But why should you be the one to put her up?'

'For obvious reasons. After all, she is my niece. She is family.'

'*Family!*' Jo gave a snort of disgust. She wrinkled her nose as if there were a very nasty smell in the room. 'The word's a con, in my opinion. It always has been and it always will. What's family ever done for the likes of us? You tell me that. Nothing!'

Hazel pondered the remark. It was the truth – or a good part of it. The word *family* had negative associations for them both. It did not conjure up the images of cosy togetherness and warmth that, to judge from the adverts and soap-operas on television, it did for the majority of the population. It evoked the opposite – images of over-work, frustrated desires, surreptitious meetings and all kinds of deceit and subterfuge. In Jo's case, it was her father who had been the restrictive influence on her life, in her own her husband. Hazel had been born in the north of England and, like most of the girls in her home town, she had married young, almost straight from school – 'Before I had the time or sense to know any better' was the phrase she generally used to explain the event. It was one that, with hindsight, struck her as thoroughly out of character. Her husband had been a school-teacher by profession and had moved to East Anglia to take up a job. She had accompanied him, settling in the village where he taught at the local primary school. The community was a typically close-knit Suffolk one, everybody in the place knew everybody else – and here, at a series of evening-classes in local history, she had met Jo . . .

The two women had been attracted to each other from the start and their friendship had quickly developed into something stronger – *love* it must be, they had decided with astonishment. Prompted by a growing desire for independence, they had made a determined effort to challenge the sexist conventions of village life and claim a space for themselves. This had been by no means easy to achieve since their situation had been beset with restraints. The struggles they had fought in their homes had been long and painful – and were now a thing of the past. The men who had been in a position to exert control on their lives were now dead. Their decease had left the two women with a sense of new-found freedom – one that Jo had immediately relished but Hazel, at first, had found difficulty coping with . . . Remembering those months, she smiled – gazing warmly at Jo. Thanks to her affection and support, that period of confusion and self-doubt had been merely a phase, it had not lasted long. Hazel leant across the table and, taking her lover's brown, weather-tanned gardener's hand in her own, clasped it tight, raising it to her cheek.

But Jo was in no mood for sentiment. 'The fact that Mandy's your niece puts you under no obligation to give her a holiday.'

'You don't understand!' Hazel frowned, irritated by her lover's obtuseness. 'It's got nothing to do with *obligation*. I genuinely want her to stay here. If things work out as I hope, it will make a link between my sister and myself, it will build a bridge between us, so to speak ...' She was talking quickly, the rapidity of her words reflecting the intensity of her emotion. Though, like Jo, she generally claimed to scorn family ties and the restrictions they imposed, in recent weeks she had caught herself experiencing vague stirrings of affection for the family she had left up north. She felt an unexpected urge, one she found difficult to articulate let alone justify, to renew contact with them – especially her sister. 'Who knows?' She changed her tone, checking the note of emotion and speaking deliberately lightly, 'I may enjoy having Mandy living in the cottage. It will liven up the place to have a teenager around – someone with a fresh outlook who isn't tied by a set of out-dated attitudes. It will encourage me to brighten up my ideas and stop me getting set in my ways. I may even find the experience fun!'

'Fun?' The astonishment in Jo's voice indicated that this was one possibility that had not entered her head. 'And if you do agree to put her up—' she spoke hesitantly as if scared to ask the question, 'what will become of us? That's the thing that really worries me . . .'

'Us?'

'Yes, *us!*' Jo repeated. She continued bravely, determined to make her meaning clear. 'You and me. Me, in particular. Our *relationship.*'

'So that's what's bothering you!' Hazel sounded startled. She gazed at Jo intently, moved by the vulnerability reflected in her tone. Eager to reassure her, she went on: 'You don't need to fret about that. You surely don't think that, after all the trials we've survived together, I'd sacrifice that and give you up? It's out of the question. Everything will be the same between us, you'll see. You'll come round here and see me of an evening, same as you do now.'

'You'll still want me to – er – stay the night?'

'Of course I will, you idiot! Whatever made you think otherwise?'

'In that case—' Jo's tone was exuberant, the expression on her face one of immense relief, 'invite anybody you like to stay in the cottage, the whole village if you wish! The butcher, the baker and the post mistress too! Invite the bloody lot, the more the merrier!' Her eyes twinkling with humour, she added formally, with an air of mock possessiveness: 'You have my personal permission to write to your niece and invite her to pay a visit.'

Hazel gave a grin, 'I'll let you into a little secret, I already have – last night, in fact – *and* posted the letter! I must get a move on, I've jobs to do in the house. There's a little matter of a room to get ready . . .'

The room Hazel had decided to give her niece during her stay in the village was an attic one, tucked away between the eaves at the front of the house. At the moment she used it as a sort of general store and the floor was covered with boxes containing bottles of raspberry jam and tomato chutney. She carried the boxes downstairs and, lugging the vacuum-cleaner up the narrow staircase, hoovered and dusted. Then, standing on a chair, she took down the curtains. They had been up in the window for years – since she and her husband had first moved to the village, in fact – and the green cotton was faded with the light. She crumpled the coarse material between her fingers, raising it to her face. It smelt of dust – reminding her momentarily of a past that was now dead and laid to rest – and, when she put it down, fine filaments of cobweb were sticking to her chin. For an instant, the thought of making new curtains crossed her mind but she decided against the idea. She found needlework a bore – a fact that only recently she had been willing to admit, even to herself. When her husband had been alive, she had always made a pretence of enjoying it. It was one of the numerous little lies and hypocrisies on which their life together had been based. He had taken it for granted that all women naturally liked sewing, she had lacked the guts to enlighten him to the contrary – and so the circle of deceit had gone on. 'It's so restful to see you sitting there with a piece of needlework in your hand,' he used to say, looking up from his evening paper and gazing at her sentimentally. She was surprised to find that the remark, one that had once rankled, irritating her intensely, no longer did. Time, as people said, healed everything, and all it did now was prompt from her a laugh – a cynical one at the self-centredness of men and their myopic view of women . . . She took the curtains downstairs, washed them and hung them on the line outdoors. So hot was the sun that by midday they were dry. She ironed them, hung them up in the window again and, to complete the decor of the room, placed a patchwork quilt on the divan. She had bought it the previous Christmas at a sale of work in the village. 'Well, do you think she'll like it?' she demanded, her eyes bright with pleasure at the prospect of her niece's visit.

'She'll be a fool is she doesn't!' Jo exclaimed. Her stocky form, clad in blue dungarees, leant against the door-frame. She had just come in from the allotment with some parsley that she had picked for the evening salad. She shuffled her feet, her shrewd brown eyes regarding her lover's face hesitantly: 'I've been thinking a bit about Mandy's visit. Look, if you like, I'll stay away from the cottage – while she's here, I mean. It won't bother me, it won't be for long – only a couple of weeks at the most . . .'

'You'll do nothing of the kind!' Hazel retorted. She gazed at her uncomprehendingly. 'If that's how you feel, then I'll write off at once and cancel the invitation. This morning you agreed to me asking her to stay here. What on earth's come over you? Have you got cold feet or something?'

'It's just I'm scared she may think it odd, me coming here so frequently. Dropping in to see you almost every day and staying the night. Her visit is very important to you, or it appears to be, and I want it to be a success.'

'Well, it certainly won't be that—' Hazel spoke vehemently, 'not if you refuse to see me and stay away from the place. I won't enjoy life at all. You know that very well!'

'I'm merely suggesting that you should tread carefully . . .'

'I'm sick and tired of treading carefully!' Hazel snapped. 'I've done it all my life – tiptoeing around the place, covering my tracks so people won't guess about us. I've done it with your Dad, my Brian *and* half the neighbours too. And if you think I'm doing it with a slip of a kid, a teenager that's young enough to be my daughter, then you're making a big mistake!'

'Mandy's not a kid, she's all of nineteen . . .'

Hazel swept the objection aside, 'You know what I mean!' She continued in a matter-of-fact tone, as if stating the obvious, 'Besides, in her case, there's no need for us to tread carefully. Things have changed a lot in the past fifteen years. Attitudes aren't as rigid as they used to be, they've loosened up. If she does find out about us, she won't react like the folks round here . . .' She paused, thinking with disquiet of the local store-keepers and the curious and disapproving looks they sometimes gave her when she went shopping. 'She belongs to the new generation, you see. She's young, she's liberated, she's lived in London. She'll behave *differently*.'

'Differently?' Jo regarded her dubiously.

'She'll accept the fact that we're lovers. She won't be prejudiced.'

Dumping her bag on the kerb, Mandy fished a tissue from the pocket of her skirt and wiped the beads of sweat from the back of her neck. The weather was stiflingly hot and the village street was turning out to be longer than the youth who had directed her to Laurel Cottage had led her to anticipate. With every step she took, her feet felt increasingly heavy and she was starting to regret not having followed her aunt's instructions and phoned her to announce her arrival. 'If the coach stops early – it sometimes does – then give me a ring and I'll pick you up in the car. There's a phone-box outside the post office' – that's what she had written in the letter. Still, the decision not to phone her had appeared right at the time, Mandy thought. It had seemed heartless to disturb the poor old dear and make her turn out, especially with the weather as hot as it was at the moment. She must be getting on now – in her sixties at least, and she no doubt took an afternoon nap, the way old folks generally do . . . With a sigh of exasperation at the heat, Mandy picked up her bag and continued on her way.

The street was a dusty grey track winding between rows of small cottages and shops – like prints from a *Country Life* calendar they looked, she thought with a grin, a bit too picturesque and highly coloured to be real. A strip of heat-haze shimmered above the asphalt and, gazing at it, she tried – unsuccessfully – to picture her aunt's face. Her failure to do so was not surprising, she thought. She had met her only once, in the company of Uncle Brian, at the christening of her baby brother. Her memory of the event – it had taken place some fifteen years ago – was extremely vague. She gave a yawn, turning from thoughts of the past to fantasising about her aunt's present surroundings. Laurel Cottage would have a thatch, she decided – almost all the houses in the village did, the public loos included, so she had discovered in the course of her walk. It would have a white-walled interior with an open fireplace and a mantelshelf cluttered with china knick-knacks and bits of brass – horse-shoes and hunting dogs, that sort of junk. A photo of Uncle Brian in a dinky silver frame would have pride of place. Poor Aunt Hazel was a widow now – and she would treasure it fondly as a memento of a perfect marriage. Though Mandy was, in fact, ignorant of the circumstances of her aunt's married life, she was an avid reader of teenage magazines and had romantic views about marriage. The prettiness of the Suffolk scenery combined with the heat had caused her imagination to soar – and she had decided that it must have been a perfect one . . . And, seated in the centre of the sitting room in front of the fireplace, would be Aunt Hazel herself – a grey-haired, apple-cheeked old lady in a lacy dress, her gnarled fingers busily occupied stitching a piece of tapestry-work . . .

'Good heavens! You're here already! Why on earth didn't you phone?'

Startled, Mandy looked up. The voice came from above her head – from a middle aged woman in faded denim trousers and an open-neck shirt perched on the top of a step-ladder. She was holding a pair of electric shears and was in the act of clipping the hedge in front of her house. Its name – so the plate on the rustic gate indicated – was Laurel Cottage ... 'Aunt Hazel!' Mandy exclaimed. So astonished was she by the suddenness of the meeting and the unlikeliness of her aunt's appearance and dress that she almost stumbled and dropped her bag ...

Inside the cottage, she looked with interest at the various features of the building that her aunt pointed out. The low ceilings and uneven floors delighted her, prompting a series of admiring 'Oohs' and 'Ahs', but certain other aspects of the place took her by surprise. There were more mod cons than she had expected. In the kitchen were a freezer and washing-machine and, though the sitting room did contain a fireplace, it looked as if it were seldom used. The radiators on the wall indicated why. 'So you don't have a fire?' she asked, disappointed.

'Not very often.' Aunt Hazel was sitting on the settee, her legs crossed. She had a magnificent tan and looked as if she spent half her life outdoors. 'I light one occasionally in the winter – for special events, Christmas and supper-parties.' She gave a mocking smile. 'This open fire lark is all very cosy – but it does make for more work, you have to admit.'

'But Uncle Brian ... He used to like a fire, didn't he? I remember mum saying so.'

'She's right about that!' Aunt Hazel sounded amused. 'The fact he did isn't surprising, of course. He wasn't the one who had to lay it. Nor did he go out in the freezing cold and bring in the wood from the shed. I generally did those chores. He didn't have the time, he was out all day at the school. Evenings too, sometimes, when he had meetings.'

'I suppose so,' Mandy murmured, nonplussed. There was some-thing about her aunt's tone that disconcerted her, making her feel uncomfortable. It had an odd ring. Not bitter exactly but sharp, suggesting a certain wry amusement at men and their ways – or Uncle Brian's ways at any rate. It did not support her fantasies of a perfect marriage ...

Her musings about her aunt's and uncle's relationship were interrupted by her aunt offering to take her upstairs to show her her room. Mandy climbed the narrow staircase, heeding the advice to duck her head to avoid colliding with the beam at the top. The room totally fulfilled her expectations, it was everything she had hoped for – and more. 'How clever you must be at needlework!' she exclaimed. The patchwork quilt had caught her eye. 'And what patience you must have! It must have taken months to put together.'

'I'm sure it did—' again the note of wry amusement, 'though it was some other woman's patience that was tried, I'm afraid, not mine. I bought it, you see, at a sale of work. I do very little sewing nowadays, as little as possible. It's one job that bores me stiff.'

'I see,' Mandy replied. She gazed gloomily at her aunt. She was depressed to discover the fantasy-image she had conceived of her still further undermined. And if the poor bereaved woman did not like sewing, then how on earth did she occupy herself? What did she do to pass the time? She had no children – and no relatives in the area. 'You must feel very lonely sometimes, Aunt Hazel, living here all by yourself.'

'Not really.' Her aunt sounded surprised by the remark. 'I quite enjoy living alone. It gives me the space to explore my own identity – to find out who I am and what I want from life.' She stretched out her hand, thoughtfully pleating the folds of the quilt. 'And there's no need for you to call me *aunt*. I don't much like it, it sounds terribly formal. Why don't you call me *Hazel*, the way my other friends do?'

Mandy frowned. 'Oh, but I much prefer calling you *aunt*. The word's so quaint, don't you think? It's got such a lovely old-fashioned ring. It makes you sound like somebody out of a television serial.'

'No doubt!' Hazel said tartly. Though she had nothing against television, she had no wish to be relegated to it for good. She folded her arms, giving Mandy the impression that she was about to make some significant statement about herself. 'Of course, the real reason I don't feel lonely is that I do have friends in the place. Not a great many, mind you, but enough. There's one in particular, one that's very important to me – Jo. We see each other almost every day . . .'

Mandy's brows lifted. The possibility of her aunt having a boyfriend had not entered her head. 'How long have you known – er – this guy Joe?'

'For a good many years!' Her aunt gave a chuckle. 'Though you've got the wrong sex. Jo is a *she*, not a *he*. You'll be meeting her shortly – on Friday evening, in fact. The two of us are going to a concert in Norwich together. I'm sorry I don't have a ticket for you. They're in short supply and I booked them some months ago before I knew you'd be staying. Anyway, after the concert she'll come back here with me. You'll have the opportunity to meet her then . . .'

Hazel switched off the car lights. The concert had ended later than it had been billed to do, and by the time she and Jo got back to the cottage it was well past midnight. She stepped out on to the gravel path – as she did so, glancing instinctively up at the window to Mandy's room. The pane was in darkness, indicating that she had gone to bed. 'I'll have to put off introducing the two of you till tomorrow,' Hazel murmured. She slipped her arm affectionately through Jo's and accompanied her into the house.

The following morning she slept later than she usually did. Whether it was the experience of sharing her home with her teenage niece that had tired her or the drive back from the concert in the dark through the winding Suffolk lanes, she had been feeling exhausted – mentally and physically. She woke up abruptly – alerted to consciousness by a shaft of sunlight falling across the bed and the sound of two voices interacting in lively conversation. She recognised them instantly as Mandy's and Jo's. At first she could not make out where they were coming from but, raising her head from the pillow, realised it was the garden.

She got out of bed, crossed to the window and looked out. The two of them were standing together on the lawn. Judging from the collection of tools at her feet – Hazel glimpsed a hammer and a reel of wire – Jo was in the act of repairing the trellis. The weight of the rambler rose had caused it to collapse and the previous night she had mentioned something about mending it . . . They were talking intently, their heads bowed. Jo lifted her arm, pointing in the direction of the village – and Mandy turned her head as if following the gesture with her eyes. They were too far off for Hazel to be able to hear what they were saying.

She stepped back from the window and briskly, with a sense of fresh vitality, finished dressing and went downstairs. The scene she had just witnessed pleased her immensely. It endorsed her faith in the younger generation, demonstrating the success of her plan to bring together the two different sides of her life – to invite her niece to her home and give her the opportunity to meet her lover. The fact the two had met without formal introductions struck her as an added bonus. It gave the event an air of spontaneity, of 'naturalness', one that augured well for the future. Any fears she harboured that their personalities might conflict and they might not get on had proved to be unfounded – totally so, judging from the animated tones of their conversation . . . 'Hi, you two!' she called, flinging open the back door and popping her head out. 'Do you fancy some toast and coffee? I'm just about to make breakfast!'

They turned, greeting her with a smile. 'Thanks but I won't bother,' Jo called back. 'I'll be getting home now. I've got a few jobs to do on the allotment. The beans need staking, for one.' She glanced up at the trellis, pointing to the lengths of wire she had replaced. 'With a bit of luck this will stand firm – at least until we get the autumn gales.'

Hazel walked with her to the gate and, on looking round, caught sight of Mandy returning to the house. 'That was a remarkably lively chat you were having with my niece!' she said teasingly, unable to contain her pleasure at the event.

Jo smiled. 'She seems to have taken to country life – in a big way! She asked me all kinds of questions about the village and I told her a bit about its history. I described the tied-cottage where dad spent his life. It's not exactly a palace – but it won't hurt her to learn how the other half lives!'

'Oh, so that's what the two of you were gabbling about!' Hazel gave a laugh, leaning her elbows on the gate. She added as an afterthought: 'I'll drop in to see you at the allotment, later in the morning when I've finished shopping.'

On returning to the house, she found Mandy curled up on the settee leafing through a glossy magazine. Hazel took two mugs from the dresser and, preparing to make the breakfast, went into the kitchen. 'I'm so glad you've met her!' she exclaimed jubilantly. She switched on the kettle and slipped a slice of bread into the toaster.

'Met who?' Mandy's voice from the sitting room sounded puzzled.

'Jo, of course!'

'Jo?' Mandy pronounced the name as a staccato question. It was as if the disclosure of identity had come as a shock – and she needed time to think about it. 'You mean, that was Jo? The woman who was mending the trellis? The one I was talking to?'

'It certainly was!' Hazel replied. She spooned the coffee into the mugs and took a bottle of milk from the fridge. 'What she doesn't know about gardening isn't worth knowing.' She was about to continue the conversation but, on entering the sitting room with the tray of toast and coffee, found that Mandy was no longer there. The sounds coming from upstairs indicated she was running a bath. On any other occasion her abrupt exit would have worried Hazel but at that moment it did not, she was feeling much too light-hearted. With an amused shrug at the unpredictable ways of the young, she ate one portion of breakfast, leaving the other one sitting on the table top. Then, having scribbled her niece a note explaining she was going out to the shops, she took a carrier bag from the drawer in the dresser and left the house.

Hazel's mood of vitality remained with her and, walking back home through the leafy, sun-dappled lanes on the edge of the village, she found herself even more conscious than usual of the short-lived beauty of the summer season and its poignantly rich medley of sounds and scents. She strode buoyantly along, holding in one hand the carrier bag and in the other a small bunch of velvety pansies Jo had picked for her from the allotment. She entered the house by the back door and – having taken two paces into the kitchen – halted. The sound of a voice coming from the sitting room took her quite by surprise. She heaved a sigh of relief, her fears of burglars allayed. It was only Mandy, speaking on the phone ... As was evident from her remarks, she was talking to the folks up north, giving them the news: 'Oh, the house is all right. In fact, it's very pretty. There's nothing wrong with *it* ...' Hazel smiled selfconsciously. She was unused to eavesdropping and the comment about the cottage amused her. Eager to play fair with her niece, she was about to speak and reveal her presence – but did not do so. There was something about Mandy's tone – a contradictory note, one censorious but at the same time furtively prurient – that prompted her to change her mind, making her remain silent: '... it's other things that are wrong. Aunt Hazel has got this friend, you see. Well, *she* calls her a friend but, if you ask me, she's not just that she's something more. The two are as thick as thieves and she did spend the night here ... No, I'm not making it up!' Mandy spoke indignantly. 'Yes, I know very well it's nasty!' She sniggered softly. 'Anyway, that's not all! You should see the way she looks, the friend I mean – and hear how she talks. Her hands are all brown and wrinkled and her accent – well, it's a bit *common*. It's no wonder, I suppose, considering her dad was a farm labourer. When I first met her, I didn't have a clue who she was. I thought she was the gardener or somebody come to do odd jobs around the place.' Mandy sniggered again. 'I can't understand Aunt Hazel allowing her to set foot in the house, let alone ... At *her* age too! It's disgusting! ... What on earth would *Uncle Brian* say?'

Hazel stood motionless in the middle of the kitchen, holding her breath. Her niece's voice droned relentlessly on, penetrating her consciousness with its insistent tones and transfixing her to the spot

– the way the butterflies and moths she had seen in cases in museums were transfixed with pins, she thought. Her head bowed, she contemplated absently the velvety blooms of the pansies. They had fallen from her hand and now lay scattered on the red-tiled floor, their little black and yellow faces gazing up at her.

CAROLINE NATZLER

Julia

In certain countries, Julia knew, her life would be a crime.

As it was she trundled through the mesh of laws patterning the
common sense of her life as an average young working woman in
London scarcely noticing, with just the occasional throb of fear that
the ticket man at Waterloo might question her too closely, or some
doubt as to whether to hand to the police the five pound note she had
once found wafting along an empty pavement.

After some years of working in a solicitor's office she tended to
weigh more the consequences of breaking the law but was alerted
also to the arbitrary divide between the criminal and the law-abiding
citizen. She realised that factors like class, race and sex determined
whether stealing from your mother's purse, smoking dope, defrauding
certain government departments or inviting sexual relations on the
street were stark and vicious crimes to be brought before the courts
or mere growing-up problems, expressions of personal or fiscal
initiative or the valid claims of a healthy (virile) sexuality.

But this was mere knowledge to Julia; a cause for concern and
debate as a responsible citizen but largely external to her, for little,
really, in her life could be criminal, though there were, of course,
things that she was careful about.

She lived comfortably, occasionally worried by her own com-
placency but generally involved in the immediate concerns of her job,
in creating a calmly expressive environment in her garden-flat, going
to films and art galleries with her friends and supporting them
through their domestic crises, and continually adjusting her own
relationships to that perfect balance of independence and security
which she knew was real love.

She knew, but it was not easy.

She had been involved with Leigh for almost three years, bracing,
glowing years of trust and excitement; from the lofty heights of their
companionship they found infinite curiosity and significance in all

the teeming details of their life together, everything from going to an avant-garde play to selecting food together in the local supermarket, gossiping or discussing a TV programme. Everything was quickened, radiant. They each had their own independent friends and interests but 'their life together was at the core, sustained by some secret of self-renewal. But perhaps Julia had secrets from Leigh, for she treasured the symbolic moments of their first meetings, almost venerating the grey pond on the heath and the park bench where she had first heard Leigh's heart beating against her cheek. Leigh took pleasure in such memories too, but was inclined to impatience at mere souvenirs, believing identity to be forged in ever new action and interaction, plunging forward and sweeping Julia on in a dynamic of self-generating love. Then, as they matured, their companionship quietened, as it seemed to Julia. She found herself cherishing the simple fact of their relationship, in solitary moods of thankfulness and self-congratulation. Sometimes, she found herself looking on.

One Sunday evening she returned home from a weekend with some friends, buoyant at the sure welcome of her own home, her own lover. Over a tin of tomatoes, half opened, and long spikes of raw spaghetti angled across the kitchen table, Leigh said to her, 'I think I ought to tell you. I spent the weekend with Anne. We slept together.' Leigh's dark eyes were suddenly hard as polished veneer. Julia could not breathe. The room was drained.

The weeping and anger during the next few weeks and the long rationalising talks they floundered through in a desperate attempt to resolve the irresolvable kept Julia going. Leigh wanted her friendship, gave her soft and glowing looks, and bodily warmth for comfort, said nothing had changed. Julia clung like a baby, craving only wordless acceptance. Sexual rejection hurt. She wanted to be loved without having to behave, regardless. She clung to Leigh's kindness and recoiled at being so patronised. She knew Leigh's mind was edging elsewhere and the image of Anne – a dull person, not worthy of dislike even, surely – hovered, vanished, re-emerged, mean and inevitable. Julia prolonged the struggle, it sustained her. Then Leigh left. Julia's breathing choked her. She wanted only to creep into a tight-fitting black box; tight, nothing.

She went to work, bought things in shops and was taken out by her friends, who gave sage, nodding advice and then talked brightly of other matters. The world was stale, crammed with hard-cornered objects, buildings, cars, upright trees, knives and forks, shut books, food in the cupboard – all there and no life. Her body was a tense weight. Grimly, she existed. Later, there was only loss, her whole life. She had forfeited her parents by a choice of life she could never afford to regret, her belief in her painting and her religion had been whittled away, she had lost her aspirations, settling for a comfortable niche in her job. She had not had children. Through absorption in Leigh she had lost her friends, mere manikins who appeared somehow to know her name. All had slipped away from under her, leaving her beached, without Leigh.

Leigh's soul was in her, she was split by such absence. And Leigh was still in the world, the same person, living and working in London.

People called friends took her to a film one evening. She sat at an aching distance in front of the flickering pretensions on the screen, and could not get involved. How to get on with life, when life was so impersonal, without Leigh? The shape of a head in front of her suddenly filled, Leigh's head, dark, smooth hair, Leigh was here, she gasped and the head turned slightly, reality flattened back to a petrified nonentity. She kept seeing Leigh – in the glimpse of a soft blue coat on the tube train, hearing Leigh's emphatic, throaty voice in a crowd, things flashing into the reality of Leigh and back to an anonymity of crowding, jabbering strangers. Every green car on the street usurped Leigh's car. A restaurant called Trattoria Venezia sliced her cold with memories of a holiday plan, and she winced every time somebody mentioned the heath, baffled at their casualness. She dreaded encountering Leigh and Anne, triumphant. She could not go on like this. She must do something. In a world so charged she felt she could do nothing, all was corrupted by Leigh. She watched her neighbours working in their garden and could not believe that people could be so engaged in anything. Always this distance. She awoke in the dull morning light of her room, and wondered why. Always this missing.

How could Leigh do this to her? Leigh loved her, had defined love for her. What were Leigh and Anne doing now? Were they laughing in bed? Was Leigh talking about some novel with Anne? What were they reading together? What should she be reading?

Something germinated; Julia began to realise that her survival might depend on hating Leigh. And she did want to survive. She would not let Leigh win. It could never have been real. A macabre, prancing charade. Leigh had been using her, biding time.

She charged herself steadily, with rage and hate, at bus stops, eating her sandwiches and clenched in front of her gas fire through the long evenings, summoning every memory and reinterpreting it, glaring at the presence of Leigh in her mind's eye and charging every utterance and every caress with indifference, duplicity, emptiness. She was vacating the past, trying to destroy it as she had destroyed the physical mementos, stamping on Leigh, spitting, tearing, forcing herself to say 'I hate you' at every little shooting memory of tenderness. For weeks she yelled silent hatred. And Leigh was still there.

One day at work she was typing a brief for a client charged with murder. The cool white paper fell gracefully back over the bar of the machine as she typed. She thought, how easy it would be to murder a person. And then there would simply be no problem. She finished the brief and folded it, tying the pink ribbon neatly.

Then gradually her own life re-emerged, the world took on substance and she grew confident. She found herself making plans and anticipating pleasures and became enmeshed in her friends' concerns, sitting intent in the red warmth of the Trattoria Venezia and discussing employment problems with Jane, parent problems with Chris. Films and novels came to her with the direct and painless indifference of ordinary perception and she could make easy judgements. The tokens of her love affair with Leigh ossified to mere facts. One halting spring morning she sat on the heath and started sketching again, enjoying the lucid world of ragged buds and sticks and rendering it clearly, with her own, undivided perception.

Leigh wrote to suggest they meet. Julia considered, calmly. She did not want the false security of a premature friendly reconciliation, some second honeymoon, and yet the time seemed ripe, now. She was self-sufficient and she trusted her own determination.

She invited Leigh to supper on Sunday, and scrabbled away in the garden during the day, pulling up dead wood, old leaves and a few early weeds, jerking with occasional fear and excitement despite herself. She found herself looking forward to seeing Leigh and imagining their meeting. Would they, should they, hug, kiss? What would they talk about? And how long could she count on Leigh staying? She determined not to dress up, she must be normal. She opened her new cookery book but balked at the demands of those highly-coloured new dishes: she need not cook so elaborately. Spaghetti bolognese was an old favourite and would suffice. She opened the kitchen cupboard, taking comfort in the familiar clusters of jars, beans, rice, flour, tins and bottles of wine, and the garden and household stuff, the iron, furniture polish and stain remover, the sleeping pills and the cool white bottle of weed-killer. Julia's heart raced.

Leigh came, she was standing there in the hall, slender and graceful as ever, a smile fluttering; she still wore her soft eggshell-blue coat and she held a bottle of white wine, tentatively. A new person, who had never gone away. They hugged in relief, there was no question. And they talked, ate and drank through the evening. Leigh had not been so happy either and Julia thought for a moment that from their separate experiences during the last few months, they could pick their way, cautiously, to a new sharing. They talked of struggle, meaninglessness and constraints on fulfilment. Julia opened a third bottle of wine. Leigh was reticent in speaking of Anne and anyway Julia could barely feel jealous with Leigh here, finally, so fulsome and real, talking, expanding in life, getting drunk, pushing back her long black hair, eyeing the kitchen and smiling softly.

'I'm sorry, you know,' Leigh's eyes querying, looking at Julia, waiting for something perhaps.

Julia looked at her, at Leigh across the table, dark-eyed and still, already softened with the drink. She poured her some more wine. 'So am I,' she said.

Leigh was not really capable of driving her own car by the end of the evening and Julia called her a taxi. She felt Leigh falling, familiar and tender, against her shoulder as she helped her into the cavernous black car.

Breakfast in Bed

I was lying on my bed reading when she tapped on the door. I called for her to come in and pretended to continue with my book. The whole point of my taking a working holiday was to have time on my own. I'd been in the hotel for ten days and now had to share my room with a comparative stranger for the rest of the summer. I would have had more privacy at home.

I'd gone to the manager to complain, but he'd reminded me that it was a double room, plenty of space for two, and implied that I could like it or lump it. He was mumbling something like, 'I don't know what you girls expect,' when I left his office – not trusting myself to stay. At thirty, being called a girl and chastised by a twenty-five-year-old college geezer was insulting.

My co-workers all seemed to like him, they took turns in delivering his morning tea and breakfast in bed. Personally, I had fantasies about spitting in his scrambled eggs or pushing him down the stairs.

My new room-mate introduced herself as Gwenn and began to unpack. It turned out that this was her fifth summer season at the Highthwaite Hotel. I was shocked. 'You mean you come back here year after year?' She looked sharply at me – 'Not much choice where I come from, better than the dole.' She lived in Manchester with her parents and two brothers. She had a nice, soft voice and was attractive in quite a glamorous sort of way.

We lived around each other quite harmoniously at first. She mixed well with the rest of the women. I kept apart, went for long walks, read a lot and brooded over my recent broken relationship.

The second week in August brought rain. Typical in the Lake District, it lasted for a week and meant more work as the guests stayed in more, apart from the hardiest of hikers who left trails of mud everywhere.

Everything was shrouded in mist. The little town of Bowness

suffered along with the rest of tourist-dependent Cumbria. I grew restless and bored. I couldn't even see Coniston Old Man from my window. I couldn't work out whether my growing interest in Gwenn was genuine or not. Maybe it was just frustration. One dull, overcast drizzly Friday morning I got a postcard from Crete from my ex-lover. She was there with my replacement, and it was wonderfully hot and romantic. I tore the card up and sulked through my morning chores.

At tea time four of the other women were planning a night on the town. Gwenn urged me to join them, 'You never go out, never socialise. It'll do you good.' I felt pressurised and embarrassed. I felt that none of the other women was particularly bothered whether I went or not. I shrugged my shoulders.

'OK.'

I felt out of place when we all met in the carpark, the others all at least had make-up on, and there I was, as usual, in jeans, T-shirt and leather jacket. They were excited at the prospect of an evening in Kendal. 'Where are we going anyway?' I asked Sally, the driver. 'Oh just to a few pubs.' That was a relief. I couldn't face a straight disco. I also felt like getting drunk.

Looking back on that evening I often wondered if Gwenn planned it – it was unusual for me to be taken so unaware.

I was on my fifth whisky when the bell for last orders went. I struggled to the bar and got myself another double and a Pernod for Gwenn. I pushed my way back through the crowd to where Gwenn was sitting. Our three companions were laughing at the bar with some pimply-looking young men. I placed the drink in front of her. She smiled, 'I've enjoyed myself tonight.' I looked up, was she flirting with me? Her blue eyes looked back at me, charming me and slightly taunting. 'You can't have had much fun with me,' I said. God knows why.

'I've never met anyone like you before.' The implication was obvious. I laughed, 'Ah, but there's a lot of us about.'

It was time to go. We sang and laughed all the way back to the car. A cold, windy night, I inhaled the fresh air, it was good and clean, so different to London. Darker, quiet.

I was a bit concerned about Sally, she'd consumed a lot of Martini, but there was little traffic and she seemed to know what she was doing. We were quite worn out I think. I felt Gwenn's hand catch hold of mine and my stomach lurched. I looked down at the space between us, yes, she was holding my hand, discreetly. I looked at her face in the darkness. She was staring at me. Dumbfounded, I just held her hand until we got back to the hotel and said goodnight to the others.

I was usually in bed by the time Gwenn came out of the TV lounge and could just look the other way while she undressed. But tonight I hurriedly stripped while she was in the bathroom and shivered when she came back and undressed at the foot of my bed. My eyes were riveted on her. She casually got in beside me in that narrow single bed.

Was this an experiment for her? 'I really like you,' she kept on repeating. We slept together every night after that. I tried to talk to her about lesbianism, but she wasn't interested. 'I'm not one of them, it's just you, I couldn't go with another woman.' Despite this, I was absurdly happy. I'd bring her back bunches of grasses from my long walks over the fells.

She asked me questions about my life in London. I asked her if she wanted to come back with me at the end of the season, she said she'd think about it.

September 1st was her birthday, her twenty-third. And what a surprise we got that morning. Christine, one of the other chamber maids, brought Gwenn breakfast in bed. She almost dropped the tray when she caught us in a passsionate embrace.

Gwenn was furious, livid. 'Why wasn't the door locked?' I asked mildly. 'I must have forgotten when I went to the loo,' she replied miserably. 'Oh God, what am I going to do?' she was crying now. 'It's nothing to be ashamed of.' I put my arm around her. 'Come on...' She shrugged me off. 'Leave me alone.' She got dressed and left the room, her breakfast congealing on the tray in the middle of the floor.

After that she never came into my bed again. In fact she hardly even spoke to me. And neither did anyone else. It was unbearable. She started going out with one of the waiters. I tried to talk to her, but she wouldn't even look at me. 'It was just a phase,' she'd say, then carry on painting her eyelids.

On the coach back to London I cried as we left the hills and trees behind. I could imagine what my friends would say, 'Well, honestly – a straight woman, what do you expect?' 'You went there to forget about Nona, not to get involved with someone else.'

I fretted and bit my nails. She'd be sorry. A waiter, for God's sake.

The Severed Tongue

This is the tale of two sisters, Procne and Philomel, and the love they bore one another, and of Tereus the Rapist who hurt them, and of the deadly revenge they took.

Procne had been married to Tereus for two long years. She was nineteen, slender and bright-eyed, with abundant black hair. He was forty-nine, heavy and strong as an ox. Each of his thighs was roughly the same girth as Procne's waist. He had coarse, gritty hair which he hardly ever washed, and small blue eyes with white eyelashes. His mouth was almost hidden beneath his sandy moustache and beard, but his lips peeped through, a livid, purplish colour.

Procne's father, King Pandion of Athens, had given her hand in marriage in return for some help Tereus had provided in driving off an invader. Needless to say, Tereus was very pleased with this prize. On their wedding night, the whole household made a hullaballoo, as was customary, to drown out the screams of the young bride. Lyres were strummed and drums were struck, while the handmaidens sang in their high-pitched voices, the age-old lament for a maidenhead, the wild hyacinth which is trampled into the stony mountainside until only a purple stain remains.

Procne was a practical young woman, and she steeled herself to receive her husband's forceful embrace.

'I will get used to it,' she told herself. But she never had. Whenever he clambered on top of her she would feel small and crushed. He would smother her with hairy kisses so she couldn't breathe, and he would bounce up and down, squelch in and out, until he was spent, and then slump like a dead man upon her. She would dream of flying out of his bed, out of the window, out of the palace into the cool dark forest. But when she woke up, she would always find him snoring beside her.

She felt guilty about not liking him more. He had always done his best to please her. She could have as many dresses as she wanted, and he had given her huge great jewels, which glinted like his eyes in an amorous mood. He never beat her, and that, she knew, was much to be thankful for. Many a time, Procne had left the party in full swing, raucous manly laughter echoing round the hall, and had come upon a woman of the court, whimpering or weeping in a corner; she had seen the bruises swell up and go down again. For the wine they drank in these parts was very sweet and very strong, and it was well known that once a man had a flagon or two of that stuff inside him he couldn't be held responsible for his actions. When Daphne, Procne's lady-in-waiting, had her arm broken by Kakos, a henchman of Tereus's, Procne had begged her husband to dismiss him. He had looked at her in disbelief.

'You've got to be joking. I can't come between a man and his wife! And in any case, Kakos is one of my best friends!'

The tears had sprung to Procne's eyes, because Daphne was one of *her* best friends, and Tereus, who hated to see her cry, had smiled and given her a hug and a kiss.

'Tereus,' she said, 'you would never hit me, would you?'

He put his hands on her shoulders, and looked straight at her from the depths of his little blue eyes. He shook his head indulgently.

'Darling, you'd never give me any cause to, would you?' Then he planted another kiss on her nose, gave her right arm a squeeze, and went off to the bathroom smiling.

She looked at his bulk, disappearing round a pillar. He was a kind man, but he made her shudder.

Procne went to the kitchen. She was a famous cook. Princes had admired her succulent roast lamb or, better still, the tender steak from the krikri or wild mountain goat, a small agile creature which Tereus and his men sometimes hunted.

She opened the kitchen door and looked out into the yard. Her little boy Itys, just over one year old, was sitting on the ground in a shaft of yellow sunlight, under the watchful eye of his nursemaid Nina. He was playing with the chickens, giggling as they clucked around him and shrieking if they pecked anywhere near his feet. Procne went and tickled his toes, sizing up the chickens. She chose her victim, carried it squawking and protesting to the blood-stained table under the vine in the corner of the yard, and chopped its head off. A screech went up; all the chickens started to scream and flutter. Itys watched his mother hang the chicken's body upside down, watched the blood come pouring out into the stone tray. Then, for no apparent reason, Itys started to cry. He screamed and bellowed until his round little face was purple, his back and his belly strained with the effort. Embarrassed, Nina passed him to his mother, but he screamed all the louder, and kicked her chest with his strong legs. She promptly gave him back to the maid and told her to take him out of earshot. Then she went back to her cooking.

She chopped nuts and onions and wild herbs for the stuffing, fresh rosemary and thyme she had picked in the mountains yesterday. When she disembowelled the chicken, its body was still warm and moist. She plunged her hand inside and pulled out the entrails, the heart, the liver, the kidneys. Later that evening she would offer these precious parts up, with the blood, to the Goddess.

Procne sang to herself. Cooking was her one great relaxation. She sang a song she had learnt at home, far away, when she was a little girl. Her voice was rich and deep, and the song gladdened her and she sang it over and over again, remembering how she and her sister Philomel had sung it together at the tops of their voices out on the mountainside when they were children. Philomel was five years younger than her, but they had always been extremely close, played together, looked after each other. They used to run about in the bright yellow sunshine hand in hand, and play roly-poly down the green grassy slopes.

The longer Procne sang – and she sang many different songs from her childhood – the more she realised what her true feelings were. She was desperately homesick.

Tereus enjoyed the roast chicken whole-heartedly. She watched him carve the bird with care, gently dismembering it, so no morsel of flesh should be wasted, and he ate up every scrap. Then he sucked at the bones and wiped the fat up with his bread.

'I've married a splendid cook,' he declared with a satisfied smile, and he patted his knee for her to come and sit upon it.

She looked up at him.

'Do you love me?' she said.

'How can you ask a question like that? You know I do,' he replied, patting his stomach.

'Will you grant me a favour?' she asked.

'Anything you like, my love,' he beamed benevolently.

'Can I go home and stay with my family for a little while?'

'Hmph. Well, I don't know about that.' He leaned back to have a good look at her. 'No, I'm not very keen on that idea.' He was rather hurt by her request.

But she begged and wheedled and pleaded with him so much over the next few days, and he saw that she was really pining, so that in the end he came to a generous compromise. He would go to her father, King Pandion, and ask to borrow his younger daughter for a little while. Young Philomel could come and stay with them for a month or two, and then everyone would be happy.

Procne eagerly agreed, glad not only that she would see her beloved sister before long, but also that she would have a short break from her huge and demanding husband. So she packed his things carefully, gave him blessings for the journey, and shut the door firmly behind him.

When Tereus's ship sailed into the harbour, Kind Pandion prepared to give him a mighty welcome, as befitted such a mighty warrior who had delivered Athens from the barbarians in her time of need. Once he had heard Tereus's errand, however, the warm glow inside him began to go cold.

'Philomel is all I have left now, you see, and I would miss her terribly if she went away. And then, Thrace is so far! The journey is so dangerous! What if something were to happen to her?'

Tereus laughed his big booming laugh.

'But, dear father-in-law, I will be there to protect her.'

'Yes, that's true, and I know she couldn't be in better hands. If I hadn't respected you I would never have entrusted Procne to your care. And how is Procne? You say she's not quite happy?'

'Perfectly happy,' Tereus reassured him, 'only just the tiniest bit homesick. That's why she wants Philomel to come and stay for a while.'

At this very moment, Philomel herself entered the room, tall for her age, and shy, with a slightly wild look in her eyes, like a bird which has been startled in the woods.

Tereus stared at her for a moment, reminded of the feeling he had had when he first gazed on her sister two years ago. Then he broke into a big grin.

'My, my, how you've grown,' he declared, and then he enfolded her in what she felt to be a most un-brother-in-law-like embrace. She submitted to this, feeling it would be impolite to try and wriggle free, but as soon as he released her she went and sat gravely at her father's feet.

Pandion was very proud of her. He pointed to a huge tapestry which hung on the wall. It showed a mountain landscape in springtime. Soft black and white woolly lambs nibbled at the emerald green grass, while in the foreground two little girls with large brown eyes and black curly hair played together among the wild hyacinths.

'See that picture?' asked Pandion. 'Philomel did that. She's the best weaver in Attica. She's won heaps of prizes,' he boasted. 'She can take any old bit of coloured wool and make it sing.' He ruffled her hair fondly.

Tereus felt a strange pang. All through the meal, he couldn't take his eyes off her. She was so like Procne, and yet so different, more dreamy-looking, more serious and reserved. But so affectionate to those she loved. When she kissed her father goodnight, he found himself wishing he could swap places with Pandion, so that he could feel her warm brown arms round his neck.

The two men stayed up drinking long after Philomel had gone to bed. The more he drank, the more Tereus convinced himself that his passion for Philomel was uncontrollable, that he must have her, at whatever cost. But even when he was drunk, he never lost his capacity for cold calculation. He just became more eloquent in his pleas – on Procne's behalf, of course – that Pandion should let him take Philomel away for the summer months.

In the end the old man agreed, but the next day, when he was sober again, he had an uneasy feeling which made him regret his decision. Just as he had been about to drop off to sleep, in the early hours of the morning, an owl had screeched right outside his bedroom window. But still, a promise is a promise, and so he had not tried to prevent Philomel from going.

She, meanwhile, was torn between her strong desire to see her sister, and her great reluctance to travel alone with her massively muscular brother-in-law, who always stood too close to her and often put his arm round her waist. She felt she must try to overcome this repulsion, for her sister's sake; but she kept asking herself, 'How can she bear him?'

Her heart felt very heavy as she boarded the boat beside the warrior, and waved goodbye to her father, who stood looking frail and small at the water's edge. It was only the thought that she would soon see Procne that kept her from crying.

She felt acutely uncomfortable throughout the voyage. Tereus rarely left her side, even for a moment, so she could never simply enjoy the wind in her face and the waves beneath her feet, and the gulls wheeling above her head. He did not talk to her much, but he would slip his hand into hers, and she would endure it, because she didn't want to hurt his feelings. And sometimes he would stare at her so hard that she felt naked although she was fully clothed, and then she would blush to the roots of her black wavy hair, and he would laugh his big booming laugh and reach for his flagon of strong Thracian wine. He was biding his time, conscious of the prying eyes of the sailors. He would try to woo her, and if not, well.

Philomel felt a surge of relief as she stepped off the ship and on to dry land. Tereus had told her that the palace was only a short drive away from the port, so she eagerly climbed into the cart which awaited them. But the journey took over two hours, and the sun was setting when they finally drew up at a little cottage deep in the heart of the forest. A servant, a sharp-eyed, unsmiling middle-aged woman, opened the door to them.

'But, Tereus, I don't understand. Where's Procne? I thought you lived in a palace?'

'Don't worry, little sister, we're going to break our journey here,' said Tereus, and he led the bewildered young woman into the dark little cottage.

Once the dinner was cooked, he dismissed the servant, who stared coldly at him before she withdrew.

'And now, my dear, it's just the two of us,' he cooed, gazing at Philomel with his beady blue eyes. 'You know I'm crazy about you, don't you? It's been agony trying to keep my hands off you all this time. You don't know what it's like, this burning fire inside me, just for one kiss of those sweet red lips, just one glimpse of that heavenly breast, just one—' But Philomel had started up and was backing towards the door. He grabbed her and forced her to sit down again, and sat down heavily beside her on the couch, squeezing against her thigh.

'Oh, don't be cruel. You don't know what it's like to be so deeply in love. For the first moment I saw you, I knew I had to have you. We're an emotional people, we Thracians, everybody says so. I can't help it if I've got a passionate nature!'

'What about Procne!' Philomel hissed.

'Oh, Procne doesn't understand me. She's a hard, cold woman. She's selfish. You're not like that. You're so sensitive; you're so intelligent.'

His breath was hot on her face. Once more she wrenched herself free, but despite his great bulk, he was fit and moved swiftly, and he grabbed her two little wrists in his great big hands.

'Don't make me do this,' he beseeched her, but still she struggled to get away, so he had no choice but to knock her to the ground. He was fourteen stone of solid muscle; she was fourteen years old, all skin and bone; and he raped her on the cold stone floor. There were no bridesmaids outside the door to howl for her lost virginity, only the seagulls, blown inland by the storm, circling above the cottage, spreading the alarm, telling the forest about a tragedy they had seen.

Tereus lay slumped on top of Philomel. He sighed deeply, and then got up unsteadily to his feet. Philomel lay on the floor, curled up into a tight little ball with her back to him.

He felt upset. Why did she have to go and make him do that? She looked awful, lying on the floor, all bedraggled. He bent down to touch her hair, to try and look at her face, to try and see if she was crying. She flinched from his hand, sat up, and edged away across the floor.

'I'm sorry, Philomel. I didn't want to hurt you, you know that. I love you.'

She flung her hair out of her face and rose to her feet, and then she found her voice.

'You fucking liar! You hate me! You wanted to hurt me! You wanted to hurt Procne as well! Just because you're the king, you think you can get away with this, but you can't! I'm going to tell everyone what you did—'

He slapped her face.

'Shut up, you stupid bitch! If you so much as breathe a word—'

'You can't stop me, you monster! I'm going to tell everyone that their famous King Tereus is nothing but a filthy rapist!'

He knocked her to the floor again.

'You're not going to tell anyone anything,' he shouted. He grabbed his sword and cut out her tongue. Her mouth filled up with blood, and he raped her again.

Procne couldn't understand why Tereus took so long to come back from Athens. She had been expecting him to arrive with Philomel at least three or four days ago, but there was still no sign of them. She was very excited at the thought of seeing Philomel again. She had prepared a splendid bedroom for her, spread a beautiful quilt upon the bed, and filled several jugs with bright yellow daffodils. But the daffodils were beginning to fade, and she was starting to get anxious in case some accident had befallen her sister on the journey. What if the ship had been caught in a storm? What if it had been attacked by pirates? She tried to comfort herself by saying that probably her father had made Tereus stay a little bit longer, because he was unwilling to part with Philomel. She tried to quieten her fears with common sense, but anxiety kept rising in her throat.

At long, long last, she heard the sound of the cart crunching along the gravel drive. She ran out of the house, and then stopped in her tracks. Only Tereus and the driver had climbed down from the cart. There was no one else.

'Tereus? Where is she? Where's Philomel?'

'Bad news, I'm afraid. She's dead.'

'Dead? What happened to her?'

'The journey was too much for her. She caught an infection. Coughed herself to pieces. Wasted away in a matter of days. I nursed her myself. Took her to a cottage as soon as we landed. Looked after her as best I could. But it was no use. She died yesterday.'

He hung his head.

'I can't believe it,' said Procne. 'My little sister is dead! She was too young. It's too cruel. She's always been so healthy, so strong. She's never ill. She never was before.'

Tereus heaved a big sigh and put his arm round his wife, to comfort her in her loss. He led her tenderly back indoors.

After the news of Philomel's death, Procne became a changed woman. She lost interest in everything – in cooking, in jewels, in her little boy Itys. She grew very silent. She never smiled, never laughed, never kept a conversation going. She drifted about the palace, sighing frequently; deep, loud, heart-rending sighs.

Tereus began to get fed up with this behaviour. He had been sympathetic at first, but Procne was taking it too far. Philomel was only her sister after all.

'It's all right for you,' cried Procne. 'You didn't love her like I did. And it's all your fault anyway.'

'What do you mean?' said Tereus indignantly. 'If you hadn't made me drag her all the way from Athens, she wouldn't have caught the infection in the first place.'

'If you hadn't been so mean she wouldn't have had to come here at all. You wouldn't let me go and visit her!'

Procne was shocked by the ugly expression on Tereus's face. She did not know what to make of it. She gathered up her skirts and stalked out of the room.

Philomel, meanwhile, was still living in the cottage in the heart of the forest. For company she had the servant Barbara, and Barbara's husband Bulbos, the wood-cutter, who had been given strict instructions by Tereus not to let Philomel out of his sight.

At first, after she had been raped and mangled, Philomel had just wanted to die. She kept vomiting. The stump of her tongue in her mouth swelled and ached and choked her. Little by little, day by day, the wound began to heal. She found she could swallow the soup which Barbara prepared for her. Philomel could not speak to Barbara, and Barbara did not speak to her, but in the older woman's eyes was a look of such deep love and anger, that Philomel knew she could trust her. Bulbos, however, did not encourage intimacy between the two women. He was paid to keep Philomel a prisoner, and he took his work seriously.

'Don't hang around with that little slut,' he would say to Barbara. 'You might catch something off her.'

Philomel could not speak, and worse than that she could not sing. She who had been used to fill the valleys with her echoing songs, could now only make a strange and mournful moan, which cost her much pain. She would sit for hours at the door of the cottage, listening to the birds chattering and crying and calling in the woods. She sat there so long, she thought at last she was beginning to understand what they were saying to each other: how men were evil and dangerous, how they take delight in trapping and hunting and killing other creatures, how they cannot tell the difference between love and death.

Philomel had lost her tongue, but gradually she remembered that there was another way to sing. Barbara brought her wool, and each day Philomel wove the brightly coloured threads together, until piece by piece a pattern began to emerge. At first the women were anxious in case Bulbos would realise what they were doing, but even when he came to look at it he didn't see. He simply scoffed at Philomel's 'knitting'.

Into the tapestry, Philomel wove every detail of her ordeal: Tereus's arrival at King Pandion's palace, the sea voyage to Thrace, the cart ride to the little cottage, her rape and gory maiming, and her imprisonment in the heart of the woods.

Philomel's fingers were busy for days and weeks. Her heart sang out as she swiftly wove the thick coarse wool – bright blue for the Aegean sea, bright green for the leaves on every tree, bright red for her blood on the kitchen floor.

When it was finished, Philomel looked at it and she saw that it was good and she folded it carefully, and gave it to Barbara. Barbara got on the donkey and rode at once to Tereus's palace, where she put it safe in Procne's hands.

Within a few hours Procne was by her sister's side; rejoicing to find her still alive, agonised to know of her suffering.

Little sister, when I see what that man has done to you, I have to weep blood. A bronze claw has grasped my heart and is squeezing the life from me.

Philomel, it is you I have cherished above all else. We two came from the same holy source, from the same red womb. The same mother gasped in agony to bring both you and me out into the light. We were suckled at the same strong breast. The same lullabies were sung to you as to me.

When you were born and I first saw you in our mother's arms, my whole body was thrilled with pleasure. I had prayed to the Goddess for a sister, and she had answered my prayer. You looked at me with eyes so thoughtful and wise that I was almost frightened. But I knew that you had been sent from heaven to be my dearest friend.

All our childhood we played together. In the long hot summers, under the azure sky, while the cicadas filled the air with their warm whispering. We picked flowers and sweet scented herbs, and made garlands for each other's hair, and sang and danced to greet each new day.

Once, I shall never forget, when you were only three years old, we were playing on the mountainside together and I lost you. The mist came down and I could not find you. My voice became hoarse, calling for you. My feet became blistered, walking across the stones, amidst the yellow gorse, and still I did not find you. I wept big tears, until my dress was wet. I felt as desolate as Demeter, searching for her daughter, Persephone. I thought you were dead. I thought the earth had opened and King Hades had sprung out to ambush you and kidnap you and take you away from me for ever.

The moon was high in the sky when I at last returned, forlorn, to the palace. Imagine my joy to find you, large as life and laughing in the kitchen. You had found your own way home. You had not even been frightened. My heart began to beat again.

It was when our mother died that we first learnt the meaning of sorrow, together. Father called us to his knee and told us that we must look after each other now. He told me that I was to be your mother from now on. Yet, in many ways, you have been a mother to me, little sister. We have mothered each other, protected each other, comforted each other. We shared our bed, our meals, our games, our secrets, our dances and our songs, for twelve sweet years, until I was taken from you.

I remember how we celebrated and made sacrifices to the Goddess on the day you first began to bleed. We offered up the sacred blood to the Goddess of life and death, in acknowledgement of the power of life and death which each woman holds within her.

It was not long after this that Athens was attacked by the enemy, and famous King Tereus of Thrace arrived on the scene to protect us, to prevent us from being raped by the barbarians. King Tereus was a civilised man, or so our father told us.

I never loved Tereus. I never even liked him. I know now that I have always hated him, because I have always been afraid of him. But I thought it was only me he would attack. I never imagined he would dare to hurt you.

You must come with me, my dear sister. We have been re-united and must never be separated again. I know you are frightened to come with me to the palace. Do not fear. I will protect you. I will make sure Tereus does not learn that you are under his roof – until it is too late.

Together we will find a way to hurt him. I will ask Hecate, the Goddess of the underworld, to show us what to do.

Come with me, little sister. Do not weep.

But both sisters fell into each other's arms, and wept loud and long, until their tears mingled. Philomel's weeping sounded strange, because she had no tongue. It sounded like the gobbling of a bird.

Tereus noted with satisfaction that a change had come over his wife. She was no longer moping about the palace, getting up late and going to bed early. She had smiled at him for the first time in weeks. Her cheeks, which had been so sallow of late, were now flushed with colour, and her eyes had regained their bright flash. He could hear her singing in the kitchen.

He was glad. It had been no fun living with her depression for the past couple of months. In bed she was like one of the statues in the temple. It took all the pleasure out of sex.

Anyway, now it seemed she had got over her sulking fit, and had resolved to be a real wife to him once again. He had gone to ask what she was cooking, but she had laughed and pushed him firmly out of the kitchen. She told him it was going to be a surprise. Savoury smells assailed his nostrils. Whatever it was, it was going to be good. He took a flagon or two of wine and went to wait in the big hall.

It was nearly an hour later that Procne brought in the best dinner service. By this time Tereus was ravenous. The meat was succulent and tender, served up in a tasty, aromatic sauce. Procne watched as he ate every mouthful, her eyes reflecting the glow from the fire. Tereus licked his lips.

'You've excelled yourself today, my darling. That was absolutely superb.'

Procne smiled.

'There's only one thing we need now to complete our cosy evening together,' Tereus added. 'Why don't we send for Itys? I haven't seen him all day.'

'He's already here,' said Procne.

Tereus looked round, puzzled.

'What do you mean? Where?' he asked.

'He's inside.'

'Inside?'

Why did icy fear grip Tereus's heart as he sat there looking into his wife's smiling, smiling face?

'You *have* seen him, you know,' she remarked casually. 'Actually, you've just eaten him.' And she lifted the lid off the last remaining dish on the tray. There lay Itys's head. Tereus felt his dinner rise up in his throat.

'You've murdered my baby boy!'

'You raped my sister.'

'You cooked him! You watched while I carved him up and swallowed him down!'

'You cut out her tongue and raped her again!'

'You unnatural monster!'

'Me!'

'You're mad!' he spluttered, backing away from her.

'And you're not,' she replied, coolly.

At this moment, Philomel appeared at the door, and glided silently to her sister's side.

Sickness overcame Tereus. He vomited and retched and retched, until all that was left inside his stomach was acid and pain.

When his body had stopped convulsing he reached for his sword.

'You'll pay for this,' he roared.

But he was wrong. For the Goddess would not stand by and let her faithful handmaidens perish at the hands of a drunken rapist.

Hand in hand, Procne and Philomel began to run. They ran the length of the hall and into the courtyard. They ran through the gate, with Tereus hard on their heels. But once they had left the palace grounds, their feet moved swifter and swifter until they were hardly touching the earth any longer. Procne found herself soaring into the air, higher and higher, as high as the treetops. She looked round. At her side flew a nightingale, singing her heart out: Philomel had found her voice again. Philomel was now a nightingale, and Procne had become a swallow.

Tereus never caught them. He turned into a hoopoe, a cross-looking bird with a lopsided crest who stamps about looking for trouble.

Procne flew off to Egypt, but she returns every summer to keep an eye on things. She watches over young housewives, and their sisters.

Philomel sings every night in the woods, a sad, sweet song that makes men want to kill themselves, and makes women want to fly out of their front doors.

This is a true story.

CAROLINE CLAXTON

The Stranger in the City

The street was almost deserted. It had long since grown dark and most people were safely indoors. Kira shivered, feeling the cold creeping through her jacket, and she turned up her collar. It was quiet, the way streets grow quiet when night falls. The odd car passed her and a bus lumbered along the other side of the road. A '30', she noted. Going to somewhere called 'Hackney Wick'.

Three men were walking towards her, hips and shoulders swinging under the street light, pendulum-style. They spread out across the pavement. As they approached, one leapt in front of her, pushing his face right up to hers. Automatically she stepped back, clenching her fists. He looked her up and down, laughed and walked on. Kira stared after him in amazement. The men stopped again and the one who laughed made to walk up to her again. She reached into her pocket, pushed back her shoulders and stared him full in the face. He stared back, then shrugged, made some comment to the other men. They all laughed. Then they turned and walked on, without a backward glance this time. Kira relaxed her grip on the bunch of keys in her pocket, breathing slowly to calm the flow of adrenalin, and started walking once more.

She heard a clicking of heels behind her and a woman passed her, walking swiftly, head down. She had a thin coat on, decorative but useless against the night chill, and a tight skirt so, although she walked quickly, she could only take short steps.

Ahead of them the lights and music of an inn spread out across the street. Several men were standing on the steps, drinking, leaning against the doorway, so that people had to jostle past them to get in. They talked to each other in low, growling voices, all talking at once. Words floated above the thud of the jukebox.

'Yeah that's what they want.'

'You should have seen mine.'

'She's a goer all right.'

The woman sensed, rather than saw, the men before they saw her and edged nearer the road, leaving a wide berth between her and the tight fingers of the men's shadows reaching across the pavement.

One of the men picked up the sound of her heels and turned sharply. He saw her and pursed his lips into a slow, shrill whistle. It shot into the air and settled. The woman glanced in his direction, her lips smiling faintly, her eyes wary, then quickly she dropped her head. Shouts followed her from the inn, all the men on the steps had noticed her now, and more came to the doorway. They all called after her and, though she kept walking, her body betrayed her. The line of her hunched shoulders, clenched arms, tottering legs showed she heard the calls. Two men left the steps, beer glasses in hand, and quickly reached her with long strides. One walked round and stood in front of her. The other caught her arm and muttered something into her ear. She pulled his arm away and his beer spilled. He swore at her, pointing to his trousers where the beer had splattered on its way to the pavement. She murmured an apology, in a voice so quiet Kira could hardly hear it, and turned to walk on – only to find the other man barring her way. He stepped closer and fingered her jacket, where the line formed a V above her breasts. He said something about the cloth and she smiled again, fear clearly in her eyes now.

Kira had stopped when the men began shouting. She stood, unnoticed, all eyes were on this strange ritual. She stood, heart pounding, wondering what to do.

After a moment she stepped from the shadows, dropping her backpack. The men turned, seeing her for the first time and looked her up and down, taking in the jacket, trousers, boots, short hair. Most were content to stare, in amusement or contempt, but some could not resist jeering.

'Hey you, you a man or a woman, huh?'

'Maybe she doesn't know.' Laughter.

'I know what you are. Dyke.'

The words fell in a jumble of sounds, but the hostility behind them was clear enough. Kira bristled as she put her arms through the straps of the backpack, eyeing the braying men coldly. As she began to move on, the woman stepped in front of her again, using the brief diversion to side-step the men obstructing her. A few remarks were called after them as they clicked and padded along the street, but no one followed.

Fewer and fewer people were on the streets now. As they came to the next corner the woman turned into a side-street. Kira glanced at her as she turned and for a moment their eyes met. The first unhostile contact Kira had made since coming here. As Kira walked on alone, she focused her mind back on her route. She reached round for her pack, to take out her map and, suddenly wary, she stepped into a doorway. The two hostile encounters warned her this city did not welcome strangers, or women, or both. And map in hand she was obviously a stranger.

The women's inn was on the corner of the road. There were several doors but Kira followed a steady stream of women filing into a side entrance. A woman sat behind a table taking money, as Kira reached her she spoke.

'Waged or unwaged?'

The words meant nothing to Kira. Maybe it was a code. She stared blankly until the woman said: 'Are you working? Do you have a job?'

'Oh. No, I do not have a job, here.'

Kira wondered if this was some kind of interview. Maybe they were checking her over before they let her in. She had been told a lot was secret in this community. From her brief walk on the streets she was beginning to see why. Before she had time to pursue the thought, the woman said: '80p then, please.'

Kira fumbled with the strange notes. Already flustered she could make no sense of them and offered a handful to the woman. She grinned. 'Just one will do.' And took one of the green ones. A woman with curly hair and an elaborate headband stared out from the green background.

The woman handed Kira a small piece of blue paper, some coins and gestured to her to walk inside.

The air was thick with smoke and heavy with music. The sound was so loud it hit the walls, floor, and ceiling, and the women in the room had to shout to make themselves heard. Kira wondered why they didn't have the music softer. Everyone seemed to be talking, and the dance floor was empty.

There was a huge wooden counter along one side of the room, where women were buying and selling drinks. Kira's throat tightened at the sight of glasses filled with amber and dark brown liquid. There seemed to be a queue, but Kira couldn't decide where it began or finished. Eventually she moved into the mass of bodies and waved a green note, as the women around her were doing. A drink seller came towards her.

'What do you want?'

'Um . . . beer.'

'What kind, lager?' What in the seas was lager?

'Er, yes. That's fine?'

'Pint? Half?'

'Pint.'

Well, she was here to learn, she commented to herself. The amber liquid arrived in a tall, straight glass. Kira sipped cautiously. Mild, slightly bitter but cool and smooth. Kira memorised the name 'Lager'.

All round her groups of women sat at small, wooden tables. Where the tables and seats ran out, women sat on the floor. Many were talking, bending close and gesticulating to get their message over the waves of music. Kira looked for a seat and spotted one grouped round one of the tables. She walked across to it and gestured to the group of women. They nodded. She sat down.

The music changed. Still the persistent beat but faster. Several women got up to dance. Kira watched them moving. Each woman moved differently, but none of them used much floor space. They shifted from foot to foot, swinging their arms, occasionally turning their heads. She could see why the dance floor was so small. They didn't need the space.

She turned to the group of women seated around her. She wanted to make contact, but didn't know where to begin. Were they as hostile to strangers as the people on the street?

One of the women was watching her. As Kira caught her eye, she smiled. Kira smiled back, hesitantly. The woman took a packet out of her pocket and pushed it towards her. Kira took a slim, white tube and studied it. It was filled with a golden-brown substance. The woman had put a tube into her mouth, Kira copied her, and she leant across holding a small, red object, which she held to the tube. The object sparked. The light dawned. The tube was a smoke. Kira drew on her tube, drawing in the smoke. It hit her throat and she resisted the reflex to cough. She was not used to so much smoke. She took her next breath more carefully, and looked up to see the woman smiling at her.

'Are you meeting someone?'

'No, I'm here alone.'

'Ah . . .' She smiled again, tossing the tight curls nestling about her head.

'Where you from?'

Kira was expecting this. She rattled off the name of the obscure Portuguese town, hoping the woman didn't know too much about it.

'Where's that?'

'Portugal,' Kira answered honestly.

'You here for a visit?'

'Yes. Yes I am.'

'Um-hum.'

'You. Are you from London?'

'Deptford. Do you know it?'

Kira shook her head.

'It's south of the river.' She looked at Kira. 'The river Thames.'

'Ah.'

Kira faintly recollected the river Thames ran through London separating north from south.

'Are . . .' began the woman, but the woman next to her bent close to her and said something. The woman nodded and turned to Kira.

'I don't know if you're interested, but we're going to a party. It's not far . . . Would you like to come with us?'

A party: a gathering of people, usually in a private dwelling.

'Yes, please. How do I . . .'

'Get there?' Kira nodded. 'I've got my bike outside. You know, motorbike?' She mimed driving a motorised machine, making sounds. Kira just held back a smile, and nodded to show she understood.

'Or you could walk . . . It's just down the road really . . . But there's room on my bike. If you want . . .'

Kira smiled and got up, finishing her beer, picking up her backpack. As they turned to leave the woman said, 'Oh, by the way, I'm Bleu.'

'You're . . .'

'That's my name,' grinned Bleu. 'Come on.'

The house was easy to find. A tall building, shedding paint and plaster. Music hummed through the open door. Bleu turned off the motor of her machine, the 'motorbike', unstrapping her helmet. Kira did the same, whirling from the speed and vibration of their journey, and the physical contact with Bleu. She offered the helmet to Bleu. 'Hang on to it,' she smiled.

They walked up the steps and went through to a large room. Like the inn they had just left, this was full of women.

'Is there any room for us?' Kira asked, half seriously.

'This is half empty,' replied Bleu. 'You wait another hour. Dee surely knows how to hold a party. I'll just put some of these on the table,' indicating the cans of beer they had bought on the way. 'And get you a glass. Be right back.'

She snaked her way through the crowd. Kira looked round the room. Like the outside, it was in need of repair. There were large cracks in the walls and ceiling, but it had been recently painted brilliant white, which emphasised its size. The white was set off and warmed a little, by brightly coloured posters. Bold slogans and pictures of women looking confident, strong. 'Women unite against racism,' one declared. Another said: 'Capitalism also relies on domestic labour.' A third: 'Porn is the theory, Rape is the practice.' Kira struggled, as she had been struggling all evening with many of the words. They stubbornly refused to translate. Perhaps, later, she could talk to Bleu about it.

The music cut through her thoughts. It was a deep, sensuous sound. It hit straight on to the emotions, the way most music does, but there was another feeling running through it. Kira couldn't place it, but it worried her. She wandered over to the music machine and picked up the cover of the disc being played. A woman stared down at her, cruelly sneering yet challenging. Disturbed, Kira tried to relate the image to the current running through the music. She slowly realised it was an undercurrent of violence. Violence when it has become pleasurable. The deep throbbing played to her sexual sensory perceptions, the woman's voice homed in on that sound but it carried the undercurrent. Do they relate sex to violence then? wondered Kira. So aware of the undercurrent, Kira could not respond sexually to the music, but looking around her she saw that women were moving in a way that could only be described as sexual. Sexual and somehow cold. In tune with the tone of the singer. The observation depressed her, but then she could not expect all cultures to be like her own. And she did not know enough about this one to make judgements.

She watched Bleu greet someone across the room. Bleu was hugging a small woman in a brilliant yellow shirt. They were both laughing, and the warmth of their laughter shone around them. Kira smiled, enjoying their pleasure, but feeling distanced. Bleu looked over and waved. With a hand she beckoned for Kira to join them and waved a glass. Kira had been drinking from the can, but she was strangely pleased to see Bleu had not forgotten her.

As she came up to them Bleu introduced the woman in the yellow shirt. 'Kira meet Alice, or Ice as she is sometimes known.'

Bleu and Alice grinned at each other. There was obviously a story behind Alice's nickname.

'Bleu tells me you're Portuguese.' Kira nodded. 'Have you been here before?'

'No. Are you from London, like Bleu?'

'Too right. It's an awful, dirty place, but I'd die of boredom anywhere else.'

Kira could well imagine. Alice never stood still for two seconds. All the time they were talking she was moving around drinking her beer in great gulps, looking all round the room.

'Oh, there's Dee. Listen I'll catch up with you later. Watch yourself, Kira.' She grinned and touched Kira lightly on the arm, before warmly hugging Bleu once more and bouncing off. Kira had a brief image of an electrical current, lighting up everything around it, moving almost faster than the eye can follow.

Bleu was handing her a glass filled with the amber beer called lager. 'I'm restless,' she said after a moment. 'I get edgy at parties sometimes.'

'Why?' asked Kira.

'I don't know,' she replied, looking surprised. She leaned back against the wall, chewing her lip. Absent-mindedly she reached for a smoking tube, offered the packet, Kira took one. As Bleu lit the smokes she went on.

'I guess it's because everyone drinks. If you're depressed you get more depressed. If you're high, you get loud and insensitive. You're s'posed to be having a fine time, so you work really hard at that. People aren't themselves at parties. Look at Patsy over there.'

She was pointing to a woman in a smoky-blue flying suit, sitting alone, staring into her glass.

'You get her on her own and she's always talking. She's lovely. But right now she feels crowded by all these people. She came 'cos Dee asked her to. Now she's feeling guilty 'cos she's hating being here. In a minute she'll look around and smile, just to show everyone she's having a real good time, you know?' As they looked across to her, Patsy looked up, smiled rather weakly and looked at her watch.

'And you see Jude over there. You can't talk to her at parties. She gets mad and shouts at you if she doesn't agree with you. That's if you can get her to talk serious.' Bleu frowned. 'Want to go for a walk?'

'A walk? OK, why not?' Kira followed Bleu out of the loud, smoky room. Outside the cool, fresh air hit them, and Bleu seemed to relax a little.

They walked, without talking. Animals scuttled away from them, slinking under hedges to stare out. Two pin-points of flame in the night's velvet. Kira cautiously threaded her arm through Bleu's. The streets, this time round, felt friendly. She felt safe with Bleu. Not because Bleu looked like she could take care of herself, though she did, but because they felt good together.

'Kira, how long you gonner be here?' They had stopped to sit on a garden wall. The quiet of the night stretched before them, broken only by the droning of cars some way off.

Kira shrugged. Bleu was looking at her intensely. 'I don't know. Really.'

Bleu frowned. 'But how much money have you got?'

Kira sighed. She really didn't want to answer questions now. She wasn't sure of herself, with emotions racing faster than the alcohol in her bloodstream. 'Oh, I'm all right,' she said, deliberately mis-understanding.

'No,' said Bleu impatiently, I didn't mean that. I meant, you'll stay till your money runs out, won't you? I mean are you staying a few weeks, or . . . what?'

'I really do not know how long I will be here. But I think it will not be a few weeks . . . why?'

Now Bleu looked uncomfortable. 'Because . . . Oh shit!'

In the tight silence they folded comfortably into a kiss, which lasted for ever, and for a few seconds. In the midst of the energy crackling and charging around them Bleu managed to croak, 'Do you want to come home, with me?'

'Yes.'

Light filtered through the blue-grey shutters, throwing speckles on to the end of the bed. Bleu stood by the door, balancing a collection of liquids and drinking vessels, pushing the door shut with her foot, as Kira looked up, stretching and smiling lazily.

'I don't know what you like, so I brought a little of all we got,' grinned Bleu, laying all the stuff down by the bed. 'Tea, coffee, juice, milk . . .'

Kira ran through the translations, peering at the different liquids. 'What's this?' she asked, picking up a pottery drinking vessel filled with a glistening copper liquid.

'Tea.'

Kira tasted the hot drink. It had a strong, definite flavour. Refreshing.

'D'you want milk in it?' Bleu was holding up a thick, white liquid in a clear bottle. Kira shook her head. Bleu picked up a clear glass filled with bright orange liquid, and settled back against the pillows.

They had made love for most of the night, and that feeling of closeness was still with them. Kira reached over and ran her tongue along Bleu's shoulder, tasting salt. Bleu sighed. A long, deep sigh of pleasure and peace. The door opened.

'Bleu, d'you know . . . Oh! Hello.'

'Patsy!' exclaimed Bleu, laughing.

'Well, how was I to know? I wanted the milk.'

Kira recognised the serious, kind woman from the party last night. This morning she had draped herself in a large, loose, T-shirt, which left most of her body unclothed, and she shuffled around, a little nervously.

'This is Kira.'

'You were at Dee's party, weren't you?'

'Yes, I was.'

Patsy looked down at the two of them. 'Well, I'll just grab the milk . . .'

'No, that's all right,' said Bleu, flashing a bright, sweet smile at Patsy. 'The rest of the house up yet?'

'Jude's well and truly hung over,' smiled Patsy, 'And Ice is cooking eggs and screaming for milk. Shall I tell her to throw a couple more in?'

Bleu looked at Kira. Kira nodded up at Patsy, and Patsy reached for the milk just as Ice yelled from the kitchen. 'What's that woman doing, or *done*, with the milk, Patsy?'

'Hang on to yerself, it's coming,' yelled back Patsy, leaving them.

Kira felt good with the sound of these women all around her. The house felt right: the women had come together and they cared for each other. Kira felt she could trust them.

They walked into the kitchen as Ice was putting food on to the table. She looked up at them and said 'Uh-huh.'

'A woman of few words,' said Bleu.

'But in them she says everything.'

All three women turned to look at Kira, as if, because she spoke with an accent, they didn't expect her to say anything startling.

'You're a clued in woman,' said Ice. Patsy grinned at Kira warmly, and Bleu hugged her hand.

'This is very good,' said Kira. Meaning the food.

'There's more in the pan, here.' Ice took Kira's plate and filled it again. 'Well. Now our happy home's complete,' said Ice to the frowning, ill-looking woman who had just walked into the kitchen.

'Don't talk to me. I have the worst headache known to woman,' said Jude.

'Known to women who drink.'

'Oh, give it a rest, Bleu.' Jude sat down at the table and lit a smoking tube.

'We're eating you know.' Ice looked sharply at Jude till she put it out.

'Tell me, Kira . . .' Patsy was saying, 'are you a feminist?'

Seas. One of those words that wouldn't translate. Kira went down the list, trying to remember which one it was. 'A feminist? Do you mean someone who fights for women?'

'Well, yes.'

'Then, yes, you could, or probably would, say I was.'

'What do you mean?' asked Ice.

'Well. I love women, and I fight for women. But there is not such a difference between men and women as there is here.'

The four women looked at her doubtfully.

'What? You mean in Portugal men and women are the same?' Bleu said.

Kira looked round the table at the women, who were all staring at her, trying to decide if she should push on with this.

'You said . . .'

'I know,' Kira broke in, trying to quiet the hurt and suspicion on Bleu's face. 'Listen, I trust you women.'

'I don't know if I can cope with this,' Jude was getting up.

'No, please stay. This will seem ridiculous and you won't believe me, but please . . . I'm asking you to try.' Kira took a deep breath and prayed silently for strength.

'Go on . . .' said Bleu, quietly.

'I am from a place called Feros. It is a small planet, thousands of light years away from here.'

The women looked at her astounded, and then all looked away.

'What you on?' asked Ice.

'Whatever it is, it's *good!*' said Jude.

'What do you mean?' Kira asked them.

'She means, are you taking something.' Kira looked blankly at Bleu. 'Are you taking drugs?'

'No,' said Kira, impatiently. 'Look. I know you find this hard to believe. You are very inward-looking on this planet, even though you have put your feet on what you call the "moon"!' They smiled at this. 'I will try and explain. I am a lover of women. On Feros we have noticed how women are treated on this planet, and we know there are bands of women trying to change this. I have come here to work among women such as you. I can learn much from you, and, I think, you can learn a little from me.'

'You're saying you're from outer space! You just walked in here and . . .'

'Jude,' broke in Kira, 'please try and forget your suspicions for a moment. I didn't "just walk in", I was, um, what you would say "transported" here yesterday.'

'And you just happen to speak English with a Portuguese accent?'

'Jude, let the woman speak,' Ice spoke gently but firmly. Kira smiled at her gratefully.

'I speak in whatever language I have chosen to speak in. You see, I think in my own language but the words you hear are in the language you know best. I always have an accent, unless I am speaking to people from my own district.'

'But how come there are words you don't understand?' Patsy asked.

'Some of the words do not translate. Some of your words have no meaning on Feros, like "feminist". On Feros there are no "feminists" and so there is no word.'

'You're saying you come from this perfect society . . .'

'No, Jude. It is not perfect. That is why I have come here to learn from you, about women and about other things – strength, caring, courage.'

There was a long silence while the women thought. It was mid-day and thin early-spring sun was falling in patches throughout the room. Finally, Bleu spoke: 'I want to believe you, Kira.'

Kira looked into Bleu's face and respected Bleu's willingness to trust her. She knew it was not easy to break away from age-old conditioning of disbelief. 'There is perhaps a way I can, um, persuade you.' The others turned to her expectantly. 'I could speak to your mind. That is, if you want me to. You have to . . .'

'Believe!'

'Now look here, Jude. You just get up and leave if you don't want to listen. Just 'cos you got a sore head don't mean you got to have a sore mouth!' Ice glowered at Jude. That electricity again, crackling, charging and spitting. 'Pay no attention to her. You go on, Kira. I want to listen.'

Jude looked at Ice, who was still glaring at her, and then across to Kira. 'I'm sorry,' she said, humbled. 'Look, I'll just shut up, OK?'

'No, you don't have to believe,' continued Kira, 'but you have to want me to come in to your mind. Otherwise, I can not make contact.' She took a breath and went on. 'I would like to speak to Bleu's mind, because I feel closest to her. Would you want me to, Bleu?'

Bleu nodded and smiled, nervously.

'Right. I will say something to your mind. Afterwards we can separate, and I will tell one person what I said, while you tell another person what you heard.'

'That sounds OK.' Bleu reached over and stroked Kira's hand. Kira took both of Bleu's hands in her own and looked into her eyes. She reached into Bleu's mind, drifting through soft and harder barriers. Clearing a path, she gently whispered: I love you , and I want you to work with me, and I with you. We are right together you and I.

Bleu was staring into Kira's eyes as Kira carefully drew away again. She looked surprised and shocked, but her lips were smiling at the warmth of their contact and Kira's mind-words.

As they had planned, the two women separated. Kira related the contact to Ice, Bleu to Patsy. The descriptions were identical.

Seated around the table once more, Jude pouring more of the infusion 'tea' from a large pot, the women flooded Kira with questions. She explained the technique of mind-speaking.

'Do you have to be close to the other person?'

'The contact does not have to be physical, Patsy. You can speak from many miles apart. But the other person must always allow you to come in to their mind. Do you want me to speak to your mind?' Patsy nodded eagerly.

Then as long as you are open to me, I can come in, Kira said to Patsy's mind.

Patsy looked round, realising that what she thought she had heard had not in fact been spoken.

'You have a very clear mind,' Kira said to her aloud, so as not to exclude the others. 'I had to thread carefully through Bleu's barriers, but your mind was open to me. It was easy to speak to you.'

'How many women do you want to work with?' Ice asked Kira.

'Well, they would have to trust me, and I them. A small group, at least to begin with.'

'I can arrange a meeting, if you like. Say the end of the week. Give me time to set it up.'

'Yes, that sounds good.'

'Well, count me in,' grinned Jude.

Ice got up, stretching. 'I can't sit around any more, women, so I'll see you later. Now, Kira,' she had already reached the kitchen door, 'You'll stay with us, won't you? While you're here?'

'I'd like that very much,' Kira called after her as she bounded up the stairs, two at a time.

In the days that followed, Bleu took Kira around London. To the tourist spots and to the women's places. They talked about their different worlds, the more Kira explained, the more she realised Bleu would have to go to Feros to understand it. Just as she was finding this planet a very different place to the world she had studied, back on Feros.

Ice had arranged a meeting of women. Some, she said, were 'spiritual', others 'radical'. The 'radicals', she said, would be interested because Kira was a lover of women (Earth word: lesbian) and because she was fighting for women.

As Bleu and Kira rode to the meeting on Bleu's bike, Kira gathered all her energy to meet the group of women who might well laugh in her face.

The meeting place was a women's centre. It was large and held together mostly by the women's efforts to keep it standing. Bleu rang a bell and spoke into a small box. There was a loud electrical brrr and the sound of a bolt unlocking. Bleu pushed the door open, telling Kira to be careful to lock it behind her. 'Men hang around, trying to get in,' she explained. 'Not that they're so interested in women's issues, just 'cos they can't bear not being allowed in.'

Ice, Patsy and Jude were already there. Bleu fetched some tea while Kira met some of the other women. Eventually Ice said they should start the meeting. 'As many women have come as are gonner come. We can't sit here for ever.'

They pulled their seats into a circle and, starting with Ice, each woman said her name and why she had come. Most of them knew nothing about the meeting and so when it came to Kira's turn – she was the last woman in the circle – they turned to her expectantly. She told them she had come to find out about women's groups and she wanted to find a small band of women, who would trust and help her.

'Now, this is the part you won't believe ...' she continued. 'Please try and forget, for a moment, what you know about space travelling ...' This was greeted with a thick silence. 'I have come here from another planet. Ridiculous as that will seem to you, I can only ask you to believe me.'

After another few moments of the heavy silence the women began asking questions. Bleu interrupted the bombardment of questions, laughter and disbelief by explaining how she had met Kira. Patsy came in on Bleu's story and related what had happened at their house. Immediately several women asked Kira to 'prove' she could 'read minds'. A woman stood up and said they should not 'ask another woman to prove herself', but Kira had anticipated this and spoke, first to Bleu, then Patsy and then to several of the new women.

There was a different atmosphere after the mind-speaking had finished. Kira needed a few moments to restore her energy. Almost all of the women were untrained in even elementary mind-speaking, and it was exhausting reaching out to them. While Kira was resting the women had a chance to talk freely.

When Kira had left the room one of the women turned to the others. 'I don't mind admitting, I find it very hard to accept this woman is from another planet. Even if she can read minds,' she said, her silver earring in the shape of a woman's symbol flashing as she shook her head.

'Five days ago, I wouldn't have believed her either, but sometime you got to reach out. I've been thinking, there's a lot we can't explain. There's a heap of religions about, but none of them explain why women are so close, and why women are "spiritual" if you want to use that word. I mean, if you think about it women have always used their powers: priestesses, fortune-tellers, witches.'

'You're right, you know, Ice,' said another woman, 'I'd like to know a bit more about this place she comes from.'

'I want to know what she wants us to *do*,' said the woman with the earring.

'We can't speak for Kira. She's the best one to answer your questions,' said Bleu. 'I'll go see if she's OK to come back.'

Kira was stretched out over two chairs, breathing deeply. Bleu gently stroked away some wisps of hair that had fallen over her forehead. Kira opened her eyes and smiled at Bleu leaning over her.

'Are you ready to come back?' Kira nodded, holding on to Bleu's hand and pulling herself up. As they went back to the meeting, Bleu told her the women wanted to know what she wanted them to do, and they wanted to know more about Feros.

'The biggest difference on Feros is that women are not thought to be inferior to men,' she told the meeting. 'I find it hard to understand why men here treat women so badly.'

'So do I,' said Jude.

'On Feros, women, and men, can chose to do whatever interests them. Of course, there are things that everyone must do to help their community, but everyone is expected to do their share.'

'Sounds perfect,' a woman said.

'I do not know of a society that is "perfect",' Kira replied. 'We are fighting, on and off, with people, other worlds, who do not like how we are. We have lived for many years in peace and now we find it hard to fight. We need to learn from others how to fight, without creating a circle of violence. That is why I say, you have a lot to teach me.'

'I asked to come here,' she went on, 'because I wanted to learn from you. You can help me by letting me work with you. And I can help you, I think, with skills I have, like mind-speaking.'

'Is it possible to learn that?' Patsy asked.

'Yes, I think so. It would take some time, but I think it is possible. There is something else. I was asked to say to you that we would welcome women from your groups on Feros. It is not a simple decision I know, and so I do not expect an answer now. You would risk everything by going, and you would be going to a place very different from your own.'

Women began talking to one another. Kira relaxed, allowing the noise to drift. She reminded herself she would have to make contact with her guide soon, and was overcome with a sudden, sharp memory of the world so far away, and so different from the place she was in.

'Kira,' one of the women was calling her. The room fell into silence once more. 'If some of us were to go to, what is it called, Feros?'

'Yes, Feros.'

'Would you take us there? When will you be going back?'.

Kira was lost in a stream of images, Feros and Earth, two worlds: one familiar, one largely unknown. Coming back to the present she found Bleu among the women, silent and serious, waiting for Kira's answer.

'If you go to Feros there will be women who will meet you, and help you in all you do. I will make contact for you and guide you from here. But . . .'

Catching Bleu's eyes and the depths of her slow, steady smile, 'I will be staying here. At least for a while.'

MARY DORCEY

A Country Dance

On the arm of your chair, your hand for a moment is still; the skin
smooth and brown against the faded, red velvet. I touch it lightly
with mine. 'Maybe what she needs is more time,' I say.

The air is dense with cigarette smoke, my eyes are tired. You stare
past me and begin again to fidget with a silver bracelet on your wrist.
I make my tone persuasive: 'Time to regain her identity, a sense of
independence, and . . .'

The words are swept from me in a sudden upswell of sound as last
orders are called. The climax of the night, and so much left unsaid,
undone. Every man in the room is on his feet, shoving for place at the
bar; the voices bluff, seductive as they work for one last round.

'Here, John, two large ones . . .'

'Pat, good man, four more pints . . .'

You ignore thcm, your gaze holding mine, your attention caught
once more by the hope of her name.

'What did you say about independence?'

'I said you need it, need to cultivate it,' I say, something perverse in
me all at once, wanting to disappoint you. Your eyes drop, slide to the
fireplace where the coal burns with a dim red glow.

'Ah, I thought it was Maeve you meant.'

And what matters after all which way I put it. In these stories aren't
all the characters interchangeable? The lights are turned up full now,
the evening over. And you as much in the dark as when we started. If
I had used less tact; if I had said straight out what everyone thinks,
would it have made a difference? I twist the stub of my last cigarette
into the glass ashtray. No, whatever I say you will hear what you
choose. Your misery safely walled beyond the reach of logic, however
much you may plead with me to advise, console. If you were not fully
certain of this, would you have asked me here tonight?

'Time, ladies and gents, please – have you no homes to go to?' The
barman turns, the great wash of his belly, supported just clear of the

crotch, tilts towards us. He swipes a greasy cloth across the tabletop, forcing us to lift our drinks: 'Come on now, girls.'

I take another sip of my whiskey and replace the glass emphatically on the cardboard coaster. You clasp your pint to your chest, swilling the dregs in languid circles.

'I don't think I can bear it much longer.'

I look at you, your dark eyes have grown sullen with pain, under the clear skin of your cheek a nerve twitches. Years ago, I would have believed you. Believed your hurt unlooked for – believed even in your will to escape it. Now, too many nights like this one have altered me. Too many nights spent in comforting others, watching while each word of sympathy is hoarded as a grain of salt to nourish the wound. On the blackness of the window I watch beads of rain glance brilliant as diamonds, each one falling distinct, separate, then merging – drawn together in swift streams to the ground. Why try to impose reason? Let you have your grand passion, the first taste of self-torment – never so sweet or keen again.

'Look, will you have another drink?' I say in a last attempt to cheer you, 'they might give us one yet.'

Instantly, your face brightens. 'Thanks, but you've bought enough, Siobáin,' you say and continue easily, 'Did you see someone has left a pint over there – will I get it?'

Without waiting for a reply, you slide your narrow hips in their scarlet jeans between our table and the bar. You reach for the pint of Harp and a half-finished cocktail. The barman swings round. 'Have you got twenty Marlborough?' you ask to distract him. While he roots on a shelf above the till, you slip the drinks over to me and turn back with a smile. Seeing it, placated, he tosses the cigarettes in the air, beating you to the catch. 'What has such a nice looking girl alone at this hour?' he asks, his voice oiled, insistent. You stand and say nothing. Your smile ransom enough. 'Go home to your bed,' he says, and throws the pack along the wet counter.

'Jesus, the things you have to do around here for a drink.' You fling yourself down on the seat beside me, close so that our knees and shoulders touch.

'You don't have to,' I say.

'Is that right?' you answer and raise one dark eyebrow. You pick up the cocktail glass and hold it to your nose. 'Is it gin or what?'

'I don't know and I certainly don't want it.'

Fishing a slice of stale lemon from the clouded liquid, you knock it back and reach for the Harp.

'Easy on,' I say, 'you'll be pissed at this rate.'

You take no notice, your head thrown back, drinking with total concentration. I watch Pat, the young barboy, guide customers to the door. A big woman, her pink dress stretched tight across her thighs, is hanging on his arm. She tells him what a fine looking lad he is, and laughs something caressively in his ear.

'Ah, wouldn't I love to, Molly, but what would Peter have to say?' Slapping her flanks with the flat of his hand, he winks across at me, and slams the door behind her. Outside, in the carpark someone is singing in a drunken baritone: 'Strangers in the night, exchanging glances, wondering in the night . . .'

'At this stage of the evening,' I say, 'everyone is wondering.'

'About what?' you ask. You run your fingers idly through your long hair, puzzled but incurious.

'Nothing,' I reply. 'A silly joke – just the crowd outside singing.'

You have noticed no singing, much less the words that accompany it. Your gaze is fixed resolutely on the uncleared tables – you have spotted one more in the corner. It's obvious now that you have no intention of going home sober, but we cannot sit here all night and I do not want Paddy to catch you lifting leftovers.

'Well, if you want to stay on,' I say smiling at you, as though it were the very thing I wanted myself, 'why don't we finish what we have in comfort, next door?' I look towards the hallway and an unmarked wooden door on the far side. You are on your feet at once, gathering our glasses, not caring where we go so long as there is a drink at the end of it.

A thin Persian carpet covers the floor of the residents' lounge. On the dim papered walls hang small red-shaded lamps with gold fringes, and two big paintings – hunting scenes – men and animals confused in the dark oils. A few of the regulars have drawn armchairs up to the fire. Pipe tobacco and the scent of cloves from their hot whiskeys, hang together in the air. A man is kneeling over the coal bucket, struggling to open the tongs. He has the red face and shrunken thighs of the habitual toper. 'What the bloody fuck is wrong with this yoke anyway?' he says.

'Here, let me,' leaving him the tongs, you lift the bucket and empty half its contents into the grate. You rattle the poker through the bars, shifting the live coals from front to back. Dust crackles. After a moment, shoots of yellow flame break from the new untouched black.

'Nothing like a good fire,' the man announces, rubbing together his blue-veined hands, 'I always like to build up a good fucking fire.'

His eyes follow the line of your flank, taut and curved as you bend to the hearth. His tongue slides over his bottom lip. 'Always like to build up a good fire,' he repeats as though it were something witty.

He looks towards me; suddenly conscious of my presence and gives a deferential nod. 'Excuse the language,' he calls over. He has placed me then as protector, older sister. And why not after all? Is it not the role I have adopted since that first day I met you in Grafton Street, walking blinded by tears, after one of your quarrels? Did I not even then, that first moment laying eyes on you, want to protect you, from Maeve – from yourself – from that reckless vulnerability of yours, that touched some hidden nerve in me? But it was not protection you wanted, it was empathy. You wanted me to look on, with everyone else, impassive, while you tormented yourself struggling to retain a love that had already slipped into obligation. Though you would not see it – you would see nothing but your own desire. Night after night, following her, watching; your wide, innocent eyes stiff with pain, while she ignored you or flirted with someone else. Waiting because at the end of the evening she might turn, and on an impulse of guilt ask you to go home with her.

'The last one, I think, do you want it?' You hand me an almost full pint of Guinness – brown, sluggish, the froth gone from it. I accept with a wry smile, why not – nothing worse than being empty-handed among drunks, and you clearly will not be hurried.

'Are they residents?' you ask with vague curiosity, looking towards the threesome on the opposite side of the fire.

'No, just regulars,' I say, and none more regular than Peg Maguire. Peg who is here every night with one man or another, drinking herself into amiability. A woman with three children who might be widowed or separated – no one asks. With her blonde hair piled above her head, lipstick a little smudged at the corners, her white coat drawn tight about her as though she were just on the point of departure, Peg – shrewd, jaunty – always careful to maintain the outward show. 'But you know country hotels: once the front door is shut you could stay for ever.' I should not have said that, of course, it encourages you. You will have to stay over with me now, I suppose, you are long past driving. I take a deep draught of the bitter stout, letting it slip quickly down my throat, and to keep this first lightness of mood, I ask you about the college. You are bored, dismissive. Second year is worse than first, you tell me – the life drawing is hopeless, you have only one male model and he wears a g-string;

afraid of getting it on in front of women. 'Anyway, I haven't been there for a week – too stoned,' you add as if that exonerated you. Tossing your head back to sweep the hair from your face. For which of us, I wonder, do you present this elaborate disdain.

'You'll come to a sorry end,' I warn you. 'All this dope and sex at nineteen destroys the appetite.' I have made you smile, a slow, lilting smile, that draws your lips from white, perfect teeth.

'Is that what happened to you?' you ask.

'Perhaps it is. I would say I have decayed into wisdom. A forty-hour week and a regular lover – no unfulfilled lust masquerading as romance.'

'Don't tell me you are not romantic about Jan,' you look at me intently, your eyes at once teasing and solemn, 'when anyone can see you're mad about her.'

'That's one way of putting it, I suppose. At least the feeling is mutual so there is no aggravation.'

'And what about Liz?' you ask. 'Was it not very hard on her?'

'Oh, Liz had other interests,' I say. 'There was no heartache there.'

I have shocked you. You want fervour and longing, not this glib detachment. Should I tell you I am posing, or am I? Is there anything I cherish more than my independence? You lean forward, the cigarette at your mouth, gripped between thumb and forefinger, urging some story of need or rejection.

'You know, it is possible for people to care for each other without tearing their souls out.' I hear my voice, slow, deliberately un-emotional. 'All this strife and yearning is a myth invented to take our minds off the mess around us Happiness distracts no one.' And what is it that impels me to disillusion you? Is it only that this intensity of yours so clearly hurts no one but yourself? With impatience you fan the trail of blue smoke from your face and cut me short.

'Ah, you are always so cynical. You would think thirty is middle age the way you go on. Anyway it's different for you. You have your work – something you really care about. It's all different.'

And so, maybe it is. What answer could I give you that would not be twisting the knife?

You stare into the fire, blazing now. The flames bouncing up the chimney throw great splashes of light about the room. Dance on the red brown of your hair. You have finished your cigarette. Your hands in your lap are curiously still – palms upturned. My own lean, fidgeting. I look about the room, at the rubber plant in the corner, the gilt-framed mirror above the mantelpiece – from it my eyes stare back at me, to my surprise still bright and sharp; a gleaming blue. I notice the faint tracing of lines at the corners. First signs. Give up the fags for good next week – get a few early nights. I look towards you. Your lips are at the rim of your glass, sipping at it, stretching it out. Do you dread going home so much?

'You can stay over with me, you know. Anna is in town – you can have her bed. Maybe you would come jogging in the morning – do you good.'

Roused for a moment, you look intently at me, from my shoulders to my thigh, appraising me. 'Aw, I'm not in your shape,' you say. 'I wouldn't last more than a mile.'

'Well, you can walk while I run,' I answer, but your gaze has slipped back to the fire, watching the leap of the flames as if they held some private message. We sit in silence, lulled by the heat and alcohol until I break it to ask – 'What are you thinking?' Foolish question, as though you would tell me. But you do, holding my eyes to yours, you answer slowly: 'I was wondering if I might ring Maeve – she could be . . .'

'At this hour? You are incorrigible.' I do not try to hide my irritation 'I thought you said you were going to keep away for a week. . .'

You begin to smile again. For a moment I wonder if you are playing with me. Then your face shuts, suddenly, as though a light had been switched off. 'You are right, of course. I'd forgotten.'

And why should I strain to follow these moods? If it were not that you look so forlorn, huddled in your chair, like an animal shut out in the rain.

'You are inconsolable, aren't you?' I say, hoping to tease you out of it. 'Tell me, have you not, even for five minutes, been attracted to another woman?'

You turn away abruptly, as though I had struck you, and ask over-loudly; 'Do you think we can get something to take away?'

'Is it a drink you want?' one of Peg's friends calls over. He has been listening to us for some time, his gaze flickering between us like a snake's tongue. 'I'll get you a drink,' he offers.

'It's all right thanks,' I say quickly.

'No, no, I insist. Name your poison, girls.' His speech is slurred. Conscious of it he repeats each sentence. 'Pat will give us a bottle – no trouble.' He hauls himself up from his chair, clutching the mantel-piece. Peg grabs at his arm.

'Pat has gone off hours ago – don't bother yourself.'

'No bother. Got to get these lassies a drink. Can't send them home thirsty,' he rolls a watering eye at us.

'And what would you know about thirst – you've never been dry long enough to have one.' Peg is an old friend and wants no trouble with me. 'Sit down, Frank and don't be annoying the girls.'

'Who's annoying anyone, Peg Maguire – certainly not you – not if you were the last bloody woman on earth.'

We have set them bickering between themselves now. Time to go. But you are edgy, persistent. 'Is there really no chance of another drink?' you ask Peg. She lowers her voice and gives you a con-spiratorial look.

'What is it you want – would a six-pack do? If you come with us to the Mountain View, I'll get you something there. They've a disco with late closing.'

'The very thing,' Frank roars. 'A disco tit. Let's all go. Two such lovely young women need . . .' he staggers to his feet once more and begins to sing 'I could have danced all night – I could have danced all night and still have begged for more. I could have spread my wings,' he wheels his arms in a jagged circle almost knocking Peg's glass, 'and done a thousand things. I'd never done . . .'

'Will you for God's sake hold on to yourself,' Peg snaps furiously, and pushes him forward.

'Are you right then, girls,' she nods towards us. 'I'll give you the lift down and you can walk back. It's only ten minutes.'

Well, that has done it. There will be no stopping you now. We will not get home 'till you are soused. And why should I try to deter you? Have I anything better to offer? All the tired virtues. Useless. I should be exasperated by you, dragging me all over the country as if a pint of stout were the holy grail. But something about you halts me. As you move to the door, something exaggerated in you – the turn of your shoulders, your head thrown back as though pulling from harness. Defiance and vulnerability in every line. Something more than youth. Something more than me as I was before I learnt – and who was it who finally taught me? – the hard-won pleasures of realism and self-sufficency. Yet if I had the power to bestow them on you, this very instant, would I want to?

In the unlit carpark we find Peg's Fiat and pile in – Frank pulling me towards his knee: 'If you were the only girl in the world and I was the only boy.' Rain slashes at the windscreen, one wiper stuck halfway across it. Peg seems to drive by ear. Wet fir trees arching over us make a black tunnel of the road. The road to God knows where. I recognise none of it, letting myself be carried forward – lapsing into the blind collective will. All needs converging in the simple drive for one more drink. 'Nothing else would matter in the world today . . .' Frank's whiskey breath encircles us. We reach tall, silver gates, pass them, and sluice through rain-filled craters in the drive, the wind snapping at our wheels. A furious night – clouds blown fast as leaves across the sky. Lights ahead – the tall Georgian house bright in welcome. Braking almost on the front steps, Peg jumps out, leaving the door wide: 'I'll put in a word for you.' We follow, our faces lowered from the rain. In the hallway with the bouncer, her blonde head bent to his ear, she is confidential, explaining that we want only a takeaway – no admission. Solemn as a mother entrusting her daughters. Then she turns back to the car and her boys waiting outside. She throws a wicked grin at me over her shoulder – why? – 'Enjoy yourselves girls,' and she is off.

Out of the night – into a frenzy of light and sound. We push through the black swing doors. Red and purple light, great shafts of it, beat against the walls and floor. The music hammers through my chest, shivering my arms. A man and woman locked together, move in a tight circle at the centre of the room. In the corner, beside a giant speaker, two girls on stiletto heels dance an old-fashioned jive. We push through the wall of shoulders at the bar, country boys shy of dancing. 'Two large bottles of stout,' I order. The barman reaches for pint glasses and shoves them under the draught tap. 'Bottles – to take away,' I call across to him. But it is useless, he has already moved to the far end of the counter to measure out whiskey.

'We will just have to drink them here,' you say, putting your mouth close to my ear so that I feel the warmth of your breath. So be it – at least we are in from the rain for a while.

We choose a corner table, as far from the speakers as possible, but still I have to shout to make you hear me.

'It's easier if you whisper,' you say, bringing your lips to my ear once more, in demonstration.

'You are used to these places, I suppose.' It is years since I have sat like this. Though so little has altered. The lights and music more violent maybe, the rest unchanging. Nobody really wants to be here, it seems. Young women dressed for romance display themselves – bringing their own glamour. The men stand banded in council, shoulders raised as a barrier, until they have drunk enough. The faces are bored or angry. Each one resenting his need, resenting his submission to this ritual fever.

You finish half your pint at one go and offer the glass to me. I down the remainder and together we start on the next, laughing. A rotating light on the ceiling spins a rainbow of colours; blue, red, gold, each thrust devouring the last. Smoke hangs in heavy green clouds about us. As though it were the fumes of marijuana I breathe it deep into my lungs and feel suddenly a burst of dizzy gaiety . . . the absurdity of it all – that we should be here. And back to me come memories of years ago – adolescence, when it might have been the scene of passion, or was it even then absurd? The pace slows and three couples move to the centre of the floor. 'I don't want to talk about it – how you broke my heart.' The voice of Rod Stewart rasps through the speakers in an old song. But a favourite of yours. We have danced to it once before – in the early hours at Clare's party two weeks ago, when Maeve had left without you. You stand beside me now and in pantomime stretch your hand. 'Will you dance with me?' You walk ahead on to the floor. Under the spotlight your white shirt is luminous – your eyes seem black. You rest your hands on your hips, at the centre of the room, waiting.

'If you stay here just a little bit longer – if you stay here – won't you listen to my heart . . .' We step into each other's arms. Our cheeks touch. I smell the scent of your shirt – the darkness of your hair. Your limbs are easy, assured against mine. Your hands familiar, hold me just below the waist. We turn the floor, elaborately slow, in one movement, as though continuing something interrupted. The music lapping thigh and shoulder. 'The stars in the sky don't mean nothing to you – they're a mirror.' Round we swing, round; closer in each widening circle. Lost to our private rhythm. The foolish words beating time in my blood.

I open my eyes. The music has stopped. Behind you I see a man standing; his eyes riveted to our bodies, his jaw dropped wide as though it had been punched. In his maddened stare I see reflected what I have refused to recognise through all these weeks. Comfort, sympathy, a protective sister – who have I been deceiving? I see it now in his eyes. Familiar at once in its stark simplicity. Making one moment of past and future. I yield myself to it; humbled, self-mocking. Quick as a struck match.

As if I had spoken aloud, with a light pressure of my hand, you return to consciousness and walk from the floor.

I follow, my skin suddenly cold. I want as quickly as possible to be gone from the spotlight. I have remembered where we are: a Friday night country dance, surrounded by drunken males who have never before seen two women dance in each other's arms. All about the room they are standing still, watching. As we cross the empty space to our table no one moves. I notice for the first time Brid Keane from the post office: she is leaning against the wall, arms folded, her face contorted in a look of such disgust, it seems for a moment that she must be putting it on.

'Let's get out of here – as soon as you've finished your drink,' I whisper.

'What – do you want another drink? Your voice rises high above the music that has begun again. I stare at you in amazement – is it possible that you haven't noticed, that you don't yet know what we've done? Can you be so naïve or so drunk that you haven't realised whose territory we are on?

And then someone moves from the table behind and pushes into the seat opposite us. Squat, red-faced, his hair oiled across his forehead. He props an elbow on the table, and juts his head forward, struggling to focus his eyes. His pink nylon shirt is open, a white tie knotted about the neck.

'Fucking lesbians,' he says at last, 'Are you bent or what?' The breath gusting into my face is sour with whiskey We look towards the dancers writhing under a strobe light and ignore him.

'Did you not hear me?' he asks, shoving his face so close to me, I see the sweat glisten on his upper lip. 'I said are you bent – queers?' He drives his elbow against mine so that the stout spills over my glass.

A familiar anger rips through me, making my legs tremble. I press my nails into the palm of my hand and say nothing. I will not satisfy him so easily.

'What were you saying about the music?' I throw you a smile.

'I asked you a question,' he says. 'Will you give me a bloody answer.' He runs the words together as though speed were his only hope of completing them.

'I said it's lousy,' you reply, 'about ten years out of date.'

He looks from me to you and back again with baffled irritation and his voice grows querulous. He asks: 'Look, would one of you lesbians give me a dance.'

A friend has joined him now, leaning over the back of your chair, a grin on his lips sly and lascivious.

'Will you not answer me?' the first one shouts, 'or are you fucking deaf?'

Drawing my shoulders up, I turn and for the first time look directly into his eyes. 'No,' I say with warning deliberation, 'we are not deaf, yes, we are lesbians and no, we will not give you a dance.'

He stares at us stupefied, then falls back into his seat, breath hissing from his chest as though a lung had burst. 'Jesus, fucking, Christ.'

You give a whoop of laughter, your eyes wide with delight. It seems you find him hugely amusing. Then you're on your feet and across the room in search of the toilet or God knows another drink.

I have my back turned to him when I feel the pink-sleeved arm nudging mine again. 'Hey, blondie – you've gorgeous hair,' he says, giving an ugly snigger. 'Did anyone ever tell you that?' It is a moment before I recognise the smell of singed hair. I reach my hand to the back of my head and a cigarette burns my fingertips. With a cry of pain, I grab hold of the oily lock across his forehead and wrench hard enough to pull it from the roots. He stretches his arm to catch hold of mine but I tear with all my force. 'You fucking cunt!' he screams.

Suddenly someone catches hold of us from behind and pulls us roughly apart. It's the bouncer – a big red-haired man in a grey suit. When he sees my face he steps back aghast. He had not expected a woman.

'I don't know what you two want,' his voice holds a cold contempt, 'but whatever it is you can settle it between you – outside.' He drops the hand on my shoulder, wheels round and walks back to his post at the door. At the sight of him my opponent is instantly subdued. He shrinks back into his seat as though he had been whipped, then slowly collapses on to the table, head in his arms.

You return carrying another drink. I wait until you are sitting down to whisper: 'We have to get out of here, Cathy – they're half savage. That one just tried to set fire to my hair.'

'The little creep!' you exclaim, your eyes sparking with indignation. 'Oh, he's easily handled – but the rest of them, look.'

At the bar a group of six or seven are standing in a circle drinking. Big farm boys in tweed jackets – older than the others and more sober. Their gaze has not left us, I know, since we walked off the dance floor, yet they have made no move. This very calm is what frightens me. In their tense vigilance, I feel an aggression infinitely more threatening than the bluster of the two next us. Hunters letting the hounds play before closing in?

'I think they may be planning something.' As I draw your attention, as if in response to some prearranged signal, one of them breaks from the group and slowly makes his way to our table.

His pale, thin face stares into mine, he makes a deep bow and stretches out his hand. 'Would one of you ladies care to dance?'

I shake my head wearily. 'No, thanks.'

He gives a scornful shrug of the shoulders and walks back to his companions. A moment later another one sets out. When he reaches us, he drops to one knee before you and for the benefit of those watching, loudly repeats the request. When you refuse him he retreats with the same show of disdain.

'What crazy egotism,' I say to you, 'They cannot bear our indifference. They can keep this going all night – building the pressure.'

For they know if they cannot arouse desire at least they can twist it into fear. And they know, too, that we have to put up with it. They have us trapped; under all the theatrics lies the threat that if we dare to leave we can be followed and once outside, alone in the dark, there will be no need for games.

'What can we do?' you ask, winding a strand of dark hair about your finger, your face attentive at last.

'I'll go off for a few minutes. Maybe if we separate, if they lose sight of us, they might get distracted.'

Five minutes later, pushing my way through the crowd to our table, I find you chatting with the one in the pink shirt and his mate, smoking and sharing their beer like old drinking pals. How can you be so unconcerned? I feel a sudden furious irritation. But you look up at me and smile warningly. 'Humour them,' I read in the movement of your lips. And you may be right. They have turned penitent now, ingratiating: 'We never meant to insult you, honest, love. We only wanted to be friendly.' His head lolling back and forth, he stabs a finger to his chest: 'I'm Mick, and this is me mate Gerry.'

All right then, let us try patience. At least while we are seen talking to these two the others will hold off.

'You know, blondie, I think you're something really special,' with the deadly earnest of the drunk, Mick addresses me. 'I noticed you the second you walked in. I said to Gerry – didn't I Gerry? Blondie, would you not give it a try with me? I know you're into women – your mate explained – and that's all right with me – honest – that's cool, you know what I mean? But you never know 'till you try, do you? Might change your life. Give us a chance, love.' He careens on through his monologue, long past noticing whether I answer or not. On the opposite side I hear Gerry, working on you with heavy flattery, admiring your eyes (glistening now – with drink or anger – dark as berries) praising the deep red of your lips – parted at the rim of your glass. And you are laughing into his face and drinking his beer. Your throat thrown back as you swallow, strong and naked.

Mick has collapsed, his head on the table drooping against my arm. 'Just one night,' he mutters into my sleeve, 'that's all I'm asking – just one night. Do yourself a favour.' His words seep through my brain, echoing weirdly, like water dripping in a cave. Drumming in monotonous background to the movement of your hands and face. Half turned from me, I do not hear what you answer Gerry, but I catch your tone; languorous, abstracted, I watch you draw in the spilt froth on the table. Your eyes lowered, the lashes black along your cheek, one finger traces the line of a half moon. Behind you I see the same group watching from the bar; patient, predatory. My blood pounds – fear and longing competing together in my veins.

And then all at once, the music stops. Everyone stands to attention, silent. The disc-jockey is making an announcement: the offer of a bottle of whiskey, a raffle, the buying of tickets – gripping them as the music and dance never could. This is our moment, with Gerry moving to the bar to buy cigarettes and Mick almost asleep, slumped backwards, his mouth dropped open. I grasp your hand beneath the table, squeezing it so that you may feel the urgency and no one else, and look towards the green exit sign. We are across the floor, stealthy and cautious as prisoners stepping between the lights of an armed camp. At the door at last, 'Fucking whoores – you needn't trouble yourselves to come back,' the bouncer restraining fury in the slam of the swing doors behind us.

And we are out.

Out in the wet darkness. The wind beating escape at our backs. I catch your hand. 'Run and don't stop.' Our feet scatter the black puddles, soaking our shins. The fir trees flapping at our sides, beckon, opening our path to the gates. So much further now. The moon will not help – hidden from us by sheets of cloud – withholding its light. We run blind, my heart knocking at my ribs; following the track only by the sting of gravel through my thin soles. 'Come on – faster.' The gates spring towards us out of nowhere – caught in a yellow shaft of brightness. A car rounds the bend behind us, the water flung hissing from its tyres. We dodge under the trees, the drenched boughs smacking my cheek. The headlights are on us, devouring the path up to and beyond the open gates. The window rolled down, I hear the drunken chanting – like the baying of hounds: 'We're here because we're queer because we're here because we're ...' 'Great fucking crack, lads ...' Gone. Past us. Pitched forward in the delirium of the chase –

seeing nothing to left or right. A trail of cigarette smoke in the air.

'All right – we can go on now,' you say, laughing – drawing me out from cover. 'Do you think it was them?'

'Yes, or someone else. We had better be gone before the next lot.'

We run on again, through the wide gates to the main road. The alcohol is washing through me now, spinning my head. My heart is beating faster than ever, though the fear has left me. You are beginning to tire. 'We are almost there,' I urge you, marvelling that you can still stand, let alone run. The rain darts in the gutter, the leaves slithering under our feet. Jumping a pool I slip towards you. Your arm outflung steadies me. You're laughing again – the long looping kind you do not want to stop. 'You're worse than I am,' you say.

The moon all at once throws open the night before us, scattering in sequins on the tarred road, silver on the hanging trees. I see the house massed and still in its light.

'We are home,' I say.

You slow your pace and let go of my hand. Your eyes under the white gleam of the moon are darker than ever – secretive.

'Are you laughing at me?' I ask, to capture your attention.

'I'm not – really,' you answer, surprised.

I lift the latch of the gate, softly so as to wake no one. How am I to keep this? To keep us from slipping back into the everyday: the lighted, walled indoors – all the managed, separating things. And what is it I fear to lose? Any more than my desire – dreaming yours. Any more than a drunken joy in escape?

The cat comes through a gap in the hedge, whipping my shins with her tail. I lift her to me and she gives a low, rough cry.

'She's been waiting for you,' you tell me.

I turn the key in the kitchen door. You step inside and stand by the window, the moonlight falling like a pool of water about your feet. I gaze at your shoes for no reason; at the pale, wet leather, muddied now.

'Well, that looked bad for a moment,' I say, putting my arm round you, not knowing whether it is you or myself I am consoling. 'Were you not frightened, at all?'

'Oh yes, I was,' you answer, leaning into me, pulling me close. 'Yes, Siobáin I was.'

And so, I have been right. So much more than comfort. I slide my lips down your cheek, still hesitant, measuring your answer. And you lift your open mouth to meet me. Desire runs in my veins. I tighten

172

my arms about you. I have imagined nothing, then. Everything. All this long night has been a preparation – an appeal. You untie the belt of my raincoat and I feel your hands, still cold from the night rain, along my sides. 'Siobáin,' you murmur again. You take my hand, and cautiously, though we are alone in the house, climb the wooden stairs.

The room is cold. The double bed with its silver and wine-red quilt waits at the centre of the floor. I light a yellow candle at the bedside. You sit on the cane chair and unlace your sneakers, slowly, knot by knot. Then stand and drop your clothes – red jeans and white shirt – in a ring about them. I turn back the sheets and step towards you. Downstairs the phone sounds, cracking the darkness like a flood-light. It rings and rings and will not stop. 'I had better answer it,' I say and move to the door.

'Who was it?' When I return, you are sitting propped against the pillow, easy as though you spent every night here. I cannot tell you that it was Jan, feeling amorous, wanting to chat, imagining me alone.

'Jan . . .' I begin, but you do not wait to hear. Reaching your hand behind my head you pull my mouth towards you. I feel, but do not hear the words you speak against my lips.

The rain drives at the window, shivering the curtains. The wind blown up from the sea sings in the stretched cables. Your body strains to mine, each movement at once a repetition and discovery. Your mouth, greedy and sweet, sucks the breath from my lungs. I draw back from your face your long dark hair and look in your eyes: you are laughing again – a flame at the still black centre. Your tongue seals my eyelids shut. Your hands, travelling over me, startle the skin as if they would draw it like a cover from muscle and bone. We move – bound in one breath – muscle, skin and bone. I kiss you from forehead to thigh. Kiss the fine secret skin beneath your breast, the hard curve of your belly. You draw me down to the scent of your hair. Your thighs gather my face.

The wind moans through the slates of the roof. The house shifts. Beneath us the sea crashes on the stones of the shore. Your voice comes clear above them beating against mine, high above the wind and rain. Spilling from the still centre – wave after wave. And then, a sudden break; a moment's straining back as though the sea were to check for one instant – resisting – before its final drop to land. But the sea does not.

You lie quiet above me. I taste the salt of tears on my tongue.

'Are you crying? What is it?'

'No, I'm not,' you answer gently, your head turned from me. Maybe so. I close my arms about you, stroking the silk of your back, finding no words. But it does not matter. Already you have moved beyond me into sleep. I lie still. Clouds have covered the moon, blackening the window of sky. I cannot see your face. Your body is heavy on mine, your breath on my cheek. I soothe myself with its rhythm. The rain has ceased. I hear once more the small night sounds of the house: the creak of wood in floorboards and rafters, the purr of the refrigerator. Then suddenly there comes a loud crash – the noise of cup or plate breaking on the kitchen's tiled floor. My breath stops – you do not stir. I hear the squeal of a window swung on its hinge. A dull thud. Footsteps?

Before my eyes a face rises: mottled cheeks, beads of sweat along the lip. A wild fear possesses me that he or his friends have followed us, come here to this house in search of us. I slide gently from under you. I creep to the door and stand listening for a moment, breath held, before opening it. Silence . . . Nothing but the hum of the 'fridge. And then . . . a soft, triumphal cry. Of course – the cat. How well I know that call. Elsie has caught a rat or bird and brought it home through the window. In the morning there will be a trail of blood and feathers on the carpet. Time enough to deal with it tomorrow.

I go back to bed. Lifting the sheet I press near to your warmth, my belly fitting exactly in the well of your back. I breathe the strange, new scent of you. A shudder goes through my limbs. I reach my hand and gently gather the weight of your breast. I feel the pulsing through the fine veins beneath the surface. You stir, sighing, and press your thighs against mine. You murmur something from sleep – a word, or name. Someone's name.

My arms slacken. I taste again your tears on my lips. In the morning what will we say to each other? Drunk as you were it will be easy to forget, to pretend the whole thing an accident. No need then to prepare an attitude – for Maeve (when she calls, as she will, as before, thanking me for taking care of you), for Jan – for ourselves. The night is fading at the window. The bare branch of the sycamore knocks on the wall behind us. Words echo in my mind, the words of the song we danced to, foolish, mocking: 'The stars in the sky mean nothing to you – they are a mirror.' And to me? What was it I said this evening about romantic illusion? I reach out my hand for the candlestick on the table. As I lift it, the flame flares golden. My movement has woken you. You regard me, for an instant, startled. How childish you look, your forehead smooth, your eyes washed clear. Was it only your hurt that set a cord between us – that lent you

the outline of maturity? 'I thought I heard a noise downstairs,' you
say.

'Yes, but it was nothing,' I kiss your eyes shut. 'Only the cat with a
bird,' I answer as you move into sleep, your cheek at my shoulder.
'Nothing.'

Far out at sea, a gull cries against the coming of light. For a little
longer night holds us beyond the grasp of speech. I lean and blow the
candle out.

Biographical Notes on the Contributors

Rosemary Auchmuty
I was born in Egypt in 1950, grew up in Australia, and have lived in south London since 1978. I earn my living mostly by teaching women's history, part-time, to women in Adult and Higher Education. I've published a couple of school textbooks, some articles on women's history and a few short stories, and I'm active in the South London Women's Studies Group and the Lesbian History Group.

Marsaili Cameron
Born in Inverness in 1951; school in Ross and Cromarty and Edinburgh; degree at Aberdeen University. Worked for a medical publishing firm in Edinburgh; then at the Open University in Milton Keynes. Contributed to the old *Gay News* from 1973 till its demise. Since 1977, freelance writer and editor, living in London.

Caroline Claxton
I was born in 1960. I am white, gentile, middle class, able-bodied. 'The Stranger in the City' is for all women who are made to feel alien, and for every lesbian everywhere.
    Come out, come out . . . there's a lot of us about.

Mary Dorcey
Born in County Dublin, Ireland, Educated at convent school. She has worked at a variety of jobs, including waitress, caterer and English language teacher. She has travelled widely and lived in Japan, England, France and America. Her first book, a collection of poetry, *Kindling*, was published by Onlywomen Press in 1982. Since then her work has appeared in journals and anthologies, including *The Virago Book of Women Poets* and *In the Pink*, published by The Women's Press, 1983. She has been active in the women's movement since

1972, a founder member of Irishwomen United and the first Irish lesbian group.

She is currently living in the west of Ireland completing a collection of short stories and working on a novel.

Berta Freistadt

I am a Londoner. I've been a teacher, an actor, a shoe-seller, a clown, a dishwasher and a women's centre worker: and I've always been a writer. But like choosing a different sexuality it took some time to organise. I've written more plays than stories and more poems than plays. I have always had an urge to translate experience into writing, life seeming more ephemeral than books. I must often describe things in writing before I can feel they've already happened, if I didn't the experience might somehow in retrospect be snatched from me. I could forget it perhaps.

I am a feminist and of course a lesbian, though sometimes I'm not sure of the order. I am forty-three, white, don't smoke, live with an Aries cat and would like to be a vegetarian, but I see my mother once a week and she cooks me sausages for lunch.

Ellen Galford

Born New Jersey 1947. Has lived in the UK since 1971 in Edinburgh, Glasgow and London. Involved in the women's liberation movement since the early seventies. Worked with other feminist writers in a writers' group in Edinburgh which produced the poetry anthology *Hens in the Hay* (Stramullion, 1980). Her first novel *Moll Cutpurse: Her True History* was published by Stramullion in 1984, and she is working on her second. She makes her living by working in mainstream publishing as a writer and editor, and lives in north London.

Kate Hall

I am forty, working class and a mother. I have a teenage daughter, called Amy, two grown-up sons and sundry animals. I have been lesbian for seven years and coincidentally (or maybe not) began painting and writing, fiction and poetry, just after I 'came out'. Recently I have been studying dance and mime.

Gillian E. Hanscombe

Lesbian/writer/mother in that order of genesis; born 1945 in Melbourne, Australia, educated at Melbourne, Monash, London and

Oxford universities; resident in England since 1969; work experience: teaching, typing, cleaning, selling, journalism, etc., etc.; politics: lesbian feminist; publications: poems and articles variously anthologised; *Rocking the Cradle – Lesbian Mothers* (with Jackie Forster), Peter Owen/ Sheba Feminist Publishers/ Alyson Publications; *The Art of Life – Dorothy Richardson and the development of feminist consciousness*, Peter Owen/University of Ohio Press; *Between Friends*, Sheba Feminist Publishers/ Alyson Publication; *Title Fight – The Battle for Gay News* (with Andrew Lumsden), Brilliance Books; *The Other Bloomsbury* (with Virginia L. Smyers), forthcoming, Virago.

Sandra McAdam Clark

I write to change the world we live in.

As a lesbian feminist, a trade-union activist, also active in the Women and El Salvador Group, I write as part of a minority, although my class and colour give me enormous privileges. As a child, my main language was French, but I now write in English, having lived in Britain since the mid sixties.

I would like to dedicate 'Distance' to Lesley, my comrade and lover.

Liz McLaren

Aged thirty-nine, has four children (two of each!) and two cats (both male). Used to be a civil servant (DHSS) until forced to retire through illness. Hoping to write more in the future, as she becomes more fluent in lesbian as well as patriarchal language.

Pearlie McNeill

I am an Australian feminist lesbian writer much influenced by my Irish working-class origins. Possibly because I am my mother's seventh and my father's first child, I have always felt somewhat ambivalent about 'the family'. There is a complex reality about my beginnings and much of my writing reflects this complexity. I also enjoy writing monologues and working-class dialogue.

Although I have been a parent to two sons for more than nineteen years now, I am being taught new ways of looking at parenthood from my partner's small daughter, who thinks I have a long way to go.

Caeia March

Born of white working-class parents, Isle of Man, 1946. Mother, Gaelic; dad, a Londoner. Grew up in industrial South Yorkshire.

Came to London, to university, in 1964.

Now a lesbian mother, and after homelessness now rents a flat in south-east London, five miles from her two sons, ages thirteen and eleven.

Now works full-time as a clerk, filing and photocopying. Ugh. Also, part-time work with women's studies group in a multi-racial community centre locally.

Very committed to the publication of writing by working-class women. Finishing two novels at present, about class and sexuality.

'Photographs' is the third of a trilogy of true stories.

Lorna Mitchell

I'm thirty-nine years old and live in Yorkshire. I've been a drop-out for about twelve years now. During that time I've been moving slowly towards becoming a 'real writer'. If you want to know more about me, read my story. I'm not a snobbish culture-vulture any more, but psychologically I haven't changed much since I was sixteen – alas!

Caroline Natzler

I am thirty-four and work as a solicitor in a south London law centre. Writing is partly a light relief from the practical politics of this sort of work. Recent experience of writing groups and classes has encouraged me to experiment with different forms, and I do think serious issues can emerge from the reworking of almost any genre (the story in this collection was written as a 'crime story'.) I think I would like to see a body of fiction developing which took lesbianism and feminism as its basic premise, without discounting the need for more polemical writing. I have been published in *Spinster* (Onlywomen Press), *Gay News*, *Spare Rib*, *Wild Words* and in *The Reach* (Onlywomen Press) and *Everyday Matters II* (Sheba Feminist Publishers).

Sigrid Nielsen

I'm thirty-seven years old. I've worked in lesbian and gay bookselling for five years and am co-founder of Lavender Menace, Edinburgh's lesbian and gay community bookshop. Before that I was a bus driver, hotel night auditor and ghostwriter. I'm editing an anthology with Gail Chester, *In Other Words: Writing as a Feminist*, which will be published by Hutchinsons in early 1986.

Paulina Palmer

I work in the English Department at the University of Warwick where I teach – among other things – a course in Literature and Sexual Politics. My home is in East Anglia and I am a member of the Cambridge Lesbian Switchboard and the Cambridge Women Writers' Collective. My chief interest is writing fiction and the themes that preoccupy me at present are *lesbian life in the provinces, aging* and *ageism*. I also enjoy researching into literature and am in the process of preparing for publication a critical study of contemporary fiction written by women. The chief influence on me has been my mother. Her sense of humour, survival skills and gifts of imagination have proved invaluable to me, both in personal terms and as a writer.

Anira Rowanchild

I live with my daughter, son and my lover in a small, isolated cottage in north Herefordshire; keep goats, chickens, an old pony and rabbits on common grazing; lived most of my life in rural Shropshire; still fetching water from the well.

Amanda Russell

I was born in London in 1954 and have lived here for most of my life. I've written for *Gay News* and *The London Lesbian Newsletter*. I've had a wide variety of jobs including dishwashing, chambermaid, kennel-maid, bookshop manager and London Lesbian Line worker.

I live in Kilburn with my lover, two cats and terrapins Butch and Femme.

Sue Sanders

Born in London of middle-class WASP parentage. An only child. Became a dyke at twenty-one and discovered the women's movement five years later. Trained as a drama teacher and worked with a wide range of women both in London and Sydney. Passionately interested in feminist theatre and have worked with and directed various women's theatre companies. 'If One Green Bottle . . .' is an attempt to share my experience of alcohol.

Lucy Whitman

I'm a Londoner, born in 1954, and I teach in a Further Education College. I have been active in various groups, including Rock Against Racism, Rock Against Sexism, Women Oppose the Nuclear Threat and, currently, Lesbians in Education. I used to write lots of articles on women and popular music (under the name Lucy Toothpaste), and I was Fiction Editor of *Spare Rib* from 1979 to 1982. Lately I have concentrated on writing fiction. 'The Severed Tongue' is one of a series of stories based on Greek myths, in which women respond to male violence with a terrible violence of their own. I find this violence frightening and alien, yet it seems to correspond to a rage I sometimes experience in my dreams.